The
Whiskey
Sea

OTHER BOOKS BY ANN HOWARD CREEL

The Magic of Ordinary Days
While You Were Mine

The Whiskey Sea

ANN HOWARD CREEL

LAKE UNION
PUBLISHING

Published by Lake Union Publishing, Seattle

www.apub.com

Amazon, the Amazon logo, and Lake Union Publishing are trademarks of Amazon.com, Inc., or its affiliates.

ISBN-13: 9781503936898
ISBN-10: 1503936899

Cover design by Rachel Adam

Printed in the United States of America

PROLOGUE

She opened her eyes to blackness. Salty blackness. She moved her arms against water, then remembered. The ocean. The flight. The flames.

No.

Now her arms and legs would not move. She was drowning, falling into the cold depths. Below her, the pull of invisible arms and no light. A silence pure and dark. Her face down, her vision gone, she was plunging fast into infinite time. She could not hold her breath much longer; she was going to die.

How predictable.

A meaningless life. More than anything, she had wanted to be useful. She had wanted to better herself and those around her. She had wanted to live as one with the sea in her soul. And she had wanted love. She had thought love would save her. She had hoped she would be worthy. She had dreamed of redemption. And for a time she believed she had found it all.

A stream of air escaped her lungs and bubbled past her lips. Her head felt compressed and rang as if a string of clanging bells was pulled taut between her ears. Not much longer. Her life almost over now.

Flashes of memories: skimming over the water into darkness, salt on her lips, big boats lingering on the horizon, crates of liquor luring them out, rolls of bills in her hands, lawmen on the take, and funerals. Desire and kisses. New York City on the arm of a man. A nice dress. Racing over the ocean. Whiskey bottles. Fear and exultation.

How had it come to this?

And where was love now?

CHAPTER ONE

1908

When death came to Della Hope, this story begins.

Della never set foot more than a few paces off the waterfront. A sweet little thing with brassy hair and misty green eyes, she made a living off being shapely and willing, with no other means to support herself. As the town whore, she lived above one of the ramshackle dockside establishments and catered to men coming in off a fishing boat, reeking of the sea. Along the way she caught a disease that drove her mad—and then killed her.

On the day Della passed from this world, Silver motored in to the docks later than usual. The day had been warm, with buttery September sun, so pleasant that after he ate some bread and cheese he'd packed for his lunch over the mudflats raking clams, he lay back on the boat deck and his eyelids closed. He woke just as the anchor was pulling free of its hold and the tide was rushing in to fill the bay and the Navesink and Shrewsbury Rivers to their banks. He extracted the anchor and coaxed the engine to life, then slowly let the motor and tide take him home.

Breathing in the familiar smells of fish and salt water, he nosed his boat into the row of mostly handmade and pieced-together craft of his fellow clammers. He heard the news as soon as he hopped onto the dock; people were milling around and beating their gums about what was to be done, since Della apparently had two little girls, who were now orphans.

Once or twice Silver had seen the older of Della's girls, about five years old, playing on the docks, but he hadn't paid much attention to her and had never known there was another. The man they called Hawkeye, who had only one good eye, which made him peer at a person real serious, was dockmaster that day, and he was pacing the wooden planks of the long pier in between cursing the messiest of the fishermen, kicking their fish heads into the sea, and shooing off seagulls.

It was a Sunday, and Hawkeye paced about as if he didn't know what to do. The sun was sinking low in the sky. "No one's gonna help them girls. They're gonna end up on the streets in the city, selling flowers . . . or themselves," he said to Silver, who reckoned Hawkeye was really talking to himself. Hawkeye pushed the gray-hazed rat's nest of black hair off a forehead that was etched with horizontal lines as deep as the river, and Silver could see that Hawkeye's eyes were bloodshot and teary. Silver figured Hawkeye had a sweet spot for Della, even though he was a married man with three or four children—Silver couldn't remember the exact number. "Who do I send for? Who's gonna decide what to do with them girls?"

The setting sun trailed a golden glow over the big city across the bay. It was Silver's favorite time of the day. Almost time to head home.

"I can't do a thing to help them," Hawkeye said, speaking more frankly than Silver had ever heard the man speak before, Silver guessed on account of his grief. "My wife, you know." He looked away. "They gonna end up like their mama, and that's what Della didn't want. Della wanted better for them girls."

Silver was aiming to stay out of this business. Though he was about the only man down on the wharves who didn't have a wife and kids at home, he'd never partaken of manly pleasures with Della. Many of those other men had indulged in Della's services, but when she took ill there was no help for her, save some Catholic women who came down to nurse her a bit, as if Della were the fallen Madonna with children. The men had vanished, except for Hawkeye, who couldn't afford to incur his wife's wrath by letting her know about his past infidelity and present concerns. Silver guessed it was the way of men. *Fine lot, all of them,* he thought gravely.

Hawkeye said, "I guess I'm going to have to go call the police. Let them take those babes away."

A wave of sadness washed over Silver, but he had no part to play in solving this problem. He hauled his day's clams to be weighed and sold, and when he came back, the docks had all but cleared out. Hawkeye was gone, too, and Silver thought that was the end of it. But as he was leaving to walk home, he passed the wharf-side bars above which Della had operated her whoring business, and there outside on the rough wooden walkway that sloshed to the beat of the incoming tide, sitting on top of a small, scarred valise, was Della's older girl, her Indian-black hair tangled, her dress stained and dirty, her feet bare, and a hard look to her jawline that said, *Leave me alone,* despite the fact that she was but a little child holding a helpless babe in her lap. And yet this small, dark-haired girl was beautiful, a heavenly mistake, as if something had blown across the ocean on an errant breeze from the shores of the Mediterranean. She could've been from some noble Italian or Greek family rather than the bastard daughter of the town whore.

The baby, who looked to be nearing a year old, was much fairer than her sister, with skin so pale and thin it looked near to transparent, and atop her head were fine threads of almost-white hair. She appeared as if blown here by some strange wind, too, though hers of Norse origins. *She ought to be growing up in the mountains of Scandinavia, not by the harsh, burning sea,* Silver thought. It was pretty obvious who'd fathered the baby, a big-time lobsterman called Whitey, who lived over in Atlantic Highlands. No other person for miles around had Whitey's near-colorless hair, except his other children. But who sired the older one remained a mystery.

The older girl stared out over the water, the sun now turning blood orange, the light over the sea a burned red, and as he drew closer, the look of the girl took hold of Silver and made him stop. Her feet were planted solidly, she held her knees together tightly, her arms were curved loosely but protectively about the baby, and she wore an expression of shattered defiance on her face, as if she'd been overtaken by some kind of stupor or shock. She didn't gaze up at him as he started to pass by.

Silver stopped for a moment, rubbed his thatch of gray whiskers, and shrugged his shoulders, first one, then the other, as he did when he found himself at a loss. The girls' story was a fitting tale for Highlands, where the rich lived across the bay in New York and in the hills above town, and those just getting by—the clammers and fishermen—lived down by the docks and the shifting deeps. There wasn't much actual space between them, yet those two places were worlds apart. Big money came to Highlands to sit on the verandas of their summer homes, slip amid clean, soft sheets in the new hotels, and comment on the quality of the clam chowder in dining establishments along the water. Big money lived in two-story, porch-fronted houses on the hills above town and traveled in automobiles and ferries. It came for the beautiful beaches, which were nearby, but at the same time far enough away from the clammers that they didn't spoil its vacation. It came to private swim clubs, beach resorts, and boats people took out for pleasure and not for work. Scant money came to the folks who washed dishes and mopped floors in the hotels, clubs, and restaurants, and to the hardy men making a living out of the rolling waters: fishermen, lobstermen, and clammers, mostly clammers. It lived packed together in small cottages and rooms near the water, where winds whipped, storms threatened, and the streets sometimes flooded during summer high tides . . . and, of course, scant money also came to women like Della Hope.

The older girl didn't move or utter a word, and yet there was something different about the light and evening breeze picking up, and it told him to wait, just wait for a minute. Don't leave those babies alone. He was aiming to stay only until Hawkeye came back. He figured the other man would show up with help soon enough, and in the meantime the little girls shouldn't be left by themselves on the wharf with the light fading. By now the sun was only a half dome cupped over the hills, and there was still no sign of Hawkeye.

"You hungry?" asked Silver, who was thus nicknamed because his hair had turned old when he was but twenty-five.

She looked at him then, the first time she'd ever really looked at him, although she had to have seen him around the waterfront plenty of times before. By God, the color of her eyes was a steely gray like he'd never seen before, and her appraising gaze was powerful. The look was neither good nor bad, trusting nor untrusting, helpless nor helpful—just a stare of pure sizing up. What he'd first interpreted as stupor was instead clearly intense concentration, as if everything in her surroundings had just transformed, and she was still trying to adjust to the altered appearance of it. Certainly her young life was now shattered.

Her eyes never moved, never watered, never told him a thing.

Clearly she wasn't going to answer. "You got a bottle for that baby?" he asked.

She reached down to her side and picked up a baby bottle, but there was no milk in it.

"You wait here. I'll be coming back, ye hear?"

Silver walked away toward Bahrs Landing, only a short stroll down the waterfront. He didn't want to go far; he aimed to stay where he could still keep an eye on the girls.

When he returned with clam fritters and a small glass bottle of milk for the older girl and another one for the baby, the older girl poured the baby's bottle. She fed that baby first, and Silver wondered how long she'd been mothering the child while Della took sick. Only a child, she was already taking care of another life on this earth. Already doing what he had shied away from doing his entire life, nearly fifty years of it.

Silver liked people to a point; he liked to hear them tell of some important news or share a laugh, but then solitude was always calling him back. Too much contact with people took things away from him—his energy, his soul, his freedom. There was something too loose and scattered about the outside world. He had taken to the sea from the moment his father taught him to clam, but even out there with all that openness of sea and sky, the one thing he craved after a day out was his own private space. Life had whittled out a little place for him and painted the sea beside it, just as he'd wanted.

After the baby had been fed and burped, the girl's face seemed brighter, as if the light of the day were opening up instead of drifting away. Still holding the baby, she started eating the fritters with one hand, picking up two, three, four of them at a time and stuffing them in her mouth, barely chewing before swallowing. Where her baby teeth had come out, there were gaps big enough to put a finger through, her lips were reddened and chapped, and she smelled musty, like a dirty room.

Silver said, "Slow down. You're gonna make yourself sick."

She kept on eating that way until the fritters were gone, and then she licked at her fingers and touched the bottom of the paper bag to pick up each and every last crumb.

"I should've brung you some more food," he said.

She handed him the empty bag and then fixed him with that gaze again.

"You talk?"

She smacked the final crumbs from her lips and swallowed them, and he saw the tendons shift in her little neck. "I talk when I got something to say." Her tone wasn't necessarily disrespectful, but it was utterly sure. She sat tall, her shoulders firmly set, and her chin level despite it all. Some people have that inner pride inside that no amount of hard knocks can ever beat out, and this girl had it in barrels. Her eyes bore through him, and they seemed to say, *I'll never belong to anyone. Not to you, not to anyone.*

Something odd, like an invisible wire, sparked and shot between him and the girl, then fizzled up his spine. Silver couldn't tear his eyes away.

Hawkeye came back and said there wasn't anyone at the police station that night, and he guessed he was going to have to walk up into the hills to wake up the judge or the mayor. "I even went to one of them Catholic ladies who used to come around and nurse Della, but she don't want 'em." Hawkeye pursed his lips. "A fair crowd gathered to watch the police take Della out of here, but then everyone went on about like nothing happened. No one paid a bit of attention to these girls."

"I'll take 'em," Silver said, stunning himself. Some spirit must have pulled those words out of his mouth. He'd never believed in ghosts, but he smelled something of Della's perfume just then, as if she'd just gone strolling by. He shook his head even as he said, "Just for tonight."

Hawkeye stared at him and started to thank him. But Silver couldn't have any of that. "I'll put 'em up for one night."

He was sure he meant it at the time.

Hawkeye said, "The girl's Frieda. The baby's Beatrice."

"Bea," said Frieda as she gazed up into the darkening sky. "I like to call her Bea."

Hawkeye said, "'Cause she's little, like a bee, yeah?" and laughed at his own joke.

The girl darted her eyes away. Silver didn't blame her. He wouldn't make a joke on a day like this.

Instead he leaned closer, laid his hands on his thighs, and studied the girl. "Well, come on. I got to get you some more food," he said, holding his breath, not knowing whether she would go with him or not.

Why did he suddenly care so much? Some kind of madness had struck him, like the sickness that smacked down so many young men when they fell into a frenzied, passionate love. He'd never fallen into that, not once, but now he was experiencing something even more profound than what he imagined that romantic love to be. Some kind of powerful longing to save something before it was too late, and that feeling was swelling solid-like in his chest.

Would she come? There was no way he could ever replace what she had lost, but for the first time in his life he believed he had something to offer, and he was ready to give it finally, as though he had awakened from a lifelong sleep.

She must have recognized the shift in him, or else she knew him as one of the few men who hadn't come to her mother, or else she saw something else she deemed worthy. After only a few seconds, she stood up and let him take the ratty valise. She carried the baby in one arm, and as they walked to his place in the gathering dark she put her free hand—a little soft creature—in his, and it changed Silver's life for good. From that moment on he wasn't going to let either of those girls go.

He knew it wouldn't be easy, and a pointed finger of doubt poked him in the ribs. Was he up to this? All he could think to do was send into these fathomless stars above an urgent plea: *Let me do right by them.* Could love reawaken an almost-dead man and save two young lives? He wanted that now as he'd never wanted anything before. But he never foresaw the future. Who would have? The storm of change still lay far away past the horizon.

CHAPTER TWO

1921

Frieda refused to show up for graduation. She'd stayed in school to please Silver and the state authorities, who'd let Silver keep the girls only if he saw them through school. But now that she had her high school diploma, she wanted nothing more to do with the school or anyone in it. At age eighteen and a legal adult, she'd reached this point in her life surrounded by a town that had ruined and shunned her mother, and the way she saw it, all the local people still wore some of the soil from the dirty life her mother had been forced to live. They were all to blame. And yet they'd had the nerve to look down on Frieda and Bea.

"Well, you've graduated even if you didn't show up today. I've been saving money so you can take a secretary course now," Silver said to her. He was sitting in his favorite chair on the front porch, squinting into the afternoon light that had settled over Highlands as soft and silky as a yellow chiffon scarf. Still wearing his clammer's overalls and shucking clams out of a bucket sitting at his feet, he was preparing for one of his lectures, Frieda thought grimly.

She stood with her feet planted and her arms crossed. "I'm not going to secretary's school. I've done what I had to do. I hated school but I finished, for you."

Silver looked up with that wary expression in his eyes he got every time they disagreed, which was often. "Then what you going to do with yourself? You're eighteen. Not a kid anymore. You got to have a future."

Frieda stepped forward to the porch rail. She wore a pair of Silver's old pants, hitched up and held at her waist with one of his belts, into which she'd carved extra holes. He'd bought her a graduation dress, which hung on a nail in the room she shared with Bea, but she'd never even tried it on.

The house, in its snug spot at the end of the road, sat perpendicular to the water, and she looked to her left toward the bay, where the breeze was lashing up little whitecaps and the late, slanting light sparkled on the swells. Out there was the only part of the earth that spoke to her.

She pushed back a tendril of long, unruly hair. "I'll clam with you."

With her firm gaze, she followed some incoming fishing boats. On the water—that was where she belonged. The sea didn't care about differences in human lives; it didn't judge. Out there the rest of the world seemed far away, and the inner emptiness she'd felt for most all of her life eased. Something else filled it, something other than her anger toward the townspeople, her fear for Bea's future, the looks people gave her, or her constant worry about getting by. When the bay was furious and churning, those frothing waters pulled the resentment right out of her and fed it to the waves. And when the tides stopped surging and the bay became silver and flat, it was as if some almighty power had smoothed her rough edges while leveling the surface of the sea with big, broad hands. She felt as if she could sail out past the land and lighthouses and float on forever.

Silver tossed the empty clamshells into a different bucket, and the loud clinking sound told Frieda he was getting ready to say something she wouldn't like.

"Clamming ain't no work for a woman."

Frieda stood tall and hinged a hand on her hip. "Why not? Any work on the water is better than something shoreside. It's been good enough for you."

"Because I didn't have no other choice."

"Well, I do have a choice, and I'm not going to any more schools. I'm done with that. Besides, remember I took a typing class junior year? I was terrible at it, and I hated every minute. My fingers didn't work when I couldn't look at the keys, when I had to keep my eyes on the paper. I have to look at what I'm doing."

He sat back. "Well, I cain't work much longer."

Frieda had noticed. Silver had always been old to her, lined with age and the sure tracks of a hard life out in the sun and sea winds. But he'd also been spry for his years. Going out in the boat every day, making runs to the school, cooking, and taking care of two girls had made that a necessity. Now he was beginning to lose stamina, move slower, and complain about aches and pains. Over the past two years his time on the water had gradually been cut in half.

Silver said, "We got to get you some working skills."

Keeping her gaze on the bay, she said, "I can take over the boat now."

She could feel his piercing stare on her back as he said flatly, "I sold it."

His words hit her like a rogue wave, fierce enough to slap her down but not kill her. *Sold* it? She spun toward him, gasping for air. "What?"

He looked down. "Like I said, I sold it."

Her heart started thumping, and her voice came out in a screech. "What are you talking about?"

"I ain't getting any younger, and I got a fair price. Fella's coming by later to pay me off."

So it wasn't sold *yet*. She pulled in a long breath. "You can't do this. I won't let you."

Silver shucked another clam. "Good fella. You know him." His brow furrowed, and he tossed the shell. "Sam Hicks."

Incredulous, Frieda asked, "How could you even think of selling the boat? If you don't want it anymore, give it to me."

"I sold it, I said."

"B-But . . ."

"I already made the arrangements. It's done now."

"I-I always assumed . . . you'd let me have it. You know how I love it out there!"

"I never made no promises. I need to get some money out of her while I still can."

Her eyes bore through him, but he was having a hard time looking her in the face. "Are you crazy? How're we going to live?"

He edged the knife around another clamshell. "I been putting away money for some time. I got enough to get by. This house is paid for, and I'll pick up an odd job here and there. Might crew for some fishermen when the weather's good. After I sell the boat, I'll have the money so you can go to that secretary school."

"I want the boat! I want to be out on the water. You know this."

"Like I said already, a life on the water ain't no life for a woman."

Frieda snorted, even as panic started to pummel her. Silver seemed dead set, not budging. "I'm not like other girls. How, how . . . ?"

"You can *marry* a clammer if you want."

A dreadful realization blanketed her brain. "Oh no you don't."

"He's a good man, Frieda. Always been a good young man. You might take a liking to him."

"How dare you!"

"I always been looking out for you. Sam Hicks could make for a good husband. And now that he'll be owning the boat, if you marry him you can still go out from time to time."

In that moment she came as close to hating Silver as she'd ever come before, despite the fact they'd always tangled. But arguing was pretty pointless with someone as stubborn as Silver. Trying a different approach, she consciously slowed her breathing and softened her tone. "Please don't sell the boat."

He clearly tempered himself a bit, too. His eyes were a tad bit sad even. "I already done it, Frieda. I'm sure sorry if it don't suit you."

"You can change your mind, can't you?"

"No," he said, and wiped the knife on his overalls. "I gave the man my word."

"Puh-*lease*, Silver!"

He shook his head and kept on shucking clams, but his rhythm was off.

"You didn't even talk to me about it!"

He pointed at her with the knife. "You won't see it this way now, but in time you'll see I'm doing right by you. You ain't never been out there in the world of men. You need some kind of skill for working indoors, and in time you're going to want yourself a husband."

"Obviously you've missed the fact that it's 1921. Everything has changed. We girls can do anything."

"Anything?" Silver squinted up at her. "I don't want you doing *anything*. I want you doing something safe, by God."

Frieda huffed. "I'm as good as any man on our boat. I figure that if you gave it to me, I'd try some new areas for clamming, and I'd find a way to make more money than all the others. I'd stay out from dawn to dusk and save up every cent for Bea's future. She loves school, loves her teachers, each and every one. She wants to be a teacher, don't you know that? And college will take money."

"You ain't never gonna make enough to pay for no college, not as a secretary or by fishing, neither one. Bea'll be better off marrying a good provider."

Rage flaming again, Frieda shouted, "Are you going to pick her husband, too?"

He looked at her keenly. "You might give the man a fighting chance."

"Silver, please don't do this. The boat has been in your family for so many years, in *our* family."

"I'm trying my best to make sure you'll always be alright."

"But you know I can take care of myself."

Silver snorted, briefly seeming to be experiencing an ounce of regret. But his tone never wavered. "I made the decision, and now you just gotta take it like a grown-up."

Frieda knew exactly how the rest of this conversation would play out. She and Silver would argue back and forth, and the one who held the power would win. She'd held the power when it came to graduation. Silver held it with the boat.

She stood in a state of exasperation, heat building inside her head. If she had to stay in his presence a moment longer, she'd explode.

"You've taken everything—everything—from me!" She let out a grunt and kicked an empty bucket, which rattled across the porch, startling some nearby gulls feeding on fish guts by the water, then took heavy steps down the porch stairs and marched away. As she stormed off, she thought hard. She had to come up with a plan. The boat hadn't changed hands yet. What could she bargain with?

Both she and Bea had the last name of Hope, same as their mother's. No one knew who their real fathers were. It didn't matter, because they were Silver's daughters. For him she had put up with the school filled with rich kids who'd sneered at her, as if she were little better than a cast-off rag doll. Not only was she poor, she was the dead whore's daughter, and many mothers didn't want their children to befriend her. Besides, the children were mean, often avoiding her, whispering behind her back, then bursting into sudden laughter over their private jokes. She couldn't make friends with the clammers' kids who had attended school either, for a different reason. Each and every one of them had something that made her think he or she could be related to her or Bea.

Each could be a half sister or half brother. Every dark-haired boy or girl could be one of hers; every blond, one of Bea's. She'd put up with it all for Silver, and now look what he'd done to her. Her escape had always been to the water, and he'd just taken that away from her.

Silver had promised to sell the boat without telling her, and even worse, he was giving up the boat to a man he thought she'd marry just so she could hold some claim to it. Sam Hicks was about twenty-five, and after growing up here he'd served time in the Great War working on engines for the navy. His age meant that he was too young to be Bea's or her father, and she'd known him to be a decent, hardworking sort who stuck mostly to himself. A few times they'd run into each other on the docks, and once he asked her to join him for a soda. She declined because Silver was waiting for her. Another time she caught him following her with his eyes as she helped Silver moor the boat. But she'd always kept her distance from boys, even those in her class. She had never been one to believe in happy endings; that was Bea's territory.

As if she'd conjured her sister's presence by the ferocity of her thoughts, here Bea was, running up behind Frieda.

"Slow down." Bea, now fourteen years old, panted out the words. "Don't go off mad. I can't stand it when you and Silver fight."

Frieda's feet kept hammering the ground, her sister on her heels, and she glanced back to see Bea's face scrunched up in agony. "Then why were you eavesdropping?"

"You were yelling!"

Still storming off, Frieda said over her shoulder, "I can't be around him right now. I swear, I want to shake him."

"It was my idea," Bea blurted out.

Frieda stopped dead in her tracks and slowly turned around. Was this whole day going to be filled with startling and infuriating confessions? "What?"

Bea leaned over her knees, catching her breath. Then she lifted her tormented face to Frieda's glare. "It's true. It makes sense—you and

Hicks with the boat together. So don't blame Silver; I was the first to bring it up. You always blame him . . ."

"And you're always too eager to shoulder the blame! Stop it, will you? I know you didn't come up with this on your own."

Sunlight trembling in Bea's silk-spun hair, she straightened, sucked in a long, tight breath, and focused on Frieda's eyes. "OK, so I might not have come up with it first. But I think it's a great idea."

Frieda harrumphed. "And I like to think for myself!"

"Look, you know me. I like to think of romantic endings."

"Good lord, Bea."

Bea wrung her hands together. "Come back home. Apologize."

When Bea set her clear blue eyes that way, Frieda was normally hard-pressed to refuse her anything. Something as pure and sweet as her sister should never have landed here. Bea was too fragile and sensitive for such a hardscrabble life. Silver had tried to make things as good as he could, but it was up to Frieda to make them better. Without the boat her chances were nil, and the boiling anguish inside her was erupting. "Why don't you do it for me? You apologize so well. Besides, I think he should be apologizing to me! You, too. Why didn't you tell me?"

"His mind is made up. It's obvious he can't keep going out anymore. He's getting tired and old. Have some mercy. Knowing he'd have to sell, he wanted to do it before the boat fell into disrepair, and he chose a good man."

"This is unbelievable. He doesn't want me to *be* a clammer, but it's OK for me to *marry* a clammer?"

Bea looked away, as if a tiny splash of shame had just run through her. She rubbed her temples. "Something like that . . . But Hicks is a veteran and a mechanic, too. He can do other things. He can always make a living."

"So now you're planning my life, too."

Bea let her hands fall to her sides. "I have dreams. I know what I want. I want you to have some plans, too, something to work toward. What, dear sister, do you want, anyway?"

"You know what I wanted! How many times do I have to say that?"

Bea's eyes pleading, she said, "Well, the boat's gone. Find something else to want. Otherwise, you won't have anything to reach for."

Frieda chuffed out a laugh. "Such flowery talk. You have promise, Bea. You have so much to offer the outside world. I'm just a regular girl trying to chip an itty-bitty pebble of my own out of a hard rock situation."

"See? You're flowery, too, only you'd never admit it."

Frieda kicked at the pieces of oyster shell that littered the road. She couldn't hold still another moment. She loved her sister, and Bea needed her. Even small slights hurt Bea deeply, so Frieda normally protected her. But not today. Her feet flying again, she yelled over her shoulder, "Leave me alone, please!"

Bea called from behind her, "Don't be gone long. Silver will worry . . ."

Frieda ran as if she could crush the day's revelations on the shell-strewn street. She ran until her breath was ragged and sweat swam down her spine. Finally walking to calm herself, she strode down the dock, where the sinking sun lit up the distant water with floating topaz twinkles. Clammers still in their bright-yellow oilskins were gathering for talk and drink after a day over the shoals. Some of them spoke to her, but most of them only glanced up, rheumy-eyed and weary, stooped over their catches or their boat engines, and didn't say anything. Some looked her over like hawks eyeing their next meal. She didn't know if they stared the same way at all young women, who were rare on the docks, or if it was because of her mother's legacy. Their stares seemed predatory and leering—the way she imagined one would appraise a whore's daughter who might be forced into the same business someday.

walked past them all, feeling lost, then trudged uphill to the cemetery to sit on her mother's grave. Some people said it was disrespectful to sit on a grave, but that was the only place Frieda could recall anything about her mother. The memory of a five-year-old is blurry, but she could dredge up a few things: her mother teaching her to make sand castles on the beach; being tucked in at night; having a cool, damp cloth placed gently on her forehead when she was sick. She remembered her mother's caring hand and missed it, and yet she never wanted to grow up to be her mother. She had to make sure that never happened to her or Bea.

The warmth of the earth seeped into her bones. Today there was a new bunch of wildflowers on the grave of the long-dead town whore. Frieda figured Silver left them from time to time. She'd seen bunches of flowers laid out here for years. At one point she thought Bea brought the flowers, but Bea denied it.

Picking them up, she curled her legs underneath her on the grave marked with only a once-white wooden cross. These flowers were fresh, and she knew that Silver hadn't been up here today. She lifted the flowers to her nose and took a sniff. Earth and nectar. Not salt and water.

Who else still thought of Della? Had anyone loved Della while she was of this earth? Della Hope: what a heartrending name for someone who'd had such a hopeless life. No one ever mentioned her, as if sad subjects should not be broached. People knew—everyone knew—but it was as if Della Hope had never existed and all that remained was her legacy of two leftover girls. Long ago, kids at school had stopped whispering about Frieda and Bea's origins, and only the occasional kid had the nerve to mention it now, then quickly regretted the impulse. Frieda had made sure of that with her thorny exterior, and Bea had accomplished the same thing with her personality and likeability. The old story had passed its prime, making her mother more dead than ever.

And what of life and love after her death? Had Della risen past clouds and flocks of dewy angels into the open arms of a kind Lord in heaven? These questions never met up with answers. Instead they floated like each of her breaths—then disappeared.

Through a break in the trees, the town, the bay, and the big city beyond spread out like a map. From that vantage point they seemed vast and unknown, and yet in a strange way small, as if in miniature. Just like her own life. At times Frieda felt the massive openness of her still-unfolding life and all its possibilities, and at other times she felt trapped in a muddled cage of smallness and mediocrity. Where was her place now in this world that surrounded her, this bustling scheme of life? Confusion about the future had always haunted her, but the one thing that had felt secure was the boat. That one small possession around which to build her life as an adult. Something to hold on to; it had sustained her and given her refuge and purpose. Out on the water she could forget about her mother's tainted past, the judgment of others, and her isolation. It didn't matter out there; it all drifted away.

She knew that Silver hadn't meant to hurt her. As she gazed out over the bay, the tide ebbing, her rage ebbed somewhat, too. The first time Silver had taken her fishing, she had been but a little thing, and somehow she got a fishhook caught in her hair. It had panicked her; it was as if that tiny hook and some fishing line could tie her up and trap her forever. Silver stopped what he was doing while the boat rolled on the swells, and he worked that hook out ever so gently. Frieda remembered his calming voice, his easy but sure touch, and his patience while she fidgeted and gulped in big breaths of air. How he had soothed her, talking to her in his low rumble; how his solid presence reassured that he would always take care of her.

So yes, Silver meant no harm; she knew that in his mind he was settling her down, but he had no idea how much his decision had unmoored her.

When she made her way back toward the waterside, the dying daylight sparkled on scales and tiny shells caught in fishing nets draped over skiffs for drying, but the approaching night already seemed the darkest in the world.

Silver had made his living on the water; he should've known. He should've understood that the sea had a way of evening out her rough edges and reviving her hopes and dreams. Now her sorrow was as big as this bay. And in her mind's eye she saw pockets turned inside out and empty piggy banks. How was she going to make money? What was she going to do with her life?

Sam Hicks was already at the house. He lounged on the porch alone, sipping on iced tea out of a chipped mug, and papers sat on the rough little table between the two chairs. Frieda strode up the porch steps, and he stood to greet her.

As she glanced at the papers, her heart fell into her gut. Silver had already signed the papers to sell Hicks the boat. Her boat. Nothing she'd said had made a bit of difference. Her defiance came seething back. Defiance was an old comrade that had kept her company for many years.

"Evening, Miss Frieda," Hicks said with a smile.

Well, well . . . He looked as though he'd dressed up for the occasion. Instead of clamming overalls or rubber boots, he wore a pair of nice pleated slacks and a freshly ironed shirt, cuffs rolled up to his elbows. Hicks was a large man with a roundish face that made him appear little older than a teenager. He was attractive in a burly, boyish way, like someone who had grown into a man nestled away in some sleepy farm town and not in the grip of a bloodbath war. Though with clean-shaven skin and not a pockmark in evidence, he still had a bit of the soldier about him. He had combed his unremarkable brown hair away from his face with oil so it lay back in wide threads. She'd never seen him in anything other than work clothes before, but it made no difference. Everyone who lived down here lay bare. They could cover themselves in different cloth, but the fiber beneath remained the same. It was pointless to try to appear anything but salt and sea stained. She rather liked herself that way.

She was not about to feign politeness. "What's the occasion?" she asked.

He smiled. Only a few little lines on his forehead and tiny etched curves in his cheeks were evident. He hadn't been out on the water long enough to show it yet, and if she didn't resent him so much for buying her boat she might have thought him comely.

"I just bought myself a boat today." He actually looked pleased with himself. Obviously Silver had not shared her feelings about the sale with this man.

She chuffed out, "So I heard."

She walked straight through the door into the house and let the screen door slam behind her. No matter how much they aired out the place in the summer, the small rooms held the smell of salt, damp wood, fried food, and smoke from the stove. Bea was helping Silver in the kitchen.

"Where you been?" Silver barked. "We could've used some assistance around here."

Frieda stopped for a moment and watched Bea—pretty, sweet Bea, helping as always. Cutting up cooked potato, stirring a pot on the stove while Silver set the table. Bea was wearing the new sundress Silver had bought her for summer, because Bea always did as she was told. If Silver wanted Bea to wear a dress, she wore it. If Silver wanted Bea to do tricks, she would do them.

Frieda did her best to shake off her anger. There wasn't an unkind thought or mean deed inside Bea. She was fresh, like a daisy, and she carried her sweet disposition like a bouquet of sunlight. Even teachers and church ladies called her an angel. Frieda truly loved her sister. Other than Silver, her sister was all she had.

Frieda shrugged. "It's not my party."

Bea interjected. "But it is. It's for your graduation day."

Silver said, "You go on and get yourself changed, will you? Dinner's almost ready."

"Let me guess: clams."

Silver winked. "My special chowder. Coney-Island style."

Bea glanced at Silver and then at Frieda. "You could try the dress, Frieda. I bet it looks good on you."

Frieda strode away and entered the bedroom she'd shared with Bea ever since their mother had died. All those years back Silver had given up his room to the girls, and since then he'd slept on the divan in the living room or on the porch in the summer. For thirteen years now she and Bea had slept in the same bed, huddled together during winter nights after the fire in the woodstove had gone out, talking and giggling until one of them fell asleep. Throughout all the years she and Bea shared secrets, Frieda had never told Silver about the stray cats Bea fed or the time she and Bea had nearly drowned, floating away on a riptide before they fought their way back.

A window faced the porch, and Frieda took a peek beyond the tattered curtains, where she could see Hicks standing tall, holding his mug and staring off into the oncoming night. Beyond him lights were twinkling across the bay and down by the docks. The full moon was rising, shooting out silver rays across the rippling waters. Taking a sip of lemonade, he then set the glass down. He seemed deep in thought, probably lost in dreams that contained a white picket fence or a bedroom with windows that overlooked the bay.

Hicks wasn't a bad man as far as she could tell. But now that he'd ruined her plans, how was she going to find a way to make things better? Silver had been making less and less money, because he could no longer stay out on the boat all day. The house needed a new roof, and the foundation was beginning to shift. They bought only the cheapest food at the grocer's and ate clams or fish most every night. Beef and pork were luxuries, along with butter and sweets of any sort. Silver had had no business splurging on the dresses.

And what of Bea? She took to books, not the sea. She got seasick on the water, and her skin burned like parchment in the sun. She believed in castles in the sky; she dreamed of things way beyond her reach. She loved literature, poetry, art, and fashion. She could barely do ordinary chores. Her hands broke out in a rash from doing the laundry. Dust made her cough and sneeze. When she tried to cook, she usually burned the food. And she came down with bad colds and sore throats every winter. She would never survive having baby after baby in some clammer's shack. The reality of a life like that would probably kill her.

Frieda turned around and touched the dress hanging on the wall. Silver had bought it in one of the dress shops that resold clothes donated by the summer crowds. But still, he'd paid too much, and it wasn't even the new drop-waist style she'd seen the fancy women wearing lately. Instead it was made of cotton in a small flowery print, fitted at the waist with a cloth-covered belt. What had he been thinking?

Frieda took it down and slipped into the thing—for Bea, not for Silver. She could've worn her school oxfords with a pair of clean socks, but instead she stuck her feet into Silver's old rubber sea boots, which she wore when he let her go out on the boat with him. She pulled the stained straw hat that she sported on the same occasions down low on her head.

When she walked into the living room, Silver, Bea, and Hicks were seated at the table, waiting for her. She stomped in and plunked herself down in the only empty chair. Silver looked up, and she could tell he appreciated her giving in about the dress and also disapproved of her ruining the effect with the boots and hat. Silver and Bea took what appeared to be a knowing glance at one another, while Bea fidgeted with her napkin, but Hicks simply sat back and laughed aloud.

"Well, well," said Silver as he likewise leaned back in the chair. "There's a girl in there after all."

Frieda grabbed her napkin, shook it open, and plopped it in her lap. "Do we have bread?"

"Right here," Bea answered, passing the bread basket. In the center of the table sat the pot of steaming clam chowder, and Frieda reached for the ladle.

"You still look lovely, even with the unusual accessories," Hicks said, his eyes all misty and annoying.

She didn't respond. Bea started urging a pleasant conversation that wasn't going to happen, Silver stared down into his chowder and ate slowly, as if he wanted to draw out the evening, and Hicks was clearly trying his best to charm her. He glanced from time to time at his food, but mostly he kept his focus on her. There was something strange in his eyes when he gazed at her, some kind of softness, but it was a highly focused sort of softness. She'd never seen this look before from anyone, and she had no idea what it meant.

He said, "Congratulations on graduating from high school."

Frieda nodded, then averted her gaze. He kept staring; she could feel the weight of it on her skin, and she wanted to shrug it away.

Hicks said, "You gotta be smart to finish."

After chomping on bread, Frieda dug into the chowder. "I barely passed." That wasn't exactly true, but she wanted Hicks to believe it. Studying and reading had been a refuge of sorts, plus it turned out she was as good a student as any. It showed she was no slacker. Her grades fell because she wouldn't participate in group assignments or stand in front of the class and read an essay. Beyond high school few opportunities awaited working-class women in Highlands. Unless one found a way to go to college, it was either a poorly paying job cooking and cleaning, or marriage and babies.

He smiled. "Still, it's an accomplishment."

She glanced over at him and registered the admiration in his eyes. Maybe what she was seeing was puppy love. But if he had a crush on her, why hadn't he approached her before? Why make some deal with Silver? His apparent actions seemed archaic and made him out to be spineless.

"I brought you something," Hicks said, and then shifted awkwardly, as if he was unsure whether to get it now or not.

Frieda glared hard.

He fidgeted, then stood up clumsily and pulled out a small box from his pants pocket. He sat again and pushed the box toward Frieda. Curious, she opened it to find an almost-round, blackened . . . something.

"It's an old coin—from a shipwreck, I'm pretty sure. I found it a year ago when I was clamming. I raked it up and kept it for a special occasion."

Picking up the coin, Frieda examined it closer. On it were some odd markings that indeed looked very old.

Hicks said, "I never took it to a museum or an expert to find out if it's valuable."

Bea chimed in, "I can ask my teacher."

Frieda rubbed the coin between her thumb and index finger.

"I cleaned it up as best I could, but I didn't want to damage it. I've heard you can do more harm than good if you don't know what you're doing," said Hicks, a hopeful expression on his face. "It could be worth something."

He seemed to be waiting for her approval. Funny thing was, Frieda did like the gift. But she wasn't about to show it. "If it's worth something, I can't accept it. If it turns out to be a trinket, then . . . thank you."

An awkward silence hung in the muggy air after that. Bea did her best to fill it, bringing up the graduation ceremony Frieda had shunned, what all the kids from her class were doing over the summer, and finally, the weather. But the conversation inevitably led back to the boat, with Hicks and Silver discussing the *Wren*'s quirks and charms, the work that needed done, and Hicks's plans for her.

Frieda could not endure that conversation. Why didn't Silver and Hicks just go join the drunks down at the speakeasy so she didn't have to hear this? She despised both of them in that moment. She imagined grabbing each of them by the head and knocking their noggins together. She wiped the chowder bowl clean with a piece of bread, stuffed it in her mouth, and left the table without a word.

CHAPTER THREE

On Monday morning Bea awakened early as usual. Rolling over to the sounds of Bea moving about the room, Frieda creaked open her eyes. Bea, donned in one of her two school dresses, was packing textbooks, pencils, and composition books into her satchel.

"What are you doing?" Frieda asked.

Bea turned around and set that clear-blue gaze on her sister. "I'm meeting with my study group."

Frieda sat up and rubbed fists into her eyes. "Funny. I thought school was out."

"Of course it is," Bea said. "But I've made plans with some friends of mine to meet three times a week to read and keep up our study habits over the summer."

Falling back on the bed, Frieda said, "Such devotion . . ."

Bea aimed for the door. "See you later."

Frieda quickly sat up and pushed back the covers. "Wait! I'll help you find something to take for lunch. Give me a minute."

"Please. I can take care of myself. Besides, Charlotte Larson's mother is making us sandwiches. Lindsay Cooper is bringing cookies.

Hazel Rogers and John LeRoy are coming, too." She paused. "I have no idea what they're bringing." Bea shrugged. "Guess it doesn't matter. We'll have plenty to eat."

After swinging her feet to the floor, Frieda raked her fingers through her hanging snarls of hair. "You shouldn't show up empty-handed." Bea was studious and smart, but not practical. It worried Frieda.

Bea passed a hand through the air as she opened the bedroom door. "Don't be silly. These are my friends."

A few minutes later the front door whisked open and the screen door whacked shut.

Frieda plopped back down. She stared at the cracked ceiling, where water stains blossomed like clouds. Could those clouds rain some kindness on her today? Please? Could some answers please come popping out of those cracks?

Nothing. Just bleakness.

After Frieda got up, she dressed and went to look for Silver. Normally he'd be up before dawn and out over the shoals by sunrise on his boat. But with the *Wren* in Hicks's hands, what would he be doing now?

In the kitchen she found him filling his Thermos with black coffee.

"Where are you going?" she asked.

He smiled and scratched his thatch of hair. "Well, hello to you, too. Good morning, Frieda."

"Good morning," she forced.

He slipped a sweater over his head, but it took him longer than usual. Frieda could see that his shoulders were bothering him. She did worry about his health, his strength, but he'd always seemed so rugged and capable to her, despite his age. Maybe she should've offered to rub some salve into his sore shoulders, but that kindness sat just an inch or so beyond her reach today. She sighed. "So where are you heading?"

"You probably don't want to know."

"Since we don't own a boat any longer, I thought you were going to take it easy."

"I'm aiming to help Hicks with some repairs on the *Wren*. Want to join us?"

Frieda rolled her eyes. "No, thanks. Why would you work on a boat you no longer own? It makes no sense."

Silver sighed. "It's called being helpful. Friendly-like. You know . . ."

"No. I don't know."

"Right," he said, and headed for the door. "You enjoy yourself, ye hear?"

Frieda crossed her arms and turned away as he, too, left the house. Then she was alone.

She made herself a mug of coffee with a little milk and sugar. She straightened up the place, then cooked herself an egg and buttered a piece of bread. Sitting on the porch in Silver's chair, she watched the sun rise high into the sky until it threatened to burn her eyes. A yellow butterfly landed on the porch rail. Birds flitted over the street in front of her, sails in the bay filled taut in the blows, gulls cried, and rigging chimed against masts down at the dock. She made herself some lunch, although she was hardly hungry.

A walk—she would take a walk. She went down to the small sand beach, where little waves broke and left lacy foam on the sand. Dainty sandpipers stepped in and around the froth like long-legged dancers. Smells of fish and salt drifted in the air. A group of summer tourists in their bathing dresses and bonnets were gathering up their things, probably to go back to their hotel for lunch. They glanced at her, studied her men's clothing and wild hair just long enough not to be considered downright rude, and then looked away.

She trudged down the shoreline, her bare feet sinking into the dense wet sand, surprised there was any weight left to her at all. A deadened, empty feeling consumed her. She was nothing more than the heat and the will of a man whose stubbornness was even greater than her own. She looked out over the water. Silhouettes of fishing and clamming boats puckered the flat horizon, ridges of black against the sunny air. Her feet landed even heavier against the sand, and her throat clogged with grief. The now-impossible opportunity beat through her body. Today on the water she could've escaped the town that looked down on her. Today she could've shown them all she was good enough to compete with all the men. Maybe she would've discovered a new shoal for clamming. Maybe she would've come back with more of a haul than even the seasoned clammers had. Or today she could've set her sights on fishing and pulled in more silvery sea life than any other fisherman. Today she could've done what she was meant to do.

She walked the beach for a while back and forth, then came home and sat through the long slog of the afternoon, listless as hell. There was a heaviness in the air, and everything made her think of what was out there in the water. She blew on her coffee and saw ripples on the sea. Laundry on a nearby clothesline flapped like white sails. Birds chirping were the cries of dolphins. She was supposed to be on the sea, where the terrestrial world could close her behind a curtain of water.

What, indeed, was she going to do now?

Two weeks later, nearing sunset, she headed out to find Hicks down at the slip for the *Wren*. She couldn't take the boredom any longer, and she'd conjured up a new plan out of idleness and desperation. She felt oddly buoyant, a purpose lifting her and keeping her afloat. On the way down the docks, she passed by the row of dilapidated storefronts that lined the waterfront and gazed up briefly at the room where she had been born and had lived with her mother. In the past Silver had always been with her, but now, alone, passing by that awful place brought on an old empty ache and mixed emotions. Sadness about her mother and also disbelief that she had let herself fall so far. How could she have chosen prostitution?

Some men stood outside one of the bars, supposedly shut down by Prohibition but still operating anyway, and they stopped to watch her pass. Disgusted, she hated the way men roved their eyes over her and probably any other woman who would venture down here alone, but she said nothing and even managed a tight smile. The door to the bar was open in the hope of a breeze, and inside the smoky darkness fishermen sat at stools, hunched over their liquor. She would have to start getting on their right side as soon as she could. Her plan depended on her ability to hide what she felt about these men. She could've fished and clammed with the best of them. She could've focused all her restless energy on working more hours than any of them did, going out in harsher conditions, finding secret harvesting and fishing spots no one else had discovered.

And then there was the hidden hope she told no one about, not even Bea—that maybe someday there would be a man who understood her, who allowed her to be untamed, who understood her love of the sea, and who might love her despite her freewheeling ways. Someday, some way . . . Torn by conflicted inner sides of herself—one that felt she could never settle down and become a man's wife, and one that secretly dreamed of romance. But who would want a woman who wanted to work like a man, who probably could never hold her tongue, and who couldn't pretend to be something she wasn't? That little flutter of longing remained, however, baffling her.

She stepped into the sunlight and continued down the docks, passing by the small, shallow-drafted skiffs and dories of the local fishermen. She smiled at a group of men working on a boat and even asked about their children and wives. Most responded softly, curiously, as if surprised by her sudden sociability but welcoming it, too.

But Hawkeye, her sworn enemy, just stared. Most of the men who'd come to her mother had become nothing but blurred faces in her mind, but not Hawkeye; she remembered him. He'd come often enough to recall. She remembered his face as he leered at her mother, how he'd had the nerve to sit down at their tiny table and share their food. He'd made himself at home, pulled her mother into the bedroom; then after he'd had his fill he'd slipped away. He had always looked both ways before he passed out of their door, slinking off like a snake. A married man. Obviously guilty over what he had been doing. Frieda knew that her mother had been his weakness but also his shame. He'd not lifted a finger to help once her mother started lapsing. Frieda would have to make herself tolerate the others, but not that one.

Still glaring, Hawkeye stopped what he was doing and wiped his fish-slimy hands on his overalls. As she strode down the pier away from him, he called, "Why you being so nice? What's got into you, girl?"

She kept walking. For some reason Hawkeye was always nosing into her business, watching her, waiting, as if hoping to find some reason to criticize.

"What are you up to?" he bellowed.

Frieda ignored him.

"Cain't be good, girl. I know that. Cain't be good."

She mumbled to herself, "None of your business."

"Seems like you might need us now that Silver's done given up his boat."

That old bastard, how dare he speak to her? How dare he pry? She tossed back over her shoulder, "Don't *need* anyone, just want something."

Hawkeye called out, "As I guessed, Frieda. As I guessed."

Frieda walked up to the *Wren*. Hicks had put a fresh coat of white paint on the hull above the waterline, painted the deck rails blue, and had outfitted the boat with a bigger, rebuilt engine. Although she was handmade, she had always been one of the better and larger clamming boats in the harbor. As Frieda had heard retold many a time, Silver and his father had built her themselves plank by plank with heavy mahogany and good ballast, and they'd bought the motor from Sea Bright Dory Works in Long Branch.

Hicks had just pulled in for the day with a haul of clams. It was true summer now; June had ushered in sun-drenched skies, and today there was barely a breeze. Hicks was dripping sweat as he moored the boat to the pier. He looked up at her, and she registered the surprise in his eyes.

She'd been forcing herself to watch him since the day he'd bought the boat. She'd tracked him as he headed out each morning to clam and looked for him when he came in. His course took him past the house and out into the bay. The first time she saw him she watched until he had disappeared into the glare of dawn over the bay, and she felt sick. And yet a form of self-torture, a desire to feel the pain, drove her to look for him each day. She noticed that Hicks knew how to handle the boat and that he worked hard, long hours. Still, she'd have to shoulder past the fact that he had her boat. The way forward had once seemed simple, but now she needed help.

Surely Hicks knew by now she wasn't interested in whatever plans he'd made with Silver, in that pitiful attempt at starting a romance. And yet he seemed aware of his appearance now, brushing away the sweat beads from his forehead and pushing back his hair. He seemed as if he was anticipating something sweet and good. As if he was actually happy to see her.

Brutal regret hit her. The way she had treated him the night of her graduation dinner. She had stomped off like a child and had also stomped on at least part of his dreams. Apparently he wasn't holding it against her. Frieda had a hard time understanding people who were that kind and forgiving. Her behavior had gone beyond rude; even when he'd brought her a gift she'd been awful. She'd taken out her rage toward Silver on Hicks; she shouldn't have reacted to him that way. It really wasn't Hicks's fault. He'd made a good deal, plain and simple. The idea that he might have gotten her as part of the deal was more pathetic than anything else.

He gave a nod. "Frieda."

She went very still. She watched him as he secured the boat, gathered up his catch, and leapt off the boat onto the pier. Surprisingly agile for a big man. Finally she said, "You need any help?"

"You wait here. Need to get this sold while it's fresh."

Sitting on the edge of the pier, she let her legs dangle close to the water's surface. She could've waited on the boat but chose not to. She knew every nick in the rails, every quirk in the way the boat handled, and she had known every sound that came from the old engine. But Hicks was already changing the *Wren*. New paint, new engine. No longer hers and never would be. Sitting close to the boat brought it all back. She'd always felt that boats had a personality and a will of their own, that somehow they forged their own ways. So why hadn't the *Wren* rebelled? Refused to run or run aground?

The tide was coming in, heavy and dark. The sun was sinking, showing only a few inches above the hills behind her, its rays sending out golden pearls all the way across the bay. She waited while the sun dragged the shadows of the piers and masts long across the water, and the sky turned salmon pink, with dark streaks of clouds skimming across it.

Hicks came back and sat down beside her without saying a word. He let his legs dangle over the water, too, and with the rising tide and his longer legs, soon his rubber boots skimmed the surface. He reached down to touch the water he'd worked over all day long, draping his fingers through it. Still not tired of it, it seemed. There was a naturalness about this moment of quiet. If Silver hadn't been so conniving, she might have found a kindred spirit in Hicks. But she couldn't admit to Silver or herself that his idea had some merit.

He sighed and snuck a few furtive glances her way. She waited for him to speak, and she knew that eventually he would. He still admired her in some strange way; that was evident, although she wished it wasn't. The way he held himself so upright made it clear that he was still hoping for something, and the way his hands and fingers had moved while he'd moored the boat made it obvious that he wished he was touching something softer. *Stroking* something softer. Glimmers of longing swam in his eyes. It was as if a storm were brewing inside Hicks, and yet the storm did not feel dangerous to her, only to him. She had an awful feeling that it would be his undoing.

He asked, "What you been up to?"

She shrugged. She'd been hunting for shells to sell to the gift shops by day and roaming around like a lost soul by the light of the moon. One night she'd built a sand castle at the water's edge and then watched as the tide came in and washed it away. She took midnight swims and then sat facing the stars, trying to figure out her future.

She felt exposed and weak, as though her as-yet-unspoken plea was already sitting out in the harsh open. She hated to ask anyone for help. Anyone. And now she had to ask the man who'd taken her boat. Hicks's face was full of shades of light, and she could not look into his longing eyes.

Finally she answered, "Trying to figure out some things."

He glanced her way. "Anything I can help you with?"

She stared down at her hands, the way they curled into her lap. Drawing them into fists, she turned to look at him. The idea had been forming over the past two weeks, but she had not yet committed it to words. "I want you to teach me about boat engines."

He gazed at her with an eager but baffled expression. "Boat engines?"

She pulled in a deep breath. "Why, when you were making a good living working on engines, did you have to go and buy Silver's boat?"

She clamped her mouth shut. She had to get the irritable edge out of her voice. Desperation had made her shrill.

He seemed to ponder her question. "I don't want to work on other people's boats my whole life. I want to work on my own. I want to have my own. I'd rather be on the water than on the docks all day long."

She could've said she'd wished for the same thing, but that he and Silver had squashed her plans. Truth was Silver would've found someone to buy the boat no matter what, though. Once he'd set his mind to something, there was no changing it.

Hicks said, "I'm still going to work on engines, too. Especially in the winter."

A gust of sudden wind leaned all the sailboat masts in the same direction. "That's what I wanted to talk to you about," she said, her mouth dry.

Slowly he said, "OK."

Swallowing, she held up her chin. "I want to learn how to work on all these boats. I want to become the best mechanic out here, second only to you." Frieda admired her idea more and more every day since it had first sparked to mind. She'd always been manually inclined, she liked to figure out how things fit together and functioned, and working on boats would keep her down on the docks. She could make money within reach of the waters.

"Why do you want to work on engines?"

"They're *boat* engines. And I love boats. It's a good skill to have, plus it'll keep me down here near the water, where I belong. I've always liked to figure out how things work, especially powerful things. Why not boat engines?"

Hicks rubbed his chin, his day-old stubble beginning to show. "I don't know how the men out here would take to a lady mechanic."

"If I know what I'm doing, they won't care if I'm a monkey."

He smiled. He had the smile of someone who didn't take anything people said to him too seriously, as if life and everything he expected from it were close to cheerful.

Frieda found it frustrating. "You got my boat. The way I see it, you owe me something in return."

"I bought the boat fair and square."

"Let's not get into what else you thought you were buying."

Hicks looked down, and she could swear he was blushing. Good. He *should* feel ashamed about that part of the deal. She was not and had never been for sale. Even the idea of that made her cringe, because her mother *had* sold herself. Oh, to have been a fly on the wall and listened to the conversation between Hicks and Silver. Based on the kind of men they were, Frieda figured that the arrangement had probably never been said aloud, only inferred, and yet fully understood.

Hicks composed himself a moment later and asked, "What do you want me to do?"

Frieda's hands clenched. "Give me your knowledge, give me lessons. Let me be your apprentice."

He waited a few moments, as if letting the idea roll around inside his head. "You'd be working with all these watermen down here. I didn't think you cared for them."

Truth was she sometimes worried each one around or over the age of forty could be her father or Bea's, but she always brushed those thoughts aside. She didn't want to know. "I don't like them. But I'll deal with it. I'll take their money for honest work."

"It's dirty work," Hicks said.

She laughed. Everything down here could be considered dirty work, and yet she loved it. Even the smell of dead fish, the heat in summer, the freezes in winter, the shabby old boats. The place had character. Where else did she belong? She had not liked school, had never enjoyed church, and couldn't stand the smell of indoor establishments. She hated to cook and clean. A secretary? What had Silver been thinking? She would have had to kowtow to male bosses, put up with flirtations from men and gossip from women, all the while confined in a small office space. Never in a million years. Nothing but an unconventional occupation would do.

He sighed again. "I have a fair number of old motors we can take apart and put back together. That's how they taught us in the navy. It takes a long time to learn what you need to know and lots of practice. I'll have to help you with your jobs for a while."

"That's what I want. That's why I'm asking."

"If you're sure . . ."

She stuck out her hand. "Deal."

Hicks took her hand slowly, holding on to it for a moment longer than necessary. "Deal."

She had to look away, staring out at the horizon at a stream of boats going out. She'd been seeing them for weeks now, boats that headed out at dusk. They made course out beyond the Hook and the bay to deep water. First a few and now more, going out most every night, especially on no-moon nights.

She gestured at them. "What are they doing?"

He followed her gaze. "Heading out to the rum boats."

She shook her head once.

"Don't you wonder how the liquor gets into bars here—and everywhere else for that matter?"

Truth was that Silver wasn't much of a drinker, and he had never once taken the girls into a bar. "I haven't thought about it."

Hicks gestured out to sea. "About five or so miles to sea are boats from Canada full of crates of whiskey and all sorts of spirits. They call it Rum Row. Some of the men around here have been going out at night, picking up liquor, and bringing it back to sell for big money. They serve as go-betweens between the large rum boats and the buyers, so people call them contact boats."

"What about the law? The coast guard?" Just across the water, Sandy Hook peninsula jutted out as a barrier between the Highlands harbor and the open sea, and a coast guard station watched over the waters right there.

"What about them?" Hicks said. "There's a lot more fishing boats than guard boats to chase them. And if a man finds himself under chase, he can hide in some secret inlet he knows is too shallow for the guard boats. Or if he's caught outright, he can throw the liquor overboard and get rid of the evidence. Sometimes he comes back the next day and gets the booze, but even if he loses one night's load he makes up for it soon enough."

"You make it sound easy."

He shook his head. "Those littler boats take all the risks. The big rum boats sail under foreign flags and hold out far enough that they can't be confiscated. Contact boatmen face all sorts of possible dangers: rough seas, engine failure, capture on the way in, and maybe even prison. Even if they dump their loads, they can still get fined for running without lights or refusing to halt on command. Fine's a thousand dollars." Hicks sat still. "But then a thousand dollars ain't much when you consider what they're making."

"How much is that?"

"I hear . . . even the smallest boats are starting to make about four hundred to a thousand dollars a night. Depends on how much they can carry."

Frieda shifted her weight as the meaning of all this sunk in. This explained the changes she had witnessed but not questioned, even though she'd been curious to know. A few people who normally had nothing had been buying used Model Ts—even a new one here and there—nice coats and dresses, and had painted their houses. Now she understood where that extra dough had come from. She took a good look at Hicks. "What about you?"

He picked up a piece of clamshell littering the pier and tossed it out to sea. "Not for me. I'll stick to what's legal."

She watched the boats heading into the fading daylight, and God help her, a burn, a strange excitement bloomed inside her chest. Those boats were going out after a different kind of catch. They were shredding through these seas for a new purpose and new riches. It took them out on the ocean, way out, much farther than she'd ever been before. She'd never been beyond sight of land. What would it feel like to look in all directions and see nothing but a watery world? Stars stretching from one horizon to the other? She closed her eyes and imagined it.

Her heart banged hard, her breath drew short, and she opened her eyes. Going against the liquor law was kind of exciting, too. Everyone hated this stupid new amendment. It hadn't changed anything; in fact, people seemed to be drinking more than before. The law had made it exciting, rebellious, and more alluring than ever to get drunk. And the money!

But it felt as distant as the dance clubs in New York City she'd heard about, the fancy verandas on the hill houses, and the hotel rooms with clean, white, scented towels. She had no way to join in. Even with the wakes of those contact boats making silvery ripples that rolled to the water below her and the new knowledge that the big rum boats were out there beyond the three-mile limit of United States jurisdiction, dancing around on the water like lures, she never guessed that it would have anything to do with her.

CHAPTER FOUR

1923

Over the next two years timing and Lady Luck were on Frieda's side. Highlands was the closest New Jersey town to Rum Row, and more and bigger boats with faster, powerful engines were harboring in Highlands and making night runs to buy booze and bring it back to sell both locally and in the city. Those men needed engines they could count on, engines that wouldn't fail them when chased by the guard.

Frieda had been a dedicated student of Hicks's and had become the trusted mechanic to many of the men who ran against the law. She could keep the old boat engines in top shape, as well as the war surplus airplane engines that many of the lobstermen had refitted for their boats for extra speed. She had been hired to work on a new Liberty, still in a crate; a fisherman had bought it for a hundred dollars from the government, and she had converted it to marine use.

In addition, new boats, built strictly as shore boats, were being launched every day, most of them flat thirty-footers with fast Sterling or Liberty engines. All the engines needed alterations to get more speed, and Frieda had a knack for making adjustments that could coax out more power. She was as highly skilled as the men doing the very same thing, and yet her customers paid her less simply because she was female. She'd had to accept that, even though it struck her as vastly unfair. Plus some of the fishermen's wives didn't want her working around their husbands. She had built a decent business since going out on her own, but she still needed more work. She had competition from another new mechanic. Despite fishing full-time, Hicks was still trying to help her. Some fishermen continued to seek his advice about their boats, and often he gave them her name. Every day she went to Bahrs Landing, which sat by the water and had become a base of operations, and she scoured for business.

Inside the restaurant well-dressed buyers from the city waited around one or more of the iron stoves for warmth, chatting, playing poker, or reading the newspaper until they received a signal that the boats were coming in. But it was the local men who made the dangerous sea runs—good seamen, lobstermen, and clammers who apparently didn't see anything wrong with breaking a law that was mostly unpopular, largely ignored, and brought in more money than they'd ever seen before.

She was pleased by her work and status as a boat mechanic, but that old longing for the sea had never left her. She knew that someday, some way, she would find a way out there. An opportunity would present itself, and she would know it when it came.

I will watch and wait. I will be ready.

A windy winter morning. Frieda packed a school lunch for Bea and tended to Silver, who'd been down with a cold. Wrapped in blankets, he sat on the divan and blew his nose into an old handkerchief. "Got work for today?" he said as he folded the handkerchief and set it in his lap.

She turned and studied him. His face was grayish, his nose red and raw, and his eyes rheumy and tired. "Not yet. Have to go see if I can rustle up a job."

"Winter's tough on the boats. Ought to be some fishermen needing repairs."

"Yep," she said.

"Yep," Silver replied, then adjusted his position on the couch and suffered through a coughing spell.

Concerned, Frieda filled the Thermos that Silver always used and brought it to him. "I might not be gone long. I'll come back and check on you, even if I land something."

"I'm OK," he said croakingly.

Frieda stood still.

Silver gazed up at her through bloodshot eyes, as if some new knowledge had just come to him; as if something had shifted. His voice soft now, he said, "Did I tell you I'm proud of you?"

She gazed down. They weren't the sort of family to heap praise on each other. Many things were known but not said.

"I hear tell you're the best mechanic out there these days."

Frieda shrugged as if it meant nothing. Only it meant a lot.

"I'm proud of you, what you've made of yourself."

Frieda studied her boots and finally whispered, "Thank you," before leaving.

Dockside, she asked around, but no one needed any repairs or maintenance that day. Bad weather was slowing things down. The winter had been brutal so far, and many of the smaller shore boats had been unable to go out. It was as if the weather itself knew strange business was stirring.

She spoke to all the locals, with the exception of Hawkeye. She'd been able to avoid talking to him for two years now, because he didn't own a boat any longer. Lost it somehow, and so he worked as relief man for the other dockmaster, something he had done before, and he crewed on other fishermen's boats. But his demeaning interest in her and in everything she was doing had not waned. Often he followed her around with his piercing eye, as if he were judge and jury presiding over her life. She'd heard from some of her customers that he'd asked how well she was working out as a mechanic. The nerve! His nickname was perfect; he was like a circling hawk, waiting to attack.

At Bahrs she sat on a stool, ordered Florence Bahrs's clam chowder, and then looked around. The tables were covered with sheet metal, and there were no tablecloths, menus, or napkins. But some of the clammers' wives sported new fur coats against the cold of winter and wore diamond rings on their weathered fingers.

When Hicks came in, he took a seat beside her. Dressed in his fisherman's coveralls, a woolen jacket and muffs on his ears, he brought with him the briny smell of the sea mixed with the scent of sweat seeping through wool. He took off the muffs and set them on the table.

Improbably, Frieda had come to like Hicks. They'd grown close over the past two years, like siblings or best friends in her view. But she had the uneasy feeling that he still had a crush on her. It came during awkward silences, when their hands accidentally brushed against each other, and when he did things like drape his coat over her shoulders when a cold wind began to blow. Sometimes she glanced up and saw that old longing in his eyes, and it made her both sad and a bit scared for him. But she pushed her concerns aside. They had so much to do, and when they worked together, which was rare now, they often found they were thinking the same things. They finished each other's sentences. Being around him made her feel warm, as if a coal lay in her core. During a few peculiar moments Frieda had felt a momentary burn, as if the coal could spark to flame, but the sensation slipped away as fast as it had come. She wondered if she was now immune to the lure of love. Her girlhood fantasies about romance had faded away over two years of grueling work. There was no room for daydreams when her mind was filled with everything about engines and building her business. Even as girls from her high school were marrying and having babies, she let her starry-eyed imaginings slide away and concentrated on learning her craft. Her focus had been on gleaning everything she could from Hicks, working beside him, and nothing else.

"You're in early," she said.

He tore off some ragged gloves. "Too rough out there in the bay. I've been fishing flounder and fluke in the river. Not much biting."

She shoved her chowder in front of him. "It's still hot."

Picking up a spoon, he stared into the steaming chowder and then at her. "What's wrong? Why aren't you eating?"

She gazed around and then gathered her sweater across her chest. She cocked her head in the direction of Hawkeye, wearing a water-stained jacket and moth-eaten woolen cap and having sat down at a table nearby. She said, "I lost my appetite."

Hicks looked over at Hawkeye. "Never understood what you have against him."

"You don't need to understand."

His eyes swam with a stricken look. Here it was again—another instance of him revealing his feelings for her. No! She could so easily hurt him. Damned if he didn't still care in the wrong way. She had to be careful and tread lightly. She wished there was a kind way to flush his attachment to her out of his system. Quickly she said, "I'm sorry. That didn't come out right. I only meant that it's personal. Between him and me. I'm not much for talking about it."

Hicks shrugged, then slurped down the chowder, and Florence Bahrs came by to ask if Hicks wanted more. He shook his head, and Florence left them alone. She was the maternal type, with a smile that warmed a round and fleshy face. She wore old-fashioned blouses and skirts, always covered by an apron, and her hair piled high on her head. An excellent cook, she fed the waterfront. Her husband, John, had bought the two-story boathouse and built bunks, filled the mattresses with straw and cornstalks, and made a living renting boats and selling bait, beds, and meals.

Hicks asked Frieda, "What else is wrong?"

"What makes you think something else is wrong?"

"I can tell when you're thinking hard on a matter. You start grinding your teeth."

She kept her eyes averted. "Do not." Then she smiled.

Their gazes met and held. Frieda had to look away.

"So, come clean. Out with it."

She sighed and breathed in, then slowly exhaled. "I've been thinking. Come better weather we should go for the liquor, too."

"Oh no you don't."

"I could work for you on the boat. We could do it together."

Hicks wiped his mouth on his sleeve and shook his head firmly. "It's not for me."

Leaning forward, she inched closer, not bothering to lower her voice. Everyone knew about the business being conducted here. There was no need for secrecy. "Everybody's doing it."

Hicks scraped the last of the chowder from the bottom of the bowl. "Not interested. And even if I was, the *Wren* ain't big enough to bring back a large load."

"It could bring enough."

He sat back. "Enough for what?"

She didn't answer. She thought it was obvious.

"What do you need that you don't have?"

"I have responsibilities. Bea's in high school now, and she's going to graduate in another couple of years. I want to send her to a real college, in the city. She's been looking for a part-time job, but so far no luck. She has no practical skills, and I'm worried . . ."

She didn't say she feared Bea would fall into her mother's footsteps someday, that she needed to get Bea away from the town's memories and lasting gossip, but Hicks gazed at her as if he understood.

She continued. "And Silver—well, you know. He's too old for this life now. He can't hardly take going out with his buddies on the good days. I got both of them to take care of."

"You're getting by, ain't you?"

She shifted in the chair. "Yeah, I'm getting by. That's the point. I'm getting by and managing to put a little money away, but it's not much. I have no security, no safety net." An image of that awful room above the bar flashed in her mind. Neither she nor Bea could end up there!

Hicks fixed her with a stern glare. But as always he spoke softly to her. "You'll worry a whole lot more if you're running against the law."

"Even the guard doesn't care. I hear the in-charge officer on the Hook gets a call that the rum boats are coming, and he sends his patrol boats and runners to look in another place, like Perth Amboy. Those men find nothing, but the officer finds a case of prime Canadian whiskey waiting for him on the dock."

"They aren't all like that, and the guard keeps moving men around so they don't get too comfortable and tempted in one spot." Hicks rose. "Want some coffee?"

"Wait," she said.

He stood still. "They're getting better. The guard. Mark my word. They've made a few big arrests. And they're learning how to spot the decoy boats, and they can light up the darkest night with tracer bullets. Some have even taken to firing warning shots across the bow of the boat they're after, and some of those shots have come mighty close. Someone's going to die, Frieda."

Around her she saw no signs of danger. She saw no death, only new lives as more people in Highlands joined the fray. Men who'd fished, worked as seiners, crewed on oyster boats, hauled lobster pots, and tonged for clams were now eating well, dressing better than they ever had before, and providing for their families as never before. Simple people who'd never been able to afford homes or new cars were pulling up in front of their just-built frame houses in cars off the showroom floor. The fishermen's children were for once as well dressed and well fed as the hill people's kids. Women could go to the hospital to have their babies. The city was growing and building up around them.

She'd never had much interest in the trappings of wealth, but the opportunities it could buy for Bea . . . ? The protection it could provide so that neither of them ever faced the predicament their mother must have faced? And the fact that it meant crossing the sea, sometimes several nights a week—that thought bloomed inside her chest. "If it's dangerous, then everyone wouldn't be getting in on the action and the money."

"No. Not everyone. Look at the Bahrs here"—he gestured around— "still making an honest living. And Hawkeye, though you hate him; he isn't doing it, either."

She glanced away. The evening was coming on, but despite the weather and sea conditions, some of the larger contact boats were still running. There was no moon, so it would be pitch-black out there, as they preferred. She had picked up on just about everything about running. The local boatmen going out to the foreign-registered, big rum boats and bringing back the liquor were essentially the middle men. They bought, ferried, and sold the offshore boats' contraband to the city men. The city men kept a lookout over on Highland Beach, where they'd get the signal from high-powered flashlights when the shore boats were coming in, and prearranged signals would tell them where to meet the drop men and the boats in Highlands, Leonardo, Belford, or other places. The city men drove to the drop site, bargained with the captain or his drop man, made their purchases, and then jumped into REO Speed Wagons or long sedans outfitted with heavy-duty springs to carry fifteen or more cases of Canadian booze into the city. The captain's drop man would take any surplus and store it in hidden barns and sheds until it could be sold.

"And me," said Hicks slowly. "I'm doing what I've always done."

Frieda straightened as she listened to some rigging clang against a mast outside and another idea hit her. "We could talk to Bahrs. If you don't want to use the *Wren*, he's got that skiff out there we could hire from him and give him a share of whatever we rake in. He'd make a lot more money than the pound-net fishing he uses it for."

Hicks shook his head. "I've heard others have tried to talk him into it. He won't rent the boat for running."

"Aren't you ever tempted?"

His face set firmly, he gazed off with a faraway look. "I fought in a war for this country. Being in the service and overseas remakes a person. I'm not going against the US, no matter what."

"But it's a stupid law."

"No matter. I'm not breaking it."

Later, still hoping to acquire some engine-fixing business, she took a walk along the piers. Pleasure yachts often pulled in at the end of the longest one, and just then a man caught Frieda's eye on board a lovely sailboat with two polished wooden masts. Startlingly handsome, the young man had sandy-brown hair that was a bit wavy and unruly, his face finely boned, his lips full and expressive. Smooth, unblemished skin like tanned chamois leather. Wearing an expensive-looking jacket and gloves, he moved about the deck working with the dock lines. Frieda's body went still. He was exquisite. Elegant and fluid. Smooth. Sophisticated.

Frieda couldn't tear her eyes away. He glanced up, and embarrassed to be caught ogling, she shot her gaze downward, turned around, and walked away. For a moment, however, she knew nothing but the feel of his eyes on her during that split second. Something precious had flowed from them and landed on her.

Mentally, she shook it off. As she strode down the pier, she wondered why the people who owned that beautiful boat would have it out in this cold weather. Probably pulling the boat on land for the winter, she surmised.

Despite an inner battle to stop it, for the rest of the day the handsome man's image kept swimming into view in her mind. If she were one to daydream about romance, he would be the perfect focus of those imaginings.

That night she fried the flounder Hicks had given her for dinner. Bea had gone upstairs to study right after school. Always studying, that girl, or flipping through discarded *Vanity Fair* magazines and dreaming of things she'd likely never have. Despite her intelligence Bea was way too idealistic. She thought that one of the fancy shops catering to the tourists would hire her to work on Saturdays, but the owners could get hill girls to do that. She could've been hired as a hotel housekeeper, but Frieda, nervous about men trying to take advantage of Bea, had talked her out of it. She also thought all she had to do was go to college and then every possible door would open for her. But Frieda knew she was the only one who could make the college dream come to fruition. She had to keep things true and tangible, and it haunted her. How was she to do it?

Silver was feeling better after his cold. He had sat on the porch until the snow began to blow sideways, hitting him in the face. He stoked a fire in the woodstove and sat down at the table that night.

He cleared his throat. "I heard you made an indecent proposal today."

So Hawkeye had eavesdropped on her conversation with Hicks. And then told Silver. She knew it had to be him; Hicks would not have snitched. That demon Hawkeye would do anything to make her life more difficult.

"Indecent?" she said. "Hardly."

Silver gave her a harsh glance. "It's a bad idea I tell you."

"It's the best idea I've had in years."

Picking up his fork and knife, Silver prepared to dig in. "Makes no sense to break the law when you don't have to."

She grasped the tablecloth. "It makes perfect sense."

Silver's eyes bored into hers. "Don't do it."

"I *can't* do it. I don't have a boat, remember?"

"You done right so far. You got yourself a good skill. You just work on the boats; that's legal. But nothing more, ye hear?"

She called for Bea to come out of the bedroom. Bea sashayed in and took her place at the table. Her presence usually put a smile on Silver's face, but not tonight. He was still fuming about Frieda, who stabbed at her food as they ate in uncharacteristic silence, the food sticking in her throat. She couldn't take Silver's disapproving stare a moment longer. Sitting up tall, she pointed at Silver and Bea with her fork. "Look at us. We don't drink whiskey or smoke tobacco. We don't make easy money, even though it's sitting five miles out on the water. If only we were churchgoers, we might qualify for sainthood."

Bea laughed. "Speaking of church," she said, "old Emil paid a thousand dollars after the raid on his speakeasy, got out of jail, and then bought some new windows for the Episcopal church. He didn't even leave town."

"See what I mean?" Frieda said to Silver.

"Where'd you hear that story?" Silver asked Bea.

"At school."

"I thought you went to school to learn about history and geography."

Bea smiled. "This is history being made, and it's all about geography around here. We're right in the hot spot. Besides, we have to gossip from time to time. It keeps things interesting."

Silver finally gave in and smiled at Bea.

Frieda took a good look at her sister. She'd grown up overnight into a young woman. Now sixteen, she still held on to some little girl's mannerisms, but she'd filled out, blooming into something beautiful amid the drabness of their existence. Paint peeling on the walls, scuffed floors, the smell of fish and cooking grease. Yellowed curtains and a sagging porch. Bea's loveliness and fragility seemed out of place here.

"And speaking of keeping things interesting," Bea said to Frieda, "I want you to cut my hair tonight."

Bea's hair trailed down almost to her waist. Every night she put it up in pin curls so that in the morning it fell in long, soft waves.

"I want that new style, short, like the girls who dance the Charleston in the city."

"I like it long," said Silver.

"I don't know how to cut hair," said Frieda, who always kept hers pulled back with a bandanna or tucked under a hat.

Bea waved a hand through the air. "How hard could it be?"

After dinner Frieda sharpened a pair of scissors and followed her sister into the bedroom, where the only mirror—a cracked one—hung on the wall. Bea always spread her books and papers, along with magazine clippings of dresses and hats she liked, all over the bed. Bea pushed aside some of the papers and perched on the edge of the bed. She'd taken down the mirror and was holding it in front of her face, peering at herself as if already imagining a new, more sophisticated girl with a chic haircut.

"Look at this bed!" Frieda exclaimed. "Always covered with your things! And last night you hogged all the covers." Frieda breathed in the smell of Bea's books, cheap lavender cologne, and the room's faint scent of mold. "I wish I had my own bed."

"No one should have to sleep with *you*! All that tossing and turning in your sleep, as if you're a boat lost at sea."

Bea turned her head this way and that as she gazed into the mirror. She flattened her hand and held it just below her chin. "Here. That's where I want you to cut it."

"That's too short."

"It's my hair, not yours."

Frieda raked a brush through her sister's hair.

Bea cringed. "Ouch! You're too rough."

Frieda didn't respond, though her hands instinctively eased back.

"Always too rough," Bea said more pensively, smiling into the mirror, as if checking to make sure her teeth still sat in perfect alignment. "Just get on with it, will you? I have a book to finish and an exam tomorrow."

Frieda made the first cut and watched tendrils of hair drift down to the bedding like feathers, its softness so in opposition to the snow that had started falling earlier and then turned to the ice now clattering on the windows. She made another cut.

"Speaking of beds . . ."

Frieda held still and sucked in a breath. "Do you have to start each sentence that way?" she said, and parroted her sister's higher-pitched voice: *"Speaking of . . ."*

"Speaking of beds . . ." Bea repeated. "You should be sharing a bed with a husband by now. You're twenty years old. Almost an old maid."

"Pipe down, and stop moving your head."

"Did you hear me?"

"Of course I heard you. You're beginning to sound like Silver."

Bea smiled at her reflection again and swept her eyes to Frieda, then brought them back to the mirror. "We all know you're going to marry Hicks one day."

Frieda harrumphed. "If you insist on talking baloney, I'll cut your hair down to your prissy white scalp!"

A grunting noise came from the other room, a *hfff* that was almost animalistic. The scissors froze in Frieda's hand. Then a thud, a muted whack. It didn't sound like Silver pulling off his boots and letting them fall to the floor. And then a sigh.

A chilling sensation gelled in Frieda's spine. She tossed down the scissors and ran out of the bedroom.

Silver, spittle foaming at his lips, lay on his side on the rug. His eyes were open and unmoving, his color close to blue. She leapt to his side and started calling his name.

Silver was conscious but couldn't speak, as if he were lost in some otherworld between life and death. Placing her hands on the sides of Silver's face, Frieda peered at him. Only his eyes seemed capable of movement, and they looked into hers with a plea.

"Bea, go run for the doctor!"

The doctor said, "A stroke."

Frieda gulped down the taste of bile in the back of her throat. "Will he get better?"

Hicks stood at her side with his arm around Bea, who was weeping.

By then they'd moved Silver into the bedroom, all of Bea's books and papers now strewn across the floor.

The doctor seemed to consider each word carefully. "Hard to know. We'll have to wait and see."

Frieda squeezed her eyes shut. *No!*

The one person who had always been their constant, their lighthouse, had now fallen.

Bea sniffled louder, and Frieda looked her way. Her sister's hair was still half-cut, the back short and the sides hanging down.

CHAPTER FIVE

Three weeks passed, and Silver got no better. One side of his body was flaccid, and he was unable to speak. He could eat and drink if hand-fed, and he could use the old chamber pot a lady from the Catholic church had brought by, but he couldn't walk or stand without someone supporting the side of his body that had died before he did. Frieda had stopped working to care for him so that Bea could return to school.

During the day she made him meals of soup and mashed food. During the night she slept on the floor, having given Bea the divan. Fighting with the blankets, she often got up to check that Silver was still there, still breathing. Only then could she summon sleep.

On those rare days when the sun came out, she bundled him into sweaters and jackets and helped him limp and drag, limp and drag, out to the porch, sitting him in the old chair, where he'd always loved to linger after a day on the sea. As she sat beside him, she remembered the kind man who had taken them home on the day their mother had died, his patience with two little girls he had known nothing about, the way he had waited while they giggled and fought, pretended to be firm, then tucked them in at night. He had gone out every day on his boat, even when the weather was brutal. She saw him trudging back to the house after a long day on the water, the red light of the sunset landing on him, bringing that last warmth of the day back with him. The way he'd tried to protect the girls by placing himself between them and the hard-judging reach of the world, but still letting them step into it on their own two feet. All to have it come down to this. She shook her head, admonishing herself, realizing that one of the last things she'd said to him before his stroke amounted to complaining.

From the beginning he'd told them the truth about their mother. Frieda had always known that her mother had lived on the edges of proper society, but as soon as she was old enough to ask in more detail, Silver had spelled it out in full, never once attempting to sugarcoat the facts. He had, of course, told them that their mother's history had nothing to do with the girls she and Bea had turned out to be. This despite the fact that he knew the things that had happened to Frieda.

It had started early, when parents of her classmates didn't want their children to get too close to the bastard child, as if she carried an infectious disease. Then the boys had offered her a penny if she would let them look up her skirt, saying, "Like mother, like daughter." The girls had been even more evil, because they were conniving in their insults. The final straw came one day when the girls had invited her to a party in the park; when she arrived, however, no one was there. After discovering a number of the girls hiding in the bushes, obviously there to witness and relish her confusion as she waited anxiously for a party that would never happen, her first thought had been to ignore them. But then something twisted inside her gut, and she chased those girls down, caught them, and pulled their hair hard. They left her alone after that. Bea had fared better. Perhaps her classmates had been nicer; perhaps the story had gotten stale, the years pushing the story to the backs of people's minds. Plus Bea's tactic had been to kill them all with kindness, and it had worked.

Silver had handled both Frieda's bitterness and Bea's extreme friend-liness with the same amount of humble grace, keeping them in rein with his love rather than with any shows of force. He'd admonished them to sit up straight and keep their room clean from time to time, but never did he lift a hand or raise his voice against them.

He looked at her now as if he could see the buzzing bees of her thoughts; as if he knew everything and still understood what was hap-pening around him; as if he wanted to console *her*. He might have lost control of some of his body, but Frieda knew that his mind was still there in full. The light of understanding still shone in his eyes. But when he opened his mouth to speak, it was like a fish gasping for life as it lay on the docks, and his face folded in on itself. His sad gaze told her that all the words he wanted to say lay in scattered piles in his mind, and that picking them up and putting them in order so they could make their way out of his mouth was beyond his bidding.

She took his paralyzed hand and worked the fingers, already begin-ning to curl upon themselves like a claw. He had small hands with large knuckles and leathery, chapped skin. After rubbing each finger, she spread them out straight and then watched them curl back again. She swallowed back her sadness and stared hard into his eyes, where she could see the apology: *I'm sorry I hurt you. I shouldn't have sold the boat.* But even stronger, there, again, was that plea—focused, querying.

"Don't you worry," she said. "I'm going to take care of everything."

A week later she hired a maid who had some experience with general nursing to stay with Silver during the day. She also went to the bank and applied for a loan against the house. Though she needed to supply some papers to the banker about her work income, she'd been assured that the loan would likely be approved. Silver was proud of owning the house free and clear, but a loan was the only way to pay for his care now.

The doctor had come again, saying that Silver had high blood pressure, something Frieda had never heard of, and telling her that had caused the stroke and could cause another one. Silver needed to eat mostly rice and fruit and no salt.

On her first day out of the house, the sun had also emerged, like a promise of better days. Still, it was cold, and she pulled her cap down over her ears. Despite her emotional exhaustion, she walked down to the docks, where the men and their boats had been awaiting her return. Many of them asked after Silver and told her about the engine work they needed done. She took all the jobs she could, worked out her pay, and then planned each job one by one in her head. She'd be caught up on her work in a week's time.

She was preparing to go buy parts when Hawkeye told her that a man named Dutch wanted to talk to her.

Looking at Hawkeye in his good eye, Frieda managed a nod of her head. Maybe Dutch needed work done on his boat, and Hawkeye was giving her a lead. She couldn't thank him, however, not for all the tea in China. He represented all that had gone wrong in this town.

She headed over to see Dutch, one of the most successful shore runners based out of Highlands. Once a lobsterman, he'd started with a twenty-eight-foot dory that could do about fifteen knots when light. But it could do only half that when fully loaded, so recently he'd bought a forty-foot Jersey sea skiff that could do thirty knots to outrun the guardsmen who were playing it straight. When Dutch saw Frieda, he moved from sitting at the helm and stepped up to the transom.

"Welcome back," he said to her. Dutch was big and blond, a man in his late thirties with huge rounded shoulders and a trim waist, a per-petually reddened face, a deep cleft in his chin, and an overall look that said, *Don't even think of messing with me.* He could've been descended from the first Vikings who had landed in America, and he also could've been a contender for Bea's father. But she couldn't think about that now. She could tolerate him. He had the pointed, squinty, farsighted eyes of a good sailor and didn't talk much unless he'd been drinking. When he did speak, he went straight to the heart of a matter.

He said, "My engineer took sick."

Frieda knew the man, a fine mechanic named Hector who had been her biggest competition for work along the docks before he started working solely for Dutch.

Dutch laughed with a smirk on his face. "Well, that's his story at least. Truth is, he's either getting cold feet or getting whipped by his wife to get himself out. He don't want to go out no more." He shrugged. "He can do OK out here working honest, but he might be my drop man from time to time."

She nodded and listened.

"We're only a crew of three, and normally I got to have men big enough to catch the bags they throw down from the rummers out there. You're too small; you won't be able to do it."

She gulped and let her eyes drift over the boat, a beauty with her square stern, bluff bow, and engine amidships, with room for cargo fore and aft. She had looked at Dutch with renewed respect when he named the boat *Wonder*, much to the guffaws and taunts of the fishermen around him. "So, what are you proposing?"

"When we go out there, we got to move fast. We pull up and tell them what we want, and they start tossing down the bags. If we get swells, we can take some hellish beatings. Water can leak down into the engine no matter how hard we aim to keep it dry."

"I know." She also knew that Dutch would not be telling her all of this without some purpose behind it. Her heart thumped in expectation, and she looked at the boat now in a new way. It was made of very thin wood—maybe five-eighths of an inch thick. Not much of a barrier between sailor and sea. And she already knew the shore boats ran at night without lights to hide from the coast guard boats in the area. If they hit a submerged log or other wreckage, it would go through the hull like a pickax through a cardboard box. And the weight of the powerful engine meant the boat would sink in mere minutes.

"Anyways, that would be your job when we get to the rummies. You have to keep that engine dry as you can and squirt pyrene if you have to. We never shut down, in case we have to leave quick. The other day some idiot's engine caught fire because the gas rags he was using to clean up oil got on the hot engine.

"We go out mostly when there's little or no moon, leave at dusk. It's close to an hour and a half out and more than two and a half back, then the drop-off, and we bring her back in. A full night's work. I need me a full-time mechanic for the runs and to always keep her in tip-top shape. You get twenty-five cents a case we sell and twenty-five dollars a week, same as I paid Hector."

She squinted back at him. "Why me?"

Dutch stood still, his eyes full of surprised reappraisal. Perhaps he thought his offer was so good he'd never considered that she wouldn't simply jump at the chance.

"You're the best man for the job."

Frieda smiled wryly. She didn't mind his choice of words. That's exactly how she wanted them to see her—as another man. She hadn't worn a dress in two years or bothered with her hair, and still it hadn't been much of a deterrent to some of the crusty old dogs who made leering remarks from time to time. It revolted her.

Finally he said, "I also know you got yourself some troubles now. How is Silver doing anyways?"

"The same."

She stood with her feet planted firmly against the sway of the tides she could feel on the pier's end. She wanted to steer the conversation back to the boat and the job. "How many cases can you carry?" she asked.

"Six to eight hundred, depending on the seas."

She did the mental math, and blood rushed to her head. She'd heard that contact boat captains were almost doubling their initial investment on each case. But men like Dutch had boat payments and other expenses resting on their shoulders. Her money would be free and clear. If they ferried seven hundred cases on a run, she would make about $175 on each night out and make another $100 or so per month. It could mean everything. It could put everything she wanted for Bea within grasp. After high school she could go to college and get away from the place where her mother had sold herself. And now with Silver's stroke, Frieda would need more money than ever to assure he got the care he needed. This money would take care of that, and she could cancel the loan against the house. Sure there were risks, and it was a bit terrifying to think of breaking a law, but finally she'd be making as much as a man did, doing the same job. She looked toward the water, where Silver's face swam into view. She recalled one of the last things he had said to her before the stroke: "Don't do it."

Was that the last advice he would ever give her?

It had been three weeks since she'd made her "indecent" proposal to Hicks, and because of Silver's stroke she hadn't even thought about joining the rumrunning business again. She'd never dreamed that any of the men would take on a woman as crew. Now this had fallen into her lap.

Dutch gestured toward the shining city across the bay. "We work just as hard as them schmucks over there, harder even, and before now we made nothing. Now that's changed. It could change things for you, too. I'm giving you a fine opportunity here. Only you got to prove something to me first."

He didn't need to say more. Frieda knew what money could do.

"So what do you say?"

Frieda stood in a quandary. Reason told her to think about the possible consequences. She had considered this a few weeks ago, but at the time it was just an idea she had no way to bring to fruition without Hicks's help. She had always been pretty sure he would turn her down, so she had never let her hopes soar high. Now she had a real opportunity in front of her. And she tolerated Dutch better than the others. Rudy Harris crewed with him. Rudy was decent, too.

Now she had to ponder whether she was really willing to break the law. Some people had been caught, fined, or, more rarely, jailed. A few had lost boats and their livelihoods, and the coast guard was cracking down. Judges were handing down stiffer sentences. Most importantly, Silver wouldn't want her to do it. It struck her: It was illegal—as was prostitution—so was this the right course for her? Her plan had always been to steer clear of anything that even remotely resembled what her mother had done. And once she started down a path such as this, would there be any turning back?

On the other hand, she believed that so many of her problems would sift away. Yes, money bought things that made life easier. She could do some repairs to the house. She could get Bea out of this town and on to the city and a better life. And money could do for Silver what she herself could not. She could hire the best possible people to look after him twenty-four hours a day if need be. It could mean restful sleep at night, money put aside, and even a few nice things this life had to offer.

If only she could silence that murmuring mouse inside her head—*Don't do it*—or could she live with it whispering from time to time?

She didn't take long to decide. "What do I have to do?"

The sea had gone silent for a moment, but now it resumed its ins and outs of life, its breathing upon the shore.

Dutch said, "Engine's not running as well as she should. It's missing, running rough and sluggish. Need to get more horsepower out of her. You fix her up and be quick about it, you got the job."

Frieda was already formulating a plan. She could adjust the timing, reset the floats in the carburetor, check the gaps on the points, and change wires and spark plugs if she found them clotted with carbon and oil. Then it hit her. "Do you have tools on board?"

Dutch's eyebrows flattened. "Hell, no. I expect a mechanic to come with his own."

Of course. Frieda had a few tools she had purchased used, but they were mixed in with Hicks's. Since she hadn't been working, he probably had the tools with him, and he had gone out over the shoals today, despite the cold winter conditions. She gazed up at Dutch, trying not to let the quivering sensation running through her body show. "I have tools. I just have to go fetch them."

Dutch pulled out a gold pocket watch and snapped it open, then said, "Clock's ticking. I need someone who can get the job done in a jiffy." He clicked the watch shut.

"I'll be back as fast as I can," Frieda said, her thoughts tripping over each other.

"What are you waiting for?"

She turned and started running.

Her head thrummed as her feet flew down the weathered planks of the pier, wood grating under each rushed footfall. *Please oh please let Hicks be back from fishing.*

She nearly collided with him while running along the wharf side.

"What's the matter?" he said as he stopped her.

"You're back. I can't believe it," said Frieda, breathing hard and fighting a sense of overwhelming fluster mixed with sudden relief.

"What the hell is going on?" Hicks demanded.

"I need the tools. Now."

He put his hands on her upper arms. "What's the rush? Tools? I thought someone had died."

"I need. To prove. To Dutch. I can fix his boat."

"What for?"

"I don't have time to explain!"

"Well, I'm not giving you the tools till you tell me."

She sucked in a long breath, and letting it out, said, "I could get the engineer job. On his boat. But I have to prove I can make his engine run better. I know what to do. I just need the tools. 'Specially the box wrenches."

Hicks looked incredulous. "You're going to start running with Dutch? This is crazy."

Her chest hurt. Each inhalation of cold air was like a blade. "Listen, I don't have time to argue. Some of those tools are mine, and I need them. I also need to go for parts. Time means everything. I gotta be fast. Will you help me?"

Hicks's eyebrow twitched and then stopped. He studied her as Frieda hopped from one foot to the other, glancing nervously around. Then she watched his face tremble, as if he were stuck in a dilemma.

"Please, Hicks."

He stood still.

"Think about what I could do for Silver. You know how I love him. And the future I could give Bea . . ."

He seemed to be going through a long decision-making process.

Frieda rocked on her feet and said, "I need to know now."

Finally he let out a long sigh. "You go for the parts; I'll go for the tools. Meet you back here."

Frieda rose on her toes and gave him a kiss on the cheek. He had never let her down. Now she'd have her shot at the job. She was already planning what she would work on first, second, and third as she rushed to see the man who sold parts. She gave him the last of her money and then ran back to the spot where she'd agreed to meet Hicks.

He was already standing in a way that told her weighty thoughts were holding him down. Without a word he simply handed her the toolbox, then turned and walked away.

"Wish me luck," she called out, but Hicks never looked back.

That was odd, but she had no time to ruminate about it now. She made her way back to Dutch's boat, where he sat wrapped in a heavy coat in the captain's chair, his feet resting on the starboard gunwale, a cigar in his right hand.

She jumped on board lugging the heavy toolbox behind her. "I'll get started."

Dutch puffed on the cigar, then exhaled in a white stream that mixed with the frosty air. He gestured down below. "Be my guest."

Frieda went down and opened the engine compartment, the wheels in her brain spinning. Now to start and be quick about it. Prove herself. She opened the toolbox and began to sort through it.

Then a white-hot instant of shock.

Inside were no box wrenches, which she needed more than anything else.

CHAPTER SIX

No! She staggered on the brink of panic, her vision clouding. It took a few seconds for her to grasp what Hicks had done.

She felt woozy, as if the boat were dipping and lifting, although it was still. This had been a malicious act to deny her what she wanted. After she'd asked for his help! A deliberate deception! A dirty trick! That's why he hadn't spoken to her and had to walk away. Probably ashamed of himself, as he should be.

Anger erupted, and if there had been something there to strike she would've punched it. But instead she sucked in some shaky breaths and willed that urge away. This was a moment for thinking, not losing control. What to do now?

She would have to come up with some explanation for Dutch, then try to find Hicks and convince him to give her the box wrenches. By then it would probably be too late. Dutch was not a patient man, and there were others he could ask, those who had their own tools and could come on board and get this done as well as she could. Or almost as well. But she could think of nothing else to do but tell him the truth and look like a fool. Quietly she eased shut the toolbox and silently tread up the companionway to the afterdeck, where Dutch still sat, smoking the same cigar. Only moments had passed, but they felt like years.

Her heart in her throat, she said to Dutch, "It seems I've been sabotaged."

"What'd you say?" Dutch said, looking none too pleased.

"Someone pulled out what I need."

After roaring with laughter, he stopped. "You're serious?"

"Unfortunately, yes."

With a cocked eyebrow he said, "Someone doesn't approve?"

"Someone always disapproves," said Frieda with a defiant little lift of her chin.

Dutch smiled wryly. "Well said."

"But I'll find them. I'll borrow if I have to. I'll be back, don't you worry."

"Settle down," he said, and slowly took his feet off the gunwale. "I got some tools on board. Always carry tools with me on the boat. Just wanted to see if you could hustle, how bad you want this. I seen you scampering all over the place. You got the energy for this work. I was looking for that and for drive, and you got both."

Frieda dared not breathe, much less say a word.

"But this disapproval, wherever it's coming from, you gonna be able to stand up to that?"

Frieda made herself stand tall, although Hicks had made her feel like a punished child. "I've always done what I wanted."

Dutch studied her, then rubbed his gloved hands on his thighs and said, "Wanting this bad and being willing to work hard for it means a lot. Plus I've heard good things about your work. Job's yours."

Frieda swallowed hard before her chest began to swell. "Thank you. I'll do right fine work for you, Dutch."

"And," he said slowly, "just to let you know, pretty soon you're going to have the best tools money can buy."

She gazed around, still trying to fathom the day's events that had led to this. The world suddenly looked so much more open and expansive. The wintry seas were splendid in their wrath and churned with opportunity. The cold air glistened and sparkled and no longer burned her cheeks. She hadn't known such happiness in . . . forever. Things were finally going her way.

"Thank you, skipper."

But what would Silver think? What would Bea say? What if, what if, what if . . . ?

Oh, stop.

"Frieda." Dutch's voice brought her back. "By God I still need you to fix the boat."

After she got Dutch's engine purring, it was late, hours past sundown. A hazy moon glowed dully through the high overcast clouds, but to Frieda the night was a cocoon of cottony glory. She spent a few moments with Dutch on deck, thanking him and assuring him that she could do the work, stand up to any naysayers, and always be ready when he needed her, day or night.

An onlooker might never have guessed that something monumental had just occurred. But as she walked away, her heart was still in her chest, its beats throbbing in her temples. No one else had any idea yet that their futures would now be linked. And that for one of them the day had changed everything.

"One more thing," Dutch called out.

Frieda turned. Dutch appeared placid, as if the day had not been even the least bit extraordinary. He existed in a constant state of seeming neutrality—not anxious, but not calm or disinterested, either. Here was a man who could deal with any adversity that befell him with complete confidence and competence. Good qualities for a captain.

He said, "You're the third man. You follow my orders and those of the first mate at all times. That going to work for you?"

He knew enough about her to be skeptical. It had always been near impossible for Frieda to follow orders, but for this to work she would have to stuff that side of her personality into a deep internal pocket. For the money it would be worth it, hard as it might be. That was the only way it worked on a boat. The captain was king.

For Bea and Silver, Frieda said, "Yes, captain."

She splurged on a Cel-Ray soda, a private celebration in one of the dockside bars, then went to tell Hicks what she thought of his ploy, even though she could hardly stay mad at him now. Nothing could tamp down the pure, sweet joy of this day. She walked down the dock to the pier where the *Wren* rocked in the water. She found him on the boat, sitting on the transom, waiting for her. By now a cold wind that prickled her cheeks had blown the clouds away, and the indigo skies were peppered with planets and stars.

"It didn't work," she said calmly as she strode up and set the toolbox on the pier.

Then she took a closer look at Hicks. He held a bottle of whiskey in his hand, and that stilled her. Hicks had never been much of a drinker. The pain in his eyes burned in her throat. He said slowly, "Figured it might not."

"I won't even bother to ask why you did it."

"You don't have to, because you already know why I did it."

Frieda said softly, "You can't save me, Hicks."

He took a swig from the bottle. "I know that."

Speechless, she realized that she had blinded herself for two years now, telling herself that Hicks was getting over her, that only fondness and friendship would remain. Now the truth sat in front of her face.

She remembered the first time she'd thought his affection for her might be his undoing. And now she was forced to acknowledge the reality of their situation. Was he unraveling now? She made her voice soft and easy, but she had to be sure never to give him any false hope. "You must be feeling pretty bad about yourself right now."

His eyebrow was twitching. "Damn right. Probably shouldn't have done that."

"I need the tools that are mine. I'll get my own box and come for them tomorrow. Dutch is going to front me the money I need for a box and a full set of tools until I can pay him back."

"How kind of him."

It was unlike Hicks to employ sarcasm. "What do you have against Dutch?"

Hicks shrugged. "He's not so bad, but he's getting caught up in a trap. They're all getting reckless."

"Seems to me he knows what he's doing."

Hicks hugged the whiskey bottle inside his heavy coat. "Whatever you say, Frieda. Whatever you say."

The sea breathed beneath her, but a stab of remorse froze Frieda. Was she doing the right thing? No matter now; she'd accepted the job. And sitting before her, suffering, was the man who'd given her the skills to do it. The quicksilver tide rushed beneath her, and she breathed heavily, then spoke tenderly: "I know what I'm doing, thanks to you. I'll always appreciate what you taught me . . ." She ran out of air, and Hicks held still and stared at her, as if he could read her thoughts, and he understood.

He gave a single nod of his head.

She turned to walk away, then thought better of it. After spinning around, she said, "Thanks for trying anyway. To save me."

He took the bottle out of his coat and raised it to her. "To your success," he said.

CHAPTER SEVEN

She spent the next few days working on engines for other runners and fishermen while they waited for the weather to improve. Others were already pulling their boats out in expectation of ice, and those men often needed help repairing their boats' hulls, cleaning them, and repainting them. She hadn't made any money on running yet and had to keep some cash coming in.

She worked with Hicks on one of the jobs and was happy to see that he was back to his old self. He avoided eye contact with her, but beyond that his behavior was the same as before his attempt at sabotage. Calm. Warm. Accepting. Hicks seemed to have the ability to get past things, to forgive others *and* himself. It was as if his anger could blow away like sand; he simply couldn't hold on to it. Or maybe it was the opposite. Maybe his blood always ran rich with emotion, only most of the time he secreted it. Frieda had noticed that many men, especially Great War veterans, were good at that. They had been through horrors they never spoke about. She also knew that the story you made up in your mind was rarely the real story. Maybe she didn't know Hicks at all.

* * *

On Tuesday, rubbing the pinpricks of blond hair on his chin, Dutch told her they were making a run that night. The recent gales had passed, but the air was bitter cold. It would feel even colder out on the water. But Dutch needed to make good on his investment in the new boat, and the ice that would put them out of the water was coming soon. Plus there was no moon.

By five o'clock the sun was almost down, and after Rudy waved her on board, Frieda followed Dutch's orders to prepare the boat for departure. She started the engine and made some final checks; then they cast off the mooring lines and pulled out slowly into the inky night, as black as a bottomless pit. Dutch took the helm, and Frieda pulled on her heaviest overcoat, one that belonged to Silver. A sense of the surreal came over her; she couldn't quite fathom that she was doing this. Finally. For years going out on a boat to make a living had been held just beyond her reach, and running for rum had been nothing but fantasy. Now here she was. It was happening. A plunge into the unknown. Her awareness sharpened, while a handful of stardust scattered around her vision. The night sparkled. Every breath she took was like a hook, but she had to concentrate on what lay ahead. They would be running dark, and she had no idea how things would go.

When she thought of Silver, she had to shift the look he had given her earlier into a hidden compartment of her mind. He knew. Instead of her usual routine of making dinner and settling in for the long winter's night, this evening she'd readied herself for the job ahead. She had decided to tell Bea the truth, and Bea in return had halfheartedly tried to talk Frieda out of it. Halfheartedly, and Frieda couldn't blame her. The lure of easy money had infected almost everyone by now.

But Frieda said nothing about it to Silver, who sat on the divan and stared at her. Probably Hawkeye had come to tell Silver already.

He was always the first to tattle on her to Silver, who followed her with that admonishing stare of his until she closed the front door behind her.

Dutch steered the boat, and Rudy picked up a pair of binoculars to scout out any trouble before it arrived. Two other boats were heading out of the same small dock area just behind them.

The water was dark except for the complex mix of red and white lights, some moving and some staying put, but Dutch knew what he was doing. He made a discreet run across Sandy Hook Bay, avoiding buoys, beacon lights, channel markers, anchored craft, and ship-wreck carcasses listing on shoals. He couldn't open up, because of all the obstacles, until they were out on the ocean. At low throttle the engine barely purred. Her four-inch exhausts were underwater and had a small silencer installed. While they were underway, there was very little for Frieda to do. Most of her work would happen in between the runs. If she was doing her work well, the engine would barely need attention. She had serviced and checked everything ahead of time, and everything was perfect. All she had to do was monitor the engine and spring into action if anything went wrong. She had time to enjoy the patina of deep waters quickening with reflected lights, the air dancing with little mists, and the stars that materialized and blinked to brilliance as the boat reached farther beyond city lights.

Rudy, a baby-faced redhead who wore circular, wire-rimmed eyeglasses like Ben Franklin's, could've passed for a teacher if his life hadn't been on the sea. Frieda remembered him as a shy boy, a few years ahead of her in high school, who had married an exuberant high school sweetheart right after graduation, and up to recently they'd lived with his parents in a rambling fishing shack, much added on to, on Fourth Street. This year, however, they'd moved into their own place, a remodeled Victorian farther away from the water and winds. Frieda had heard that Rudy's wife was pregnant again, and she congratulated him now. Their firstborn son was as redheaded as Rudy, and Frieda imagined a whole baseball team of little redheads in his future.

As they swung past several anchored sailboats, Rudy asked her, "You ever sailed? I mean, on a sailboat."

Frieda answered, "No."

He lowered the binoculars and gazed out over the black bay as if every swell was magical. "I learned when I was a kid. It's different. No engine sounds. Just wind and sea." He glanced at her. "Peaceful, you know?"

"And slow."

"Fast enough to have gotten the first explorers here."

Frieda smiled, but the tension of the night, her first night out, made her lips tremble. "I was just thinking earlier that you look like a teacher."

"That so? Well, thank you, I guess."

Frieda gulped. She couldn't believe they were having a casual conversation while on their way to commit a crime. It was obvious Rudy was used to this.

Rudy said, "OK, so you're right. Sailing's a lot slower. But the quiet makes up for that. It's like you're a part of the sea, gliding where the wind takes you. Using nothing but nature's breath. It's more relaxing." He grinned. "You have to understand, I've got a kid at home and a baby on the way. I need peace and quiet sometimes." He stretched before taking his post in the bow. "When I've put up enough money for the kids' future, I might buy me a little sailboat. Teach the kids while they're young, you know?"

She nodded and then finally smiled a real smile. Rudy was nice. She wished she had known him better before.

Farther out beyond Sandy Hook Bay, the lights of New York City to port, Frieda could see that hundreds of boats, out of every large and small dock, pier, and inlet along this section of coast, were headed for a similar soiree. Dutch opened the throttle, and soon they were gliding along the sheer surface of the water at close to thirty knots, sending up white water on either side like the wings of a bird, a third of the keel fully up and out of the water as they raced along.

They cut a wide course around the lightships on the way out to sea and then dove full throttle into the rolling swells of the Atlantic. The sea spanked the hull, and Dutch kept up the pace until they smacked face-first into a dense fog. Dutch turned to starboard, skirting the shore, and yelled out to Rudy, "Watch out for breakers!"

A few minutes later Rudy shouted back, "Breakers ahead, sir."

Frieda said, "How do you know?" after she had swallowed the knot forming in the back of her throat. She had to put her faith in Dutch's abilities. The fog felt like a premonition of doom, but she'd placed her life and fate into his hands. What else was there to do?

He said, "I feel it in the swell."

Dutch grunted his discontent but whipped the boat back toward open waters and kept pushing. Even with the fog it was clear he had a plan and appeared to know exactly where he was. Rudy spread out flat on his stomach in the bow, searching through the thick air for any dark patches, indicating boats. She sat next to Dutch and kept an eye on the engine compartment. He seemed to sense her questions before she asked them.

"No turning back now," Dutch said in his hoarse voice. "I got lots of thirsty patrons to feed, bless their bloodsucking souls."

She had no idea how he planned to find a boat five or so miles out to sea in the midst of this gloom. Frieda knew how to work engines to their maximum potential and tong for clams near the shore, but she was as much a novice to the deeper seas as any other landlubber. But Dutch kept on, as if his eyes and will alone could cut through the dense curtain.

Frieda raked away long strands of hair that were sticking to her face and lips.

Dutch continued: "I had to know where the waves were breaking. I'm thinking thirty-five to forty minutes from the breakers; that's what it usually takes. Then we'll stop and listen for the yachts' bells. They should be ringing all the time in this fog."

The engine needed no attention, so Frieda simply sat and shivered as they plowed ahead into near-zero visibility, and she hoped to high heavens that nothing was out there to run into. Her stomach clenched as the wraiths of mist twirled before her, and she tucked her face back into the collar of the big overcoat. Something sharp caught in her chest as she thought of the two lives entrusted to her care. Bea. Silver. And then the crawl of shame. She'd never fathomed an existence that included heading out in dangerous seas in search of contraband. She was breaking the law and aiding others to break it, too. Now a part of keeping the liquor flowing, she was old enough to know that liquor was often overused; it erupted in bar fights, left wives and children behind, and could even fell the strongest of men.

Except for the low hum of the engine, all was silent, and they flew over the thick, black sea, a small boat racing away from the rest of the world. Far from shore and at the appointed time, Dutch slowed down, and they listened. About ten minutes later they heard ships' bells, and Rudy exclaimed, "Hot damn."

Frieda peered through the fog as they drew closer to encounter one of the strangest scenes she'd ever witnessed. The ships—big black birds in the mist—were surrounded by hundreds of other boats of all sizes and designs, everything from slow old tubs to speedboats built just for running. They drifted about and fended off the others like goslings surrounding the mother goose, and Frieda was stunned to realize that the atmosphere was something akin to a party. Here was a flotilla of boats strung together to break the law and make money, and no one seemed to have a care in the world. A floating liquor establishment out in the middle of the dark ocean, like some kind of magical, mythical circus. It made Frieda think of pirates, mermaids, gods, and sirens of the sea. No one acted the slightest touched with doubt, even with jellyfish, like flowers, floating in the water about the boats and danger from the coast guard boats looming. Transactions were at hand, and the booze was in demand. She was stunned again to find they had to wait their turn. Now *this* was a story, a real story.

As they drew closer, she could see hand-lettered wooden signs hanging in the large boats' rigging listing the prices and the types of liquor for sale. Champagne was thirty to forty dollars a case, depending on the label and quality, and whiskey and most others were thirty to fifty dollars, depending on the same things. Dutch pulled their boat closer as other boats loaded and left, while Rudy kept watch for the coast guard. Although the fog was still hugging the water, it seemed to be thinning. Frieda didn't know how to feel about that; it made the return safer but also made them easier to find.

Dutch pulled up to the Canadian three-masted schooner named *Eva Marie*, where about fifteen other boats were conducting their business, their engines running and ready for immediate departure, their hulls thumping cheek to cheek around the big boat, all of them rolling and bumping and lowering cargo into their holds. The schooner was all burly men, gleaming faces, low lights flooding the deck, full of people and crates, and a sense of enthusiastic purpose. People worked quickly, determinedly, and zealously. She blinked several times. She could scarcely believe it. She had tried to imagine this moment ever since Dutch had hired her, but nothing she'd pictured had come close to this energy and the feel of this orderly chaos. These people had a burning fire in their bellies, and the scene felt as if it could at any moment combust into flames. She had no other way to describe it but to say that out here these people were alive. More alive than landlubbers. More alive than people playing it straight.

The crew of the big boat threw out lines, and Frieda helped Rudy put over the fenders. Dutch was deciding what label liquor he wanted, while some of the men got off their boats and scrambled aboard the *Eva Marie* to stay for a while. This close, Frieda could hear music and saw some couples—the men wearing striped blazers and Oxford baggies, the women wearing chemises and T-bar shoes—dancing on the deck, as though this were a party. Some people had obviously come out here just for the excitement, and she could understand why. The vitality was catching, and she wished she could scoop it up in her arms and carry it back with her. People seemed mesmerized, as if under a spell, and everything hinged on these incandescent moments. Men moved the liquor with eager agility and handled the sales untiringly as if there was nothing else in the world as important, while someone strummed a banjo and women danced and sang. Laughter, smiles, and music reigned over a sense of avid determination. This was a place of business after all, but the most jubilant of businesses. Maybe it was the lure of wealth, the excitement of breaking the law, the glory of success.

For a few long moments it was as if she'd left her body and was hovering somewhere above the water looking down on this pandemonium, peering down on a play acted out by newly redeemed people. If that were true, then who or what was the redeemer? She found she didn't care. She loved all of these people now as she had never loved people before. What was happening to her? She was shocked to find that she wanted to belong here, she wanted to be a part of it. She had joined their fray, their slinky and illustrious private club, and she breathed deeply in elation. She rubbed her upper arms to make sure it wasn't a dream, that she was really experiencing that unbelievable sight and huge tide of emotion.

She made herself go below deck to check that the engine stayed dry, but she wanted to know everything that was happening above. She could hear Dutch order three hundred Johnnie Walker Black, two hundred of Dewar's, and a hundred of Booth's High & Dry, then others she couldn't remember. She had no idea what kind of liquor Dutch was ordering, and it hit her how sheltered a life she had led so far. Silver had kept her and Bea away from anything like this.

All was well with the engine, so she peered up from below to watch the action. Dutch paid by pitching his money—a roll of large-denomination bills held by a rubber band. The men on board were so busy with loading and keeping the boats coming and going that they didn't even count it. Even in this shady business there was a code of ethics. Dutch told her that other boats didn't even require payment in advance; instead, they let the contact boat captains pay the next time they came out.

Before they began loading, the crew of the *Eva Marie* threw down a mattress for the crew of the *Wonder* to place on the deck against breakage. Crew on board the big rum boat tossed the bags over without taking the time to aim carefully. It took another hour for Rudy and Dutch to load 750 cases—burlap sacks holding six straw-wrapped bottles each—from the deck into the holds.

"My first time out," Dutch said to Frieda, who was now helping load the cases into the boat, proving to Dutch that she could indeed do more than just engine work, "I smashed fifteen cases."

Even with the mattress a few cases ended up broken, but the boat slowly filled, and the *Wonder* began to settle lower and lower into the sea, until they were only about a foot above the water. Rudy told her the most popular liquor types were scotch whiskey, French brandy, and

Cuban or other West Indian rums, but buyers on shore had a taste for everything. Scotch had a particularly swanky allure.

Throughout the loading process, Frieda kept checking the engine compartment, which was supposed to be watertight. She had covered it with a canvas tarp just in case and listened and smelled for any signs of overheating or any unusual noises. The swells amounted only to low rollers that night, and the two boats rubbed against each other just occasionally, the fenders groaning under the pressure and the wooden sides of the old *Eva Marie* creaking.

Everything was going smoothly. She was doing her job. Although she had only just begun, the idea that this could ever be taken from her was unfathomable. If it was possible to fall in love with a job, she had done it at first sight. Here she was out on the water doing work that was a perfect fit for her strengths and desires. Could such happiness come out of the unexpected? Or was unexpected happiness the best happiness of all?

Dutch chatted with the crew on the other boat as he caught and stacked the cases fore and aft, but Rudy remained mostly silent as he, too, worked. Frieda kept her head down, not wanting to call attention to herself. At one point she caught one of the rum boat's crew peering at her, and she quickly turned her face away, put up her collar, and tugged down her woolen cap.

When all the business was completed, Dutch swung the rudder around, and the heavily laden boat struck out in the fog for shore. Loaded down, they couldn't go as fast as before, but the fog also wasn't as thick anymore. Almost two hours later, just offshore they left the murky gloom as suddenly as they had entered it. The change was like a heavy curtain being lifted. The lights of the city looked like diamonds tossed against a palette of black velvet, and the Sandy Hook Light and then the Twin Lights called them home. Now that he could see, Dutch pushed the boat faster, and as they cut through swells, the sea spray blew into Frieda's face, waking her again and again to this new reality.

Her mind and body felt so free. She was reborn, filled with freshness and the possibilities of the future. Her life would never be the same. Frieda began to breathe normally. She hadn't realized that something had been caught in her chest until she let it go, and then she found she could take in full breaths and release them all the way to the bottom of her lungs. Her head cleared; her heart filled with exhilaration. They had done it, and she had been an essential part of it. She finally fit somewhere, and until that night she hadn't known she had wanted such a sense of belonging.

"Picket boat in pursuit, sir," Rudy said calmly.

Exhilaration changed to panic in one held breath. She turned and saw the coast guard picket boat running dark in their wake. *No! It couldn't be.* The guard boat shot tracers that lit the sky like fireworks over the river on the Fourth of July. If there was any doubt they'd been spotted, it no longer remained. She clenched the edge of the bench seat and held on for her life. Here she was, her first time out, and she was going to get caught, maybe go to jail. She imagined the confines of a cell, the look on Silver's face, Bea's disappointment. Her body became flimsy and weightless; she could have slipped over the side of the boat and let the sea suck her under.

Dutch sped up, but the boat rode too low in the water, and if they went any faster they risked being swamped. The boat thumped heavily over the swells as they drew closer to shore. Still, Frieda hoped, the *Wonder* might run faster than the older, typically slower guard boats. She wasn't the praying type, but she looked up at the stars and closed her eyes. *Please, no. I've only just started. Give me a chance. Don't take it away just when everything is finally at my fingertips.*

Only a trace of worry on his face, Dutch remained surprisingly calm. "Don't put up a fuss if we get caught," he said to Frieda. "Go along with it. Worst thing that can happen is you get a fine and a year's probation. They could take my boat, but there's ways to get her back."

Trying to swallow, Frieda found her throat had gone dry. How could he remain so unfazed? Rudy seemed amazingly calm, too. Maybe because they had been through this before and were better prepared for it. She had no money to pay off a fine. Rudy and Dutch had already had the chance to put money away for something like this. She began to feel sick, her heart thumping as her throat constricted. She managed to force out, "Do we have to dump the liquor?"

"Not yet. I'm not sure what she's up to," he said, meaning the coast guard boat.

The guard boat was gaining on them. Dutch stood solemnly at the wheel, stealing occasional glances over his right shoulder to check on their pursuer's progress. Frieda's knees were turning boggy. She thought she might fall, even though she'd always been as steady as the ballast in a boat. "They have to identify themselves, and they can't shoot at us," he said over the sound of the boat thwacking down in the troughs between waves. Dutch was taking the same way in as he'd come out, and now he eased past the same buoys, beacons, and anchored boats he'd carefully maneuvered around before. He shouted to Rudy, "Take a look-see."

Rudy took the binoculars. The guard boat was allowed to traverse the waters blacked out until it was time to identify herself. A small hand lamp normally used in the pilothouse to take a quick glance at a chart was shined upward at the coast guard ensign on the picket boat's halyards. Next it was shined onto the face of the skipper, who smiled in a manner that Frieda didn't know how to interpret.

Rudy laughed. "It's Parker."

Frieda had no idea what that meant, and with the guard boat within earshot now, she didn't want to ask for fear of saying something wrong. Though Dutch and Rudy's tension had subsided, her panic would stay for a while. Dutch throttled down and let the boat come to a drift. After a little skirting about the *Wonder*, the skipper of the guard picket boat pulled alongside, came aboard, and gazed around.

"Boys, where have you been?" He shook Dutch's hand, and Frieda got a look at his face. Even in the darkness she could see his high-bridged nose and its hooked tip, like that of a falcon, and she wondered if he had always had that air of arrogance about him, or if it was something he had acquired along with his commission. "And what have you for me tonight?"

Dutch told the skipper to take his pick. What else could he say? As the guardsman started passing cases back to the other men on the picket boat, he said, "I heard there's some French perfume out there on some of the boats tonight. Didn't happen to get any, did you?"

Dutch shook his head, remaining pleasant, and said, "What's the matter? Don't like the smell of your own armpits?"

The skipper laughed, and his men then knew it was alright to laugh, too.

"I was thinking about the wife. Wouldn't hurt her to learn some French ways in the fucking department."

Everyone laughed except for Frieda.

The skipper strolled toward her. "What do we have here?" he asked.

She stood up. She had no idea what to say.

Dutch answered for her. "My engineer skedaddled on me. This here's my new engineer. Name's Frieda."

"Well, I'll be . . ." the skipper said, and reached out to touch Frieda's hat. He removed it from her head as she stood in the rocking boat without flinching. Her hair fell in a long mess of tangled waves past her shoulders. The skipper said in a more soothing voice, "You should've warned me, Dutch, on account I wouldn't have been so crass."

"Don't worry about me." Frieda finally spoke, but her voice did not come out as firmly or as strongly as she had wanted it to. "I've heard it all," she said, even though that wasn't exactly true. She'd never been treated completely like one of the boys before. Even the hard men who'd been her mechanical work customers had minced their words around women, including her, most of the time.

"You're the engineer?" he asked.

"I can do anything with an engine. I could take it apart and put it back together again blindfolded."

He stared at her briefly, as if she were some new breed of bird that he had yet to catch in his talons, then continued about his business, while all around them other boats went in toward the shore with their hauls.

After the guardsmen had taken about 150 cases, they sped off, and Frieda sincerely hoped she had seen the last of Parker and his sorry lot.

The rest of the return journey was uneventful. The engines were purring, so she scampered up to the bow to sit with Rudy, whose job was to keep watch for obstacles and other boats at all times. The *Wonder* put in at Highland Beach, where transport cars from the city were waiting, and Frieda helped unload the cases while Dutch sold the booze. It was better to be moving about in the cold than sitting and suffering. Her body warmth was oozing away, but by the time the liquor had been unloaded and sold and they had tied back up at the dockside, a new warmth entered her body, and she found herself enlivened with unexpected energy. She had been awake all day and most of the night, too, and yet she had just awakened to a new life.

Dutch said good-bye and left, but not without giving Frieda her night's pay and a wink that let her know she had passed the second test he'd given her. She had performed well; she had done it.

"You're smiling," Rudy said as he looped the excess mooring lines on the dock.

She hadn't realized she had been smiling. Stuffing the money into her pockets, she blew a stream of frosted white breath into the coldest air of the night so far. Memories of the night's events came in vibrant flashes, and she knew she would never forget them. Now, she, too, had a part to play in all the tumultuous change around her. "I guess because we made it, and it was . . . except for a moment or two . . . it went well, don't you think?"

Rudy stood up. "Yeah, it went well." He grabbed his things and started to walk down the dock. Then he stopped and turned around. "Are you coming?"

She hurried to catch up.

"Listen to me," Rudy said as they walked. "Next time it might not be one of the guard boats on the take. Next time it could be real trouble, or worse, it could be a go-through man."

"What's that?"

"A go-through man. A hijacker. A pirate. Criminals, I mean real criminals, not like us dabbling in it for a while. They'll kill every one of us to get the money we have on board going out, or the booze we have on board coming in."

Frieda walked close by his side. "Can't anything be done?"

He laughed at the obvious irony of it. "What are we going to do? Call the law?"

Frieda looked ahead as they reached the place to go separate ways.

"Tonight we were lucky," said Rudy. Under the dock lights she could see that his eyes were shadowed behind his glasses, and his face was cheerless. Rudy had a quick mind and a sense of righteousness about him despite his business. He was making money—but maybe not without incurring costs of other sorts. She had the sense that no one really knew what they had drifted into.

"Why are you telling me this?"

"Didn't Dutch?"

"Not the way you just did. He probably assumes I know all about rumrunning, including all of the risks."

Rudy sighed. "Dutch doesn't like to think about the risks, much less talk about them. But I want you to know it's not all fun and games. It could be dangerous."

"If it's dangerous, then why are you doing it?" Frieda asked him.

He looked at her as if he wanted her to understand. What do most people do when a better life, usually beyond their reach, is suddenly sitting at their doorstep, or in their case, sitting right out at sea? Even Rudy had worn a thick new sweater tonight, and he drove a newer Model T to the docks.

Rudy answered, "Same reason as everyone else."

CHAPTER EIGHT

1925

At the bar on a May afternoon, Frieda sat surrounded by locals, who had come to celebrate the birth of Rudy's third son, Martin. Another redhead, as she had predicted. Frieda sat hunched over her shot of whiskey, willing the kinks out of her neck and waving away approaches from men who didn't know her and her ways. Her new life had transformed her; she belonged down on the docks, she belonged with the runners, and she had money for the first time in her life. She had done what she wanted, and she had done most of it on her own. The engineer's job on Dutch's boat and its success had made her a young woman to be reckoned with. She had grown to trust Dutch and Rudy like family.

The bar was without a single window, and a bright beam of sunlight pierced the gloom each time the door was opened. Men stood outside on the lookout for police, but most everyone in the bar glanced up anyway when the door banged open. To Frieda's surprise it was Bea who burst through the door, waving an envelope in her hand and searching for her sister through the dense smoke.

"Frieda!" she called out over the sounds of people laughing and shouting, music blasting, and the clinking of glasses. Frieda waved her sister over. Bea weaved her way through the throng of people trying to get to the bar for service.

"What are you doing here?" Frieda said as she stood up.

"My acceptance," said Bea, and held out an envelope. "It came in the mail."

"You don't belong in here," Frieda said. Although Bea was now eighteen and had graduated from high school second in her class, Frieda still viewed her sister as sheltered. Bea didn't belong in this seedy shoreside establishment; she belonged at home with her books, magazines, and dreams. Frieda had seen to that, just as Silver had seen to it before the stroke had knocked him down.

Bea was wearing a straight, low-waisted, *garçonne*-style dress and a smart cloche hat on her head, and she smelled of soap and cologne, not of salt and seawater. Clothes and toiletries that Frieda's rumrunning money had provided. It had also paid for a hairdresser's professional cut in the shingled style that Bea now sported, and even more importantly, a new roof on the house, work on the foundation, and anything they wanted from the grocer's.

Bea squeezed into the space between two barstools and handed the acceptance letter to Frieda. Bea had applied to NYU, and Frieda had socked away the money to pay for her to live and study in the city and earn her degree.

Over the past two years Frieda had served as the full-time ship's engineer on Dutch's boat. In April of 1924 the United States had increased the limit of jurisdiction to twelve miles instead of three, making it harder for them all, especially the smaller boats. Now the offshore boats had to wait about twenty miles out, and the contact boats' trips took longer.

But the *Wonder* was up to the task, and her crew had gone out about twelve nights a month, depending on the moon and the weather—more in the warmer months and less during the winter. For the most part the runs went smoothly, and their roles were clear: Dutch was captain and took the helm, Rudy was first mate and lookout man when they ran dark, and Frieda was in charge of the engine, helping out with other tasks as needed. Several times they were chased by guard picket boats bent on arrest instead of collusion, and twice Dutch had to dump the cargo over the side of the boat, though he did so with the booze connected to strong Manila rope lines tied to semisubmerged buoys. Then the next day, with Rudy keeping watch for any reappearance of the picket boat, they went back to the spot, hauled the load, and sold it in the usual way.

Rudy had grinned at her when they found the stash. "It's too easy," he said.

Other boat captains used a flashlight in a weighted and stoppered five-gallon glass jug. Dropped a foot or so below the surface and set with a rock anchor, the jugs could be found by crews the next night by the glow of the dim underwater light.

Once Dutch had to jettison the cargo before any lines or buoys could be attached, because the guard was firing so heavily, tracer bullets landing all around and almost hitting the boat. But he took bearings on shore landmarks and he knew the depth of the channel, so the next day they returned with a clamming rake and some oyster tongs and retrieved most of it. Another time, when this happened close to shore, locals had watched the entire chase from shore, then went out first thing in the morning in rowboats and canoes and took the booty for themselves.

Dutch had grumbled, "Stealing sons of bitches."

"Not like we're legal," Frieda said back.

"Whose side are you on?" he asked with a laugh.

Some boats used rifle fire to shoot out coast guard searchlights during night chases, smashing the lenses and even once killing the man at the beam. Others deliberately tossed aside wooden whiskey cases that could potentially sink or damage guard boats. Yet others sent out phony distress signals that the guard had to answer; after all, their duty was first and foremost assistance at sea and rescue. The government tried to crack down with a blockade and add more boats to the coast guard fleet, yet still the runners and the shore boats were slipping in so much contraband that liquor flowed in restaurants and bars across New Jersey, New York, Pennsylvania, and beyond. Frieda's rolls of money grew.

One bitterly cold winter night they had to dodge floating ice, and Dutch was more nervous than Frieda had ever seen him. Each time they passed another ice floe, he said, "Another damn sinker. They're as thick as fleas on a mutt."

Suddenly, the boat had flooded with light. A guard boat had found them with its searchlight. Normally Dutch would simply outrun them, but with all the ice floes around it was too risky to go full speed ahead. Yet still he had to throttle up somewhat to get out of the range of the searchlight, and Frieda held her breath, preparing for collision.

Once out of the light's reach, Dutch said, "Change of course." He made a slow, wide, arching turn in the opposite direction, back toward the guard boat.

Frieda said through chattering teeth, "What are you doing?"

"The last thing they'll expect is us turning around and getting near 'em again. They'll keep going in, hoping to trap us." He gave her a rigid look. "Don't question me, Frieda."

And she had no choice but to say, "Aye, captain."

The ploy worked. Aided by the cover of snow that had begun to fall, the *Wonder* thwarted her would-be captors and passed the guard boat so silently and slowly the guardsmen had no idea she had slipped away right under their noses.

Another time, on the way in the propeller hit something, most likely a big piece of driftwood or a lobster trap buoy, and the prop was bent so badly that the boat's speed was cut in half. They limped back to the shore, while the boat vibrated from bow to stern. On that night they could've been caught handily, and the slow slog back was endless.

Dutch had said then, "Keep your fingers crossed. Or if you're the praying sort, pray."

Well inside the bay a boat came near, and it didn't take long to see it was one of the guard picket boats. Frieda and Rudy prepared to dump, even though the guard boat was gaining on them so fast they probably couldn't have tossed all the cases in time. Because of the damaged prop, the *Wonder* couldn't try to outrun them, and all seemed lost until they recognized the captain, who happened to be one they knew was on the take. As they had done several other times before, they let the guard captain off-load what he wanted.

By now they knew which guard boat captains could be paid off with booze and which ones wanted money. They knew the cops in town who turned a blind eye to the goings-on in exchange for some of the proceeds. They knew the best judge to go before if they were ever charged with anything. They also knew the guardsmen, policemen, and other authorities who were playing it straight. And there were plenty of strict law enforcers, too, so on that night they were lucky.

One night the fog was so thick that Dutch couldn't find his way back into the bay, and they had to toss out the anchor and spend the rest of the night at sea, but near enough to shore so the anchor would hold. Dutch, Frieda, and Rudy took turns, with two sleeping while the third kept watch, but when it was Frieda's time to sleep, all she could do was listen to the sound of powerful breakers colliding with the shore, the full force of the fathomless seas behind them, and nothing but one small anchor separating them from the same fate as those waves. She had stared into the murk, looking for even the faintest blink of a star, while doubts played out in her mind. What was she doing? The sea could eat alive even the strongest soul. But by morning she had decided that the dangers on the sea were not as frightening as the dangers of being poor.

Occasionally they took their chances and went out during the day. On her first daytime run, Frieda was overcome by the bright new world of blue sky and blue seas, lacy froth and stomach-lurching swells, lemon sun, and bulging clouds. Dragonflies had skimmed the surface of the water as the Hook slowly slid away.

Frieda was seldom frightened, but what truly did scare her were the go-through men. Their name came from the fact that they would go through anything to get what they wanted, and they were a merciless, lowlife group of men who preyed on the inshore contact boats. Typically they advanced in powerful, black-hulled boats just after dusk, when the contact boats were heading out, an hour or so before the coast guard began any pursuits, so there would be no witnesses. No one knew who they were or where they came from, but they were rumored to carry Thompson submachine guns they didn't hesitate to shoot. The *Wonder* found herself under chase one night, but that time the other boat was no faster than theirs, and Rudy tossed overboard a contraption of wood, junk, and wires he'd made just for this possibility, and the go-through boat's prop hit it and their speed slowed to a crawl. Others weren't so lucky, however, and Frieda had heard that along Long Island, dead men had been found on contact boats—and other boats had simply vanished.

On the other hand, they'd made close to two hundred runs without any problems whatsoever, which explained why more and more shore boats were getting in on the action and the money.

When they weren't running or retrieving, the threesome often spent time together in the local speakeasies, where Frieda finally partook of some of the cargo they ferried. She downed shots of whiskey with the men and finally understood the allure of alcohol as she let the worries that had always plagued her slip away for a few hours.

* * *

Frieda shook her head and said again to Bea, "You don't belong in here."

Bea's eyes bright, she said, "Look at all the other women in here, for God's sake. It's a new era for women! I wish you didn't belong here so clearly among the *men*! You know, you could buy yourself a nice dress for a change."

"Sit down," Frieda said, and gave Bea the stool.

"Am I allowed a drink in celebration?" She looked up and down the bar in search of the bartender.

Frieda's lips pursed. "Maybe one. Just this once."

Bea flagged down the bartender. "What should I order?" she whispered to Frieda.

"Something weak."

As the bartender approached, Bea said, "I'll try a Bee's Knees." Then she sat back and waited, looking very much like a young lady poised to take her first dance. Frieda asked, "How's Silver today?" Frieda hadn't seen him since the night before, since she'd arisen and left the house early to work on the *Wonder*'s engine. Despite treatment from a specialist paid for with Frieda's money, Silver's condition had remained virtually unchanged. He needed assistance with all activities and had not regained the ability to speak. Frieda and Bea had encouraged him to communicate by writing with his good hand, but Silver had never been able to write much more than his name, anyway; instead, now he let his feelings and needs be known through gestures and expressions. Frieda had bought him a gramophone, and he loved to listen to music or have one of the girls read to him. His favorites were classical music and Walt Whitman's poems.

Bea answered, "The same. Polly and I got him up this morning, fed him, and settled him out on the porch. He sits there, you know, and looks for you."

After one of the men gave up his seat, Frieda slipped onto the barstool next to her sister. She mumbled, "Thanks," to the man and just sat there, ignoring Bea's comment. Nothing Bea could say could compare to the stares Silver often sent her way. *I know what you're doing,* his eyes said, *and I don't approve.* How she hated what those eyes did to her. They looked right through her.

Hicks appeared over her shoulder. "He checks to make sure you're still alive, Frieda." She turned around to take a good look at Hicks. She rarely saw him now. He clammed and fished during the day; she worked primarily at night. Sometimes he picked up an odd job on an engine, and a few times over the past two years he and Frieda had worked together to fix a more complex engine. But it had been a long time since their last joint job.

So had he come over just to make her feel bad?

He looked unchanged, with the same concern in his eyes, a certain tenderness Frieda could not face. He said, "It must worry Mr. Silver to no end, what you're doing."

Frieda remembered the day Silver had sold the boat and told her that he wanted her to do something safe with her life. Safe! It was true he never would've sanctioned her rumrunning. But safety? How could one ever feel safe without money?

Bea nodded. "He can't go to sleep most nights you're out unless we give him a sleeping powder."

Why was Bea doing this, too? Frieda fumed.

Bea said, "I'm going to college now. You can quit, can't you? I'll get a summer job to help."

After spinning around to face the bar, Frieda folded her hands together on the bar top and stared straight ahead. The money she'd made running had paid for the nurses, the clothes, the good food, and now was going to pay for Bea's education and housing in the city. Frieda had worked on a budget late into the wee hours of many nights. She probably had enough for Bea's education and life in New York City. She probably had enough for Silver's care for several years into the future. But what if something unforeseen came up? She needed excess savings to feel secure. Didn't they know that?

Hicks placed a hand on her shoulder ever so gently, as if to say he understood. Over the past few years Hicks had continued to be a clammer and fisherman plain and simple, while most everyone else glittered in some newfangled way. Now many of the fishermen turned runners drove to the docks in new Cadillacs, Moons, Auburns, and Pierce-Arrows, and their families wore clothes from the city. Over the years many men had slowly surrendered to temptation—but not Hicks.

He continued to stand behind her—a bit too close, she felt. Perhaps he still harbored hope that she would go back to being the girl who only wanted her own clam boat and might marry him and settle down. But she had changed irrevocably, and that was no longer possible, if it ever had been.

Frieda said, "Enough, please." She sipped her shot. She had never liked to gulp it and didn't like the sudden rush that happened the few times she had tried. Rather, she liked the slow ease into a peaceful hum that blocked out the looks, the advances, and the recriminations from people like Hicks and the secret voice inside her head.

Nearby a heated discussion had ensued between a local fisherman and a couple of young men who clearly didn't belong there any more than Bea did. They weren't local—of that Frieda was certain. Too well-dressed—wearing Panama straw hats, cuffed trousers, and two-toned shoes—and too sure of themselves, too cocky to mind that they stood out. They had well-cared-for hands, pressed clothes, and moved with a certain elegance that no local man would ever be able to emulate.

The fisherman, Tom Cleary, was saying in a heated voice, "Sure, I'll rent you my boat, but don't even think of going out for a load of booze. If I find out you've gone within ten miles of a rum boat, I'll wring your blue-blooded necks. Remember I warned you."

It wasn't the first time a group of weekend playboys had come down and tried to enter the business for nothing but a night of fun and adventure. One of the young men, a thin fella with a manicured moustache and horn-rimmed glasses, lifted his glass in the air. "We've been properly scolded," he said to Tom Cleary. "We only wish to take a moonlight ride on the bay."

Didn't they know that nights with a big moon were the worst time to go? *Fools,* she thought. Tom said as much. "Moonlight ride? If you're aiming to head for the rum boats, you couldn't've picked a worse time. You'll get caught, and I could lose my boat. If I find out that's what you're up to, I'll shoot you and leave you on the beach for the crabs."

The other young man stepped up. "Forget it, mate," he said to the fisherman. "I wouldn't want to deceive you."

The second young man came into view, and Frieda froze. She had seen him before. But how was that possible? He wasn't from around here; he smelled of old money. No matter how much the rich tried to dress down in their "casual clothes" and fit in, they reeked of another upbringing, just as hothouse roses always smelled different from wild-flowers. It was in the looks, movements, and mannerisms; Frieda had always distrusted anyone who oozed wealth. But at least this man was honest. Then it hit her: she had seen him on a sailboat about the time she'd started running with Dutch and Rudy. His beauty had stunned her then as it did now.

He said, "We'll find another way of entertaining ourselves."

"You do that," said Tom.

Hicks was telling her about a new speedboat he'd been working on for a customer and how difficult it was to handle in rough seas, how hard to steer while pounding over the waves. But her eyes had never left the face of the rich young man. An Ivy Leaguer if there ever was one. He had a simple but astounding beauty. Tall, with a confident stance. Clever, self-assured eyes. She studied the way his lips moved as he continued to chat with the fisherman and watched the curve of his wrist as he held a bottle of gin by its neck.

He turned and met her gaze, staring with open curiosity right back at her, as if she were a strange and rare bird on display in a cage. Frieda's heart tripped.

She pulled her eyes away and set them on Hicks's face. She knew the boat he was talking about. "If Carl can learn to handle her, he'll be able to outrun anyone out there."

"He got double-crossed by a scoundrel coast guard captain who handed him a rotten deal. Lost his other boat because of it."

"Why, Hicks," Frieda said with a smile. "I thought our business didn't interest you."

He shrugged. "Just sharing a story, that's all."

Bea handed him her acceptance letter. Hicks looked it over, congratulated her, and passed it back. Then he said to Frieda in a low voice, "You've done what you set out to do. You can get out."

Frieda blinked hard. "There's room and board to think of. Plus she'll need clothes and books. And don't forget Silver."

"Silver would want you out of this tomfoolery more than anybody. Look, I listen to all the stories. It's getting harder, more dangerous, and you know it. Get out with what you have. Get out while the getting's good."

She looked at him more closely. He seemed in the midst of some sort of personal loss. So she said as gently as she could in a voice that few ever heard her use, "I know you mean well, but this conversation is as old as two-day fish."

Hicks sipped his drink slowly, just as she did, but he didn't comment again, nor did he leave. Never willing to give up on her, it seemed. The bar was getting more crowded. A few couples started dancing on the old plank flooring, and the lights flickered off and on as if the energy of the place had drained electricity from the wires. Hicks kept glancing her way, and to her dismay his eyes were lit with that old familiar flame. For a terrified moment she thought perhaps he might ask her to dance. Dreading how to refuse him, she was relieved when the opportunity was lost. Relieved only until she saw that Hawkeye was approaching. He broke into their little group, bringing with him the stink of fish and an unwashed body. Frieda tensed. Why would he come near her? He knew she despised him. Hawkeye was verging on drunk, and he slurred his words. "I hear congratulations are in order."

She had just taken a sip of whiskey, and the burn in the back of her throat shot back into her mouth. How dare he congratulate Bea when, more than anyone else, he would love to see both girls fail, would love seeing them used as he had used their mother? Frieda's eyes turned to slits as Bea looked up and accepted his well wishes. When Frieda was able to speak, only four words made their way out of her.

"Get away from her," she said tersely through her teeth.

He grabbed ahold of the bar. "I only wish the best for the girl," said the white-haired old cur, his eyes reflecting pain or remorse or something else. Guilt, Frieda decided.

Frieda hissed, "She doesn't want to hear from you."

"I don't?" piped in Bea.

Hawkeye said, "Let the girl speak for herself."

Bea quipped, "Yeah, Frieda."

Now Frieda was fuming at the both of them, but she focused her rage on Hawkeye. Bea was too young to know better. "How dare you try to come between my sister and me!"

Hawkeye rocked on his heels. "What?"

"Haven't you done enough? We all know what you did to our mother." Stunned she had said that, Frieda tried to gulp back her words. She never mentioned her mother, nor did anyone else for that matter, at least not in front of her. The liquor had given life to her anger and loosened her tongue, and Bea and Hicks held still from the shock of the mention of Della Hope. They had no idea she had almost said, *"And now you have your eye on my sister and me!"* She bit down on her lip and breathed in and out a few times in large gulps of air.

Bea said, "Old business."

Hawkeye took off his hat, revealing oily white threads smeared onto his forehead, and he appeared sobered by her words. "I always wished the best for your mother, God rest her soul." At that moment he looked more pitiable and penitent than ruthless and cruel.

But once her rage had shown itself she couldn't plug it, couldn't stop the rushing flow. "Where were you when she was sick?"

Hawkeye never lowered his sharpened gaze, as if Frieda's words had awakened him from a deep sleep. "I done what I could." He pointed a finger at her. "Now listen here, young lady. You don't know as much as you think you do."

"You did what you could? Guess that wasn't much, was it?" Hicks placed a calm hand on her shoulder, but Frieda shrugged it off.

A line of distress ran down the center of Hawkeye's greasy forehead. "I did more than the others did."

Those words, like daggers. "The others?" The sting festered and made the room seesaw. Why did this still hurt so badly? "Aren't you the devil, so good at rubbing salt into an open wound?"

"I meant no harm, not to your mother, your sister, not even you, though you're the mean one." He wagged his finger again. "You need to learn how to watch that mouth of yours, because someday someone's going to—"

She grabbed his finger and twisted it so hard she heard a crack. Hawkeye let out an alarming wail, Hicks gasped, and then the bar went silent. Doubled over, Hawkeye clutched his finger, and Frieda heard Bea breathe out an astonished, "Frieda . . ."

"Go to hell," Frieda said to Hawkeye, although she hadn't meant to hurt him badly. She might have been small built, but she could summon an almighty strength when she needed to.

Around them the bar remained frozen like a photograph. Frieda didn't know if the bar was really as silent as it seemed, or if nothing could be heard above the pounding of her heart.

Hawkeye looked in agony, and for a moment she felt regret. Still holding his finger, he straightened up. "I hope," he began, as his eyes misted over, "that someday you know the pain of loving someone you can't have, Miss Frieda. I don't wish harm on no person, but I wish for you to know this."

How dare he? "I wish to amend my comment." She stood up and plunked down some bills on the counter. "Go *straight* to *bloody* hell."

She pushed away from the bar and took long strides toward the door. People parted for her. Her vision was blurred from held-back tears or the smoke in the place or her anger, but she did see well enough to notice the handsome Ivy Leaguer with the beautiful lips as she passed him by. She paused and stared at him—the scent of worldly experience wafting, charms abounding, face handsome-ing. He held her gaze with what looked like a bit of awe and respect, lifted the bottle in a little salute, and gave a single nod of his head.

Outside the night was soft and silky. The beam of the lighthouse was making its sweep; the distant lights of the big city were in sharp view. The clanging of some boat's bell hammered through her bones. A brisk night wind was blowing in off the water, and she pulled her sweater across her chest. She began to walk briskly toward home and then heard footsteps behind her.

"That was quite a show," Hicks called out.

She continued to stride away.

"This life is roughing you up, Frieda," he called out just loud enough for her to hear him. "It's making you hard."

She said over her shoulder, "I've always been hard."

CHAPTER NINE

Two days later Carl, the man who had bought the big speedboat Hicks had told her about, sold it to Dutch. Carl had been scared off by reports of go-through men murdering entire crews, but his boat left no doubt as to what his original intentions had been. The *Pauline* was equipped with two compartments for carrying cargo, one in the engine room and one between the engine room and crew's quarters under the pilothouse, meaning that she could carry more than a thousand bags of cargo. Fifty feet long, she was a beauty, and Frieda quickly inspected the engine room. Fitted with three engines capable of three hundred horsepower each, and all fitted with silencers, the boat could make thirty-five to thirty-eight knots even with cases on board.

Dutch stood aside as Frieda completed her inspection. It was midday, the sun at the top of the sky. "My oldest son got his college acceptance letter, too, and my wife wants a new house up in the hills. We already bought the plot, and she's working with an architect to kit it out with all the frills," he said. "I figure we can go out more nights on this one. We can handle rougher seas. We'll get out and back faster. And we won't even have to wait for dark nights if we don't want to."

"I won't dare ask how much she cost," said Frieda.

"I aim to make it back in six months' time," answered Dutch.

They motored her out for a test run in the bay, and Dutch let Frieda take the helm. There was a flat calm, and the sun was a bright coin hanging in the sky, raining down warmth. Frieda realized she had forgotten how nice it was to be out on the water with nowhere to go and nothing to fear. The boat, with her V-shaped hull, cut through the water as if it were a sheet of spread oil. Dutch squinted into the sunlight, his face turning redder by the minute; even with his fair complexion, he was one of the only watermen who rarely wore a hat.

Dutch said, "Lucky for you Hawkeye's finger ain't broke. He could've pressed charges. But I hear he's willing to let it go, because it's just a sprain."

"Oh, that's big of him. He's such a lying scoundrel. I bet I only cracked his knuckle."

Dutch laughed harshly. "Remind me never to cross you."

Frieda shrugged. "It's worked out pretty good for us these years. I pledged never to cross *you*, captain, remember?"

"That you did." Dutch rubbed his chin and they flew onward.

"One thing I didn't tell you yet," he shouted over the wind a few minutes later.

Frieda tossed a glance his way but kept her focus on the water ahead.

"I took on another man."

She shot him an inquisitive look. "Why do we need another man?"

"I figure with this boat our chanciest moments'll be when we ain't moving a knot, when we're loading up off the rummies. He's a big guy; he can help get her loaded up fast."

Frieda shrugged.

"We'll all still be making more money. This fella don't even want part of the take."

"What?" she said, and almost let off the throttle.

"Yep, that's the truth."

It made no sense to Frieda until she saw who the new man was. The next night the handsome Ivy Leaguer from the bar made his way down the pier just as the sun was beginning to sink low in the sky, and Frieda had to catch her breath. Sauntering in that way that only the rich could saunter, panther-like, he wore sufficiently faded khaki pants and a plaid shirt that showed wear yet couldn't disguise that it had been purchased in a fine shop. The new canvas tie-ups and smart boater hat were dead giveaways, too. He approached the boat without an ounce of hesitation and tossed down a small rucksack. She noticed the line of white skin on his wrist where he must have normally worn an expensive wristwatch.

"Princeton," said Dutch. "Meet Frieda."

She fought not to gasp as he tipped his hat. She leapt to her feet and felt herself blush.

"I've already met the lady," he said. "Well, I guess we've not formally met, but I've seen her alright." He addressed this to Dutch, although his eyes never left hers. So here he was standing right in front of her: the beautiful rich boy who had paid his respects as she had shoved her way out of the bar. She was surprised he remembered her. She looked deep into his face; it was a youthful face, but the elegant, angular bones suggested he would fit in among English nobility. Snobbishness was saved by gentle eyes filled with eagerness, and something even more extraordinary, an innate sadness. She found herself momentarily mute.

A crazy feeling came over her that she'd somehow mystically beckoned him here, that she'd pieced together snippets of her secret fantasies into this perfection. Her hidden loneliness, her needs, her wants had come to life and bid him here.

"Frieda, ain't you going to speak?" asked Dutch.

She offered her hand to the man, brushed away her wild thoughts, and let herself return to her more normal state of annoyance. Just a rich boy, probably college educated—there had to be a reason Dutch was calling him Princeton—and most likely handy on board because of summers by the shore on daddy's boat. Here was someone who wanted adventure, someone who didn't need to do this. Someone out for a bit of fun.

"I don't hear 'welcome aboard' from you, little miss," Princeton said with a dynamic smile. Perfect white teeth gleamed from a face tanned most likely by holidays; certainly not by work out in the sun.

Did that smile ever fail to charm? Did he know how handsome he was? Of course he did, but she told herself it had no effect on her. She tersely said, "Welcome. There's work to be done."

"I've never been afraid of work."

We'll see about that, Frieda thought.

Only a scratch of silver moon hooked the sky that night, and the seas were dark and hypnotically still as they made the run out to the rum boats, and the stars seemed to rise from the sea. The rush of adrenaline that came with going out had never simmered down for Frieda. And tonight there was the additional tension of not knowing for certain what this singular new man was doing here.

Princeton sat as close to the pilothouse as he could, while Dutch explained the rules. No lights, no smoking, and no loud talking. Keep your eyes peeled at all times. Rudy took to the bow with his binoculars, and Frieda remained in the engine room to familiarize herself further with the engines of that fine boat, listening to her hum. She would care for it as she had cared for the *Wonder*, draining every drop of oil from the engines after each trip, refilling the pan with top-quality oil, pouring the gasoline into the tanks through a chamois leather to filter it for purification, and adjusting the points and plugs clearances to within a thousandth of an inch. Below deck was a complete set of tools, with spare plugs, batteries, flashlights, and other engine parts she might need in a clutch.

They made the run out with no problems, and when Frieda came above deck for air, she turned her face into the wind off the bow and let it pour over her face. Every run was a little different, every run a new adventure. Although she loved taking care of the engines on land, nothing could compare to the journey out to sea. This was the best part of the job. All the moments in port were but a prelude to these. She loved Bea and Silver, but her life with them had remained rather drab. They lived much as they had before so that most of Frieda's money could be stocked away. All concerns, however, soared away out here.

At the rum boats their cases were loaded uneventfully. With Princeton helping, the loading phase went faster. The coast looked clear for a return journey. On the slower run back to shore, Frieda came up for fresh air and found Princeton sitting by himself, gazing out to sea as the wind whipped his hair and his eyes gleamed with an excited contentment. It was the same way she felt each and every night. But her first night stood out. That night, now so long ago. She recalled those feelings that Princeton must have been experiencing now.

"Join me," he said, and Frieda moved to his side. Something about his presence, that longing look in his eyes, along with its sadness, drew her near.

"I didn't know Princeton boys were interested in boats—other than pleasure yachts, of course."

"I've always loved the ocean," he said quietly without moving.

The sea had already changed. Now the curved moonlight fluttered through wispy clouds, and some chop scudded across the bay, sculpting ridges on the surface. "What do you know of the sea?"

He paused. "I don't know it like you do, I suppose. But I've crossed this ocean," he said with a gesture toward the Atlantic.

"As a passenger, of course."

After he smiled, he said, "As a passenger. On my first crossing I was just a kid going over with my parents. It was only a year or so after the *Titanic*. To tell you the truth, I was scared to death, even though I had to put on a brave face."

The boat cut across the ridged swells and settled into a nice rhythm. Frieda was surprised to find herself relaxing in Princeton's company.

She sensed life experience, intelligence, and a worldliness that he didn't flaunt. "So how long are you planning to do this?" she asked after they had sat in silence for a few minutes.

"The summer."

"Then what?"

"Off to Harvard Law."

"Oh," Frieda said through a sigh. "This is a summertime adventure. What happened? Parties at the beach house and dinners in the city weren't enough for you?"

He laughed. "As a matter of fact, no. They weren't—they aren't—enough for me."

"You need a little danger in your life," she said flatly.

His eyebrows shot up. "Hmm, maybe so." Then his eyebrows flattened, and his eyes filled with curiosity. "I wonder why that is."

She laughed. "There's no doubt why that is. If you don't know danger otherwise, if you don't have to worry about having enough money or food or shelter, maybe you have to go out and find it. Maybe it helps you feel alive."

At first his face was blank, and then it softened into what seemed to be admiration and a bit of amusement. "That's a very interesting theory."

She said no more.

Holding still, his head cocked, his gaze firm, he seemed to absorb every detail of her and what she had said. Then, "A very interesting theory. One that I frankly hadn't thought of before. And it might just be true."

She turned her head and caught his eye. "What happens if you get caught?"

After shrugging he said, "Plenty of lawyers in the family."

She looked ahead. "I see."

He put his hands between his knees, and his voice lowered and surprised her with its solemn timbre. "You don't want me here."

Her breathing halted. "It wasn't my decision. It's Dutch's boat."

"You didn't answer my question."

"I didn't realize it was a question. It sounded more like a statement."

After leaning back, he smiled. "Ah, you either want to challenge me . . . or dismiss me. It could make for some interesting conversations. Nothing about colleges and money and society girls my mother wants me to marry."

"Oh, poor you, bless your heart."

A laugh burst out of him. She was surprised—and relieved—that she could speak freely. It seemed he could match her banter without being combative or the least bit defensive. Instead of barbs, it was as if they were giving each other easy nudges. It wouldn't help to be at each other's throats, especially if trouble came their way. "So what's wrong with Princeton and Harvard Law?" she asked.

"Human beings have a natural tendency toward ignorance," he said with a smile. "I don't want to interfere with that too much."

Frieda had to let that settle. Almost everything Princeton said was a surprise. "So, knowledge is a bad thing?"

"Ignorance, or a certain amount of it anyway, might just be the key to happiness."

"Ah, so you're spending time among the ignorant masses to uncover our secrets of lifelong delight."

"If you're so fond of education, then why aren't you in school somewhere instead of out here?"

"I'll have you know I had a wildly successful high school education."

The grin on his lovely lips had not left. "Clever girl."

"My father saved enough for secretarial school, but I wouldn't be happy sitting in an office surrounded by gossiping women and cigar-smoking bosses."

"You're making my case."

She shook her head.

His smile faded. "Princeton and Harvard Law, you see—none of it was my choice."

"Come now. Nothing about your life was or is your choice? You're here right now, and I doubt you asked anyone's permission about that, other than Dutch's."

"You're right. This is one of the first decisions I've been able to make on my own."

She glanced around. "Now, where oh where is my tiny violin when I need it?"

He cupped the back of his head in his hands. The ease of his movements and his confidence shook her. "You don't get it, and you never will. But you amuse me, Frieda. You're an unusual girl."

She relaxed. He was . . . genuinely likable.

"I'm not asking for anyone's sympathy or even their understanding. But I had to ask my parents' permission to take this summer to myself. They had decided I needed more time in Europe to experience the culture, but I wanted to strike out and do something different and of my own choosing."

"Mingling with the lower classes."

"As you keep saying."

"And you think you'll find that 'something different' here? It gets tiresome. And winter can be brutal. But never mind about that. This is just a summer soirée for you. Nevertheless, we'll get chased; you wait and see."

He looked out over the water. "You aren't going to scare me off, if that's what you're after."

She faced ahead, into the wind. "Where are you living?"

"I found a summer house to rent up on Portland Road."

"Of course you did."

"So what's wrong with summer houses?"

She shook her head.

The boat slowed as their conversation came to a halt.

"We're coming in for the drop now."

"OK. Tell me what I need to know."

She was impressed that he seemed to want to learn, and by his eagerness to dive into even the most menial of tasks. The drop could be as risky as the runs. "We never land at the same place back to back. We have five favorite drop zones, and we always rotate. And we always know where we're going to drop before we go out. Our drop man signals us from the beach when everything looks clear to come in. He used to light bonfires on the beach, but now he uses flashlights of different colors. Dutch also uses the radio when he needs to, but always in code. The guard is getting better at intercepting and deciphering the runners' radio transmissions. So we have to change things from time to time. The drop man's nickname is Cobra. He's been with us from the beginning, and Dutch trusts him with our lives."

"Sounds like an important job."

"He has to be able to defend the drop zone from thieves and pay off police if necessary. If he wanted to, he could stage a fake holdup and run off with the whole lot of it before the buyers come."

Now it was his turn to say, "I see."

There was a brief silence.

"I saw you once before. Down here," Frieda said. "A couple of winters ago. You were on a sailboat."

He seemed to be searching his memory. "I was here helping out a friend then, but I would've remembered seeing you. It must have been someone else."

"No. It was you."

"I doubt that."

"No. It was you."

As they pulled into shore, Frieda remembered back to when she had first seen Princeton. All along his image had been lingering somewhere in the back of her mind. Had the strength of her will beckoned him to return to this place and enter her life?

CHAPTER TEN

The drop went smoothly, but because the boat had a V-hull instead of a flat bottom, the men had to wade in waist-deep water to bring in the haul. In the winter they would have to use a rowboat. Princeton joined in the cool-water slog to shore, slinging bags of liquor as if he had been born to it and occasionally smiling at Frieda. Absolute silence was a must at the drop, as there were houses and roads nearby and they couldn't call any unwanted attention to themselves. The cars holding buyers came and went slowly without headlights, and some of the loot was sold that night, then and there. The rest went into storage sites that Dutch had arranged. He'd found locals with sheds who were willing to risk storing the contraband for five dollars a case for freight, one dollar for storage. If they took two hundred cases from him, they made twelve hundred dollars for twelve hours' work—more money than those fishermen usually made in a year battling the sea and the elements. The exchanges between all the men onshore were made in whispers absorbed by the soft sand underfoot.

After they had arrived back at the docks, it was well past two in the morning but still earlier than they'd ever made it back before, so they decided to go to the dockside juice joint for a drink before calling it a night. The usual feeling of elation and relief after the run ended was still there, but another kind of adrenaline surge had set Frieda's nerves zinging. She could scarcely feel her feet as they walked the long pier, the four of them sliding into the speakeasy.

Unexpectedly, Frieda became aware of her appearance. Behind the bar was a scratched and smudged mirror, but it gave her enough of a sense of how she must look. Sea-blown hair, too long and out of style; her lips wind chapped; freckles on her cheeks from too much time in the sun; not a trace of pancake makeup or lipstick; dressed in a shirt and pants, like a man. Her nails bitten down raggedly, with engine grease underneath, and her hands red, raw, and probably repulsive, the skin calloused and chafed from pulling on mooring lines and handling engine parts.

And still Princeton's eyes focused on her. He had found a way to wiggle in close beside her while Rudy and Dutch became engrossed in conversation with two other runners. In the mirror she caught stolen glimpses of him through the haze and then quickly averted her eyes.

Blood thrumming in her neck and breath threading in her chest, she whispered, "What is your real name?"

"Charles John Wallace the third."

"The third? Why is it only rich men pass on their names?"

He took a swig of his whiskey. "Damned if I know."

"I suppose Princeton was just awful."

He ordered another round of drinks. "Is this the only subject in which we're allowed to engage?"

Frieda shrugged with one shoulder.

"No. Princeton was not awful. I was able to take a variety of courses there. Art, literature, sciences. But once I get to law school, it's just law. Nothing else."

"Why do you have to go?"

"Ah," he said. "That's a long and tedious story. But the short of it is that almost all the men in my family have law degrees. It's expected. A rite of passage. But enough of this!" he asserted, but in a pleasant way. "All that family duty is downright boring compared to this." He gestured around the bar, but he obviously meant the entirety of running against the law. "Out on the boat you don't know what's going to happen from one night to the next. And that's what I want. I want to be surprised. And what you said earlier about the danger is probably true, too," he finished.

Charles laid his hand on hers on top of the bar.

Frieda pulled it back. "What are you doing?"

"At the moment I'm trying to get your attention."

"Ha!"

"Don't laugh. I have to work hard to hold your attention; I know that already. I have to impress you somehow."

Frieda blinked and tried to fathom what was happening. "Because I'm a female in close proximity? Because I'm convenient?"

He set those lovely seeking eyes on her. The laws of biological chance had been breached when Charles was born. Not fair for one person to get so much.

"You're more than just a female in close proximity. And you're hardly convenient. I came here for a simple adventure with no complications. I never planned on coming across you." And then the swim of sadness in his eyes, captivating her. "I haven't been able to get you out of my mind since you stormed out of the bar the other night."

His words, his panther-graceful body, and his admiring gaze made Frieda feel as if she'd suddenly been lifted off the floor. She had no idea what to do with all of this. Could he really be interested in the likes of her? She breathed out, "I'm an odd bird."

"How so?"

"Isn't it obvious? I don't wear dresses. Don't do my hair. Don't wear perfume."

"Don't bathe?" he said with a grin.

She laughed. "Of course I bathe. But things girls are supposed to care about don't mean that much to me."

"So, what *do* you care about?"

He reached for her hand again, and Frieda was loath to deter him for a minuscule moment. A small bolt attached to her heart turned loose a notch, allowing a little leak of feeling to pass through. What meant most to her just then was Princeton's approval, and she hated her vulnerability. She was never vulnerable. She was entranced by his every movement and expression and enraged at herself. How was this happening to her? She sensed compassion in this man who sat before her, vulnerable himself. But this . . . this she knew nothing about. She was the proverbial fish out of water.

She looked away and slowly reclaimed her hand. "I care about boats."

He appeared a tad . . . hurt. "Good answer. It's a good thing to have someone who cares about boats on board a boat. But you're avoiding the question."

Frieda held her breath. "Yes." She exhaled. "I am."

He studied her a few moments longer, then gazed back toward the bartender and said, "Fair enough."

When they had drunk their fill, they left the bar. Princeton placed his hand at the small of Frieda's back as he opened the door for her to step through. From anyone else the gesture might have maddened her, but from him it was as simple as the lack of guile in his eyes or the casual poise of his posture. Princeton offered to escort her home, and she almost laughed at him but held herself back.

"There's no need," she told him. Her mouth was dry from the liquor or from nerves, and her hands were sweaty as she pushed them tightly into her jacket pockets. She was dumbstruck by the beauty of his chiseled face when he was serious, maybe even lovelier than when he smiled. She told herself that his offer to escort her home was nothing more than what his sort of gentleman offered to do for a lady and that it fell perfectly within the confined manners of his world.

"Are you sure?" he asked, and then amazingly seemed to be seeking *her* approval. He lifted a curious eyebrow, an air of longing about him.

"Talk about no surprises. I know every inch of my way around this town. I know just about everyone who lives here, too. So yes, I'm sure."

She was almost certain she saw disappointment in his face, only a few inches away.

Slowly he said, "I'll see you tomorrow, then?" followed by that dazzling smile.

She nodded.

"Good night, Frieda."

She waved and backed away, but even after she turned she sensed that he stood there on the wharf, watching her go and sending into the air the silky ribbons of his sweet thoughts. As she continued to plant one foot in front of the other, she forced herself not to turn around and instead let the first brightening violet light of dawn touch her face. During the night she had lost all track of time.

When she let herself into the house, all was silent except for the sound of Silver snoring in the bedroom. Bea lay asleep on the divan, an open magazine across her lap. Frieda tidied up and lay down on the floor, for the first time admonishing herself for not buying a couple of regular beds for her and Bea, though where would they have put them? She could have rented a bigger house, but she didn't think Silver would take well to the idea of moving. He'd lived in this house most of his life and loved the view from the front porch.

Frieda couldn't sleep. Instead she reviewed everything about the night. Tonight she had done nothing to improve the upper class's impressions of working-class people.

She settled under her sheet and remembered the way it felt when he sat next to her, the heat of his body beside her as the night cooled, the way his eyes searched the sea in longing for something, the way he swung the bags with such gusto and enthusiasm, the way he freely shared his disappointment in his rich boy's life. She tried to bring his face into full focus, and she could recall the line of his lips, his broad, flat forehead hovering over a heavy brow, and the jaw that seemed just slightly undersized for the rest of his face. She wanted desperately to pull all of those pieces into a clear vision of him as a whole, but she could not put it all together, like a puzzle with pieces that didn't quite fit. But why was she doing this? She had never been one to swoon over a man. She had made a free life for herself; she didn't need a man. But what was this odd and unnerving pull? *Dismiss it,* she told herself. Besides, how crazy was it for her—twenty-two years old, daughter of a whore, rumrunner's boat engineer, sleeping on the floor of an old house—to give a moment's thought to a man like Charles John Wallace the third?

CHAPTER ELEVEN

They made three more successful runs that week, each one filled with that familiar elation, and only during the last run was there a moment of danger. One of the larger coast guard cutters, seventy-five feet long, with a white hull and housing gold-braided patrol officers, gave chase on the way in. The *Pauline*, even with her speed, was so loaded with bags of booze that the cutter was gaining on her. Dutch, always confident, looked annoyed, but Frieda feared the worst. She was relieved when Dutch ordered the dump. They began to toss out the liquor three bags at a time.

Princeton sprang into action, along with the rest of them. He tossed over the bags as ordered but never seemed scared. Terror seized Frieda's heart each time they were chased. She had everything to lose. But what of Princeton? Did he know that his family would always get him out of any trouble? Or would he claim to have hitched a one-time ride and feign complete ignorance of the boat's purpose?

But when the coast guard saw the crew dumping, they made a slow turnaround. Their captain knew that by the time he chased the inshore contact boat down, no evidence would be left on board. Parker and the other guardsmen on the take were long gone, and these new boat captains were out to catch them. But they also knew when to give up.

So as the cutter glided away, Dutch ordered the crew to stop dumping and then continued on course. Now that the threat had dissipated, Frieda's heart rate was ticking down to normal. She sat next to Princeton, as had become their new habit. "Was that enough of a surprise for you? Enough danger and excitement?"

"I don't know yet," he answered with a gleam in his eyes. "I still don't know how the night's going to end."

Sighing, Frieda sat up straight. "Well, I for one hope nothing else happens."

He looked at her. "Are you sure?"

What else did he think she wanted? They'd been chased by a guard boat. Wasn't that enough? His eyes peered into hers as if seeking something else, as if he was actually seeking more with *her*.

Each night Princeton had kept a gentlemanly distance. They were there to do a job, after all, and he had become as focused as the rest of them, but even when they were in the middle of a fast and near-silent run back or forth, the gleaming gift of his gaze always found her and drew her to his side. He took every opportunity to sit next to her. He scooted up close and pointed out the landmarks of New York City as they sped past the lights, and his eyes sought her out as if she were the one who needed protection and not the other way around. If she were an odd bird, then he was a rare bird.

She finally answered him: "I hate getting chased. It scares me every time."

Leaning back, he peered at her, his eyes playful. "I knew it."

She turned to look at him. "Knew what?"

"Tough cookie has a soft inside."

"Tough cookies never have a soft inside." She glanced down, then back up, while a smile twitched on her lips. "But you're conceding that I'm a tough cookie?"

"I'm saying that you hide the softer side of yourself well." He tapped his temple. "But I know."

"Oh, I get it. Now you're going to analyze me. After all, we've been acquainted for years."

He laughed. "You're no dumb Dora, that's for sure." His voice changed. "In fact, I think you might just be an old soul."

Frieda's brow creased. "I've never understood what that means."

"It means," he said, leaning forward and peering even closer, "in some religions followers believe in reincarnation. An old soul is one that has been reincarnated many times, gaining a certain amount of innate wisdom from past lives."

"I never knew that," Frieda said. "Now, that's the kind of thing I would've liked to learn in school."

"Just as I thought."

He was clearly studying her, and Frieda wasn't sure how to feel about that. She wasn't a specimen! But his attention, his focus . . .

"And I'll find out more about you in time."

She had to look away. Even a tough cookie could be crumbled in the hands of someone like Princeton. She eased out, "I have nothing but time."

He gave a little nod, as if their time had already begun.

They continued on to the prearranged drop site and simply sold what they had left.

She was helping Rudy get the boat moored and secure back at the pier. In some ways Rudy had the most important job of the four of them. He had to keep a constant watch for other boats. Since they and many others ran completely dark, the fear of collision was always on their minds, and Rudy was their lookout man. The waters they ran were heavily traveled with commercial fishermen, coastal tankers, passenger vessels, and deep-sea boats bound into or out of New York harbors. In the summer there were pleasure yachts, too. He had worked as the first mate with Dutch for three years now and with Frieda for over two, and never did he complain. Never did he pry into either her or Dutch's private worlds, either. But now he looked at her strangely. "Do you know what you're doing?" he finally asked as he adjusted a fender.

She glanced up from the stern of the boat, where she had been coiling some dock lines, to where Princeton stood waiting for her on the end of the pier. The stars were out, and there was no wind, only the sounds of boats gently rocking in the water and the soft slaps of the waves landing on shore.

Rudy was one of those sensitive souls, attuned to every nuance in the air around him, every tilt of the planet. And he was concerned for her; that meant something. She thought she could read his mind and its prediction: big-city rich boy comes to small town and woos local girl, then leaves her heartbroken.

Frieda looked away from Princeton as he stood waiting patiently, rock solid on the pier while an unexpected crashing wave heaved against the pilings and sent up a little burst of spray. She already knew that the seawater had a tendency to curl his hair, that he liked to sit facing the city on a run, that he liked his coffee black, that he didn't wash his own clothes.

She said to Rudy, "I haven't done anything yet."

Rudy glanced at Princeton and then back at her.

"I'm not talking about him," he said, "although that could be something worth examining. I'm talking about this, what we're doing here."

She wiped the droplets of salt water from her face. Rudy hadn't spoken to her like this since the night two years ago when she'd first joined the crew. What was bothering him now?

As if he'd read her mind, Rudy said, "That cutter knows who we are now. We're not such a small operation anymore; we have one of the biggest boats. We'd be a great success story for them if they caught us. They'll be back."

"Guess so."

"It doesn't bother you?"

"Not as much as it should."

Rudy, finished with his chores now, took off his glasses and cleaned them with the tail of his shirt. "Just want you to know the risks you're taking before you get in too deep."

"Too deep? It's been two years! I appreciate your concern, but where is your worry for all the others involved?"

Rudy shrugged and smiled. "They're not dames."

Frieda laughed. "You can't include me in that lot. I've never been girly."

"You're still a dame. We men need to look out for the womenfolk, you know." His face sobered. "Besides, haven't you made enough?"

Frieda finished coiling and storing extra dock lines, then stuffed her hands into her pants pockets. "I have Bea to put through school, Silver to look after. You know that." Her voice changed. "And what about you? Haven't you had enough?"

"I got me a wife and three kids, but yeah, I'm thinking I've got just about enough. I'm thinking that after the summer's over, this . . ." He gestured around. "This is gonna be over for me, too."

He confused her. There was too much money to be made. And how much is ever enough? What if Silver's condition worsened and he needed round-the-clock professional nurses or hospitalization for years to come? What if he had another stroke that affected the other side? He'd be completely helpless. How long would her money last then? And what if Bea's tuition went up? What if Dutch quit running and she couldn't find enough work?

But over the years she'd gained a lot of respect for Rudy and his opinions, more so than Dutch. Dutch was getting cocky. Just tonight he'd whooped and hollered when the cutter gave up, whereas Rudy had been sweating, even though the night was cool. Rudy might have one drink in the speakeasy after work, but then he went home to his family. Dutch, on the other hand, was sometimes staying out all night. His blond hair was turning more white every day, and his face was now dotted with what looked like permanent age spots. He spent a lot of time shuffling between the boat, the shore, and his storage sites, and often he carried a flask of whiskey under his coat. But she never asked any questions; this was a most unusual conversation.

She said to Rudy, "Summer's just started."

"How well I know this, Frieda. I'm just saying that once the weather turns foul again and we've saved up all summer long, let's you and me get out of this thing. Let's go back on the level. We're not in it for fun."

She knew his comment about "fun" was aimed at Princeton, and she didn't argue with the truth.

CHAPTER TWELVE

Two nights later they went out on a run again, and their boat moved like a stingray in slick waters. They were making great money, and when they pulled in earlier than usual, Dutch said, "The night is young. This calls for a celebration."

It was a lovely night, with millions of stars splattered across the sky and only a curved blade of waxing moon cutting across that dark velvet. The wind hushed like someone sighing, and music drifted down over them from dockside bars. Normally she and Rudy headed home or each had a drink at night's end, but both agreed it would be nice to stay out for a while. Princeton offered no objection either, so while they put gear away and secured the boat for the night, Dutch set up something of a makeshift bar on the afterdeck and started mixing.

Frieda, Rudy, and Princeton settled in, lounging about. Now that they were back in port, Princeton did not wait for her on the end of the pier. Not like when they were on the boat running in. Princeton made no effort to speak with her, and his eyes did not chase her around tonight. What had happened? Maybe she had held her distance too long and pushed him away. Disappointment settled over Frieda. She pored over the night's memories for a clue as to what could have made Princeton change. He'd sat beside her as before and conversed in his casual, teasing manner, but now there was a sense of remoteness, as if he'd dug a gulf between them. Maybe he'd had his fill of her already; maybe she'd simply been a way to kill time on board the boat. Maybe that was all he'd been after: to conquer and then withdraw. Then again, nothing much had actually happened between them. She felt burning shame for ever having imagined that they could have become a couple. No one else in his or her right mind would ever think they could have been together. How foolish had been her feelings.

Dutch, almost finished making his concoction, paused for a moment, tilted his head upwards, and then said, "I heard that some of those stars out there, by the time their light has got here they're already burnt out."

"I heard that, too," said Rudy, but Frieda kept quiet. Her eyes kept drifting to Princeton; she found herself sadly studying his stance and movements. The loss of his attention was like having something precious, which you held secretly in your hands, suddenly snatched away.

"What do you say, Princeton?" Dutch asked.

Princeton shrugged. "Don't know much about space. I'm not a physicist."

"A *physicist?*" Dutch barked. "I'm talking about being a person. Most *persons* find that kind of thought pretty damn amazing."

Princeton shrugged again. With his education he had to know a great deal more about space than she, Dutch, or Rudy did, and she would've liked to hear him share some of that knowledge. But it was obvious that Princeton didn't want to seem superior to his current peers. He didn't flaunt.

Dutch invited a few other runners to join them, as he had by now blended his brew—whiskey with champagne, topped off with dollops of brandy and green-mint liquor. When he started passing drinks around, Frieda said, "None for me."

Dutch reared back, feigning offense. "Don't want to sample my magic?"

Frieda removed her cap and shook out her hair. "Sure and steady course to sickness, looks like to me."

"Ah, come on. Thought you was one of the boys."

"Not tonight."

He lowered his voice. "It ain't because of Princeton, is it?"

Frieda stiffened as a stab of fear poked her in the sternum. Did everyone see what had come over her? Were they as shocked as she was, and were they feeling the need to protect her? Dutch's way was with glibness; Rudy's was with kindness. Was her fondness so obvious? And now her disappointment? Thank God Princeton was out of earshot, chatting it up with the other runners on board.

She fixed her eyes on Dutch's. She could do this. She could pretend to be completely at ease. "It's because I want to leave here tonight standing on my own two feet."

Dutch jerked his head to one side. "Suit yourself."

All the men finished the first round and then started on another. Frieda sipped on champagne. Rudy stopped after two drinks and came to sit next to her. She figured he had enough alcohol in his system that he wouldn't notice how her eyes yearningly followed Princeton as he kept up with all these hard-drinking sailors.

But he did. He followed her gaze as she watched Princeton gulp down another tumbler full of Dutch's madness, and Dutch said to him, "You sure can swig hefty, Princeton old boy, cain't you?"

Princeton answered, "I've been known to hold my liquor. One of the first things you learn in college."

Dutch whooped out a laugh and fixed them both another drink. Frieda wondered how long Princeton could take this.

After delivering the next round to the others, Dutch sidled up to Princeton and said, "Must be good for you with the ladies, you being an Ivy Leaguer and all."

Frieda listened hard. She didn't want to miss this. She had no clue about Princeton's romantic past.

Princeton shrugged, took a slug of the fresh drink, and said with a devious grin, "So many dames, so little time."

Another slight. But then again, what was he to say? Princeton had become expert at dodging questions about his personal life with flippant remarks. She had witnessed this kind of thing before when Dutch tried to pry. Maybe that was all it was. She'd always admired his ability to be friendly and comfortable with everyone but not take anyone too seriously, either. But all the rationalizing she could muster didn't relieve her pointed sense of loss. She slumped and looked down at her hands. Better now rather than later.

Dutch snorted out another laugh and clasped Princeton by the shoulder. "Let me teach you something you might not have learnt already, only you should've. You always make time for the dames, my man. You always make time."

Another man joined them and blocked Frieda's view.

Rudy turned to her. "What do you think of him?" he said just loud enough for her to hear. The music from the bars was pounding now, pulsing down the pier and over the water, while the rest of the town had gone from a few twinkling lights left on by night owls to black and still.

"I figured you'd ask," she said, and lifted her head to look up the pier, where more men were striding out, coming to join their party.

"None of my beeswax, but I'm asking anyway."

"It doesn't matter. I'm not even remotely on the same level. What do *you* think of him?"

Rudy gave a chuckle. "I was prepared to find him a fool, but he seems like a good enough guy."

Frieda nodded. Yes, a pretty great guy, in her opinion, but she had been nothing but a passing fancy.

"Listen here," Rudy breathed out as he scooted closer. "I want to tell you a love story."

Frieda smirked. "You?"

"Yeah, I know it's not like any of us here to tell love stories, but I think you'll find it fitting."

"O-K," Frieda said hesitantly.

Rudy sat taller and looked out to sea. "My wife was the prettiest, most popular girl in our high school class. Came from a family with some money, too. Everyone wanted her and told me she was out of *my* league. But I got her anyway."

Frieda took her last sip of champagne. "How?"

"I insulted her."

Managing a laugh, Frieda wiped some champagne from her lips.

"Yeah, I insulted her. Everyone else treated her like a princess, complimented her all the time, and followed her around. She could say the dumbest thing, and everyone acted like it was brilliant. So one day she was reading aloud a poem she had written. Everyone else was oohing and aahing, but I told her what I really thought. That it was more sap than substance. She was so impressed that anyone would tell her the truth, she started going out with me. From then on we were as thick as thieves. She moved to the wrong side of the tracks to marry me, gave up her inheritance, too. Her daddy wrote her off because he couldn't stand the idea of her being with me."

Frieda sat dumbfounded; all the while a little light of hope began to shine behind her eyes.

"Too bad about her father, but you're right. That's a great love story."

Rudy gathered his things to leave. "I'm turning in. Just wanted you to hear that first."

Now the afterdeck was swarming with men getting drunk on Dutch's giggle water, and their laughter and shouting had risen to a roar. She couldn't hear any individual conversations, but every time she caught sight of Princeton, she strained to hear what he was saying, what he was talking about to all of these men whose lives were nothing like his. But he seemed fine. If he didn't look so damn gorgeous, he would fit right in. Just a glimpse of him swayed the boat under her feet, even though the water was still. What a fool she had been. And yet she couldn't just walk away. Despite it all she worried for Princeton, even though he was holding his own for now.

Few of the men noticed her sitting off to the side, and only once did one of the drunks try to cozy up to her. After shooing him off, she heard someone make a remark about her being the babysitter.

She should leave. But something protective, almost motherly, kept her sitting there. Babysitter indeed. Would he be able to deal with this as the night wore on? Dutch had a cruel streak. Maybe he just wanted to revel tonight, or maybe he wanted to get Princeton drunk just to make sure he knew his place, to take him down a notch. If Princeton got sick, who would help him?

She saw him stagger, then quickly make a correction and plant his feet again.

One of the latecomers produced a ukulele seemingly out of nowhere, then strummed and belted out, "How You Gonna Keep 'Em Down on the Farm?"

Everyone found it hilarious, including Princeton, and the drinks poured on.

Surrounded by intoxicated people, coupled with her confusion over Princeton, she began to wonder about everything. The liquor. The running. People drinking more than ever, getting foolish about it. She now played a part in providing the stuff of so many people's woes. There had always been some known drunks in town who had ruined their lives and families, and she'd heard tales of many others. Drunks had likely been patrons of her mother's services. And the other day down near Bahrs, someone had hung an old Anti-Saloon League poster that read, "The

Saloon or the Boys and Girls." She'd understood it as a message to the runners, and moments such as this hit Frieda with sudden qualms. Was it a sign? But what was she to do about people drinking? She could not save people from themselves.

Princeton was not the first to leave. Earning himself some respect, she supposed, he waited until a few others had called it a night before he did. When he tried to step off the transom onto the pier, however, he stumbled. Dutch gave him a hand. "You're looking a little green about the gills, ain't you?" Dutch said with a sloppy smile.

Princeton nodded and managed to smile back. He jumped off and made an awkward, lurching landing but kept on his feet. As he walked down the pier, Dutch called out, "Don't fall in," and laughed.

Frieda watched Princeton wobble down the pier, turn on the dock, and then disappear into the deep-indigo shadows. He never looked back at her. Not one glance.

Her feelings turned dark. She wanted out of here. She wanted to curl up in her blankets and sheets on the floor and try to make sense out of what had transpired tonight. Maybe in the still of night she could find some light. She waited a little longer so it wouldn't be obvious she'd waited because of Princeton. Dutch made another round with his brew, even though the men left on the afterdeck were slurring and staggering, laughing at nothing, and grasping at anything. They wouldn't stop until they could go on no longer.

By the time she stepped off the boat, Dutch was vomiting over the side.

Before she walked down the pier, she said under her breath, "Serves you right."

CHAPTER THIRTEEN

The next night Dutch was obviously still hungover and not at the top of his game. He stood a bit rockingly at the pilothouse as he started the engines, and the sea was churning. Surprisingly, Princeton seemed unaffected by the drink he'd suffered the night before. Maybe he had learned how to hold his liquor in college after all.

And more surprisingly, the other Princeton was back. When he first came on board, he gave her that gleaming slash of a smile, and sweet fondness shone in his eyes. Relief spread through Frieda like the softest of touches. Her dour mood switched to a joyous one in a matter of moments. She breathed in the night with expectation and happiness, all the while wondering what had happened. Why had he ignored her the night before? It no longer mattered. He was paying attention to her now. He was back to seeking Frieda out, sitting next to her, talking about the city, and anticipating the pickup and the drop. Maybe last night had been all about proving himself to the men and had meant nothing about her.

This by-the-sea living clearly suited Princeton. His skin was tanned and smooth, and she had to check herself from reaching out and touching his face.

They made another slick run to the rum boats and back, and it felt glorious. The wind and sea had never tasted sweeter. Rolling waves undulated across the open ocean and careened onto Sandy Hook with weighty wallops on the bar. Frieda took off her hat, let her hair fly free, and closed her eyes to feel every ounce of the power beneath them. Princeton had come around to her again, and that, taken with a roller-coaster passage on heaving seas, made for a night of ecstasy, even though the process took a little longer due to Dutch's sluggishness and the rough conditions.

When it was over and they were back at the dock, Dutch went below to catch a rest, and then Rudy left. After preparing the boat for the night, Frieda looked for Princeton. He had waited for her. Coming to the edge of the pier, he offered her a hand up. She let him take her hand, although she didn't need any assistance. Perhaps she wanted to feel the touch of his skin after all those gazes had gone by without ever being turned into something else.

That night he hadn't worn a hat, and his hair was tousled in a beautiful way, as if he'd just awakened on some sunny morning. "Let's walk down the beach," he said with that silkiest of voices. "I don't want to deal with the crowd in the bar tonight."

He kept her hand in his as they left the dockside, and this time she didn't pull away. She let him lead her. *Don't let go. Oh, please . . .* They walked toward the tiny stretch of beach north of the harbor. On the way she could see Silver's house—her home—sitting dark in the distance. No lights on. Bea and Silver surely already in bed. No awareness of how much her life was changing at that moment.

The beach was deserted, and the sand was soft. Small waves kissed the shore.

"So we're off for a while," Princeton said as he looked toward the moon that had been growing fuller every night.

She had to smile. He'd said, "We're off," as if this were a real job for him.

She simply nodded, and both of them stopped, facing each other in the middle of the beach, a few feet from the water.

"Let's go to the city tomorrow," he said.

"The city?"

"Yeah, you know, the big city over there," he said with a smile.

The lights of New York twinkled, as if in teasing or dancing. Her eyes tried to make connections between all of those blinking signals. What had Dutch been trying to say to her when he'd asked her, "It ain't because of Princeton, is it?" Was he messaging, *Don't let him do this to you?* But she saw something in Princeton, something the others didn't see. Maybe it was the sadness that hung around him. Maybe it was his frankness. Maybe it was the way he made himself fit in. But the most important thing was that he had shown himself to her and no one else. She was ensnared, as if she'd been tied up in chains. She had not foreseen this. She of all people; feeling vulnerable was a foreign thing to her. Yet she had started to like the liberating sensation of her walls coming down. But the other part was terrifying. Any weakness was mortifying. Should she walk away now? This was her chance. *Refuse him*; that's all she had to do.

He whispered, "Don't tell me you've never been."

She looked at him. "I've never been."

His smile faded. "That's almost a crime."

She shrugged. "I have responsibilities here."

As if letting that sink in, he stood still. "So . . . maybe it's time you took a night off from all of those 'responsibilities.'"

"Oh, I don't know . . ."

"Come now. You have to go to the city. And hey, you've got an expert to show you around." That smile again . . . "Don't tell me you're afraid of a little 'danger' in the city? I can tell you it's a lot safer than these seas."

"Before running I never found the sea frightening. I loved it out there. Still do, but it's different now."

"You're a girl with a lot on her shoulders. Let me show you another side of life. Don't worry; I'll take care of you, I promise."

She looked at his high-boned face and into his eager eyes. In some ways he seemed more innocent than her. Innocent in that he didn't know that he could hurt someone. Was this just another game for him, another way of entertaining himself? Maybe he was hanging out with a local girl to go along with running the rum. Maybe it was another way of showing he wasn't his father's son. Was it a bit of rebellion that he longed to taste, just for the difference in flavor? Did he have any idea what his attentions had done to her?

"Please say yes, or I'll die and scare away all the fish," he said.

She gulped. "I need to know . . ." Her mouth had gone dry, and her voice had simmered down to a whisper. "I need to know . . . what you're doing here with me."

She waited as if life and death lay within his words. A flippant answer would lead her to despair, whereas a sweet one would slide her to a place she had never swum before.

He stood completely still as the onshore breeze ruffled the waves of his hair and the light of the moon caught in the cups of his curls.

He eased out his words. "I suppose I could say that you deserve a night of fun, that you deserve to get away from all this for once. But that's not what you're asking, is it, Frieda?"

His face was close and clear. Very close. She studied the tightly woven fabric of his shirt collar and shook her head.

"Look at me."

She did.

"I'm just a guy like any other out here. I know you don't believe that, but it's true. I've stumbled upon a girl who interests me. So there it is." He spoke with a soft surety that moved her. "I'm fascinated by you."

He touched her face with his fingertips along her jawline, light as feathers. Frieda froze from a combination of fear and yearning. He moved his fingers to her lips, and he pressed them gently, as if kissing her with his touch. She stood on the edge of the unknown, and in that moment she didn't care if he meant one iota of what he said. Her heart was fluttering, and her will was lost, lost, lost. He moved to her neck, where her pulse throbbed, and then down, where breaths could scarcely pass.

The planet clicked just a tiny notch on its axis, but her world did a somersault. Perhaps her surrender had always been inevitable.

The next day she pulled out Bea's dresses after bathing with some of Bea's lavender-scented soap. Wrapped in a towel, she perused the dresses that Bea had bought from sales racks.

"What are you doing?" Bea said as she made the bed. The two girls had already helped Silver out to the porch and fed him his breakfast. It was the nurse's day off, and Bea was dressed in a simple cotton dress for cleaning, cooking, and washing.

Frieda said, "I have a date."

Bea's eyes flashed. "You? A date?" A knowing smile then. "I bet it's Hicks."

Earlier that day, when Frieda went to the grocer's she'd seen Hicks, and he gave her a hopeful, friendly wave. Unreasonable guilt had filled her for a moment. "It's not Hicks."

"You're kidding. Then who is the mystery man?"

Frieda was not in the mood to banter back and forth with her sister. Her movements were slow and measured, and Bea must have sensed the change. Bea sat down on the bed, crossed her legs delicately at the ankles, and said nothing more.

After a few minutes of watching Frieda look through the dresses, Bea finally said, "I know the one." She got up and selected a sleeveless, dark-blue sheath dress with a low waistline, scalloped neckline, and flowing fabric that fell to midcalf. She held it out to Frieda.

"It's new, the latest. It's simple, understated, and it moves like silk, although of course it's not the real thing."

Frieda donned one of Bea's slips and then slid into the dress. She sat on the edge of the bed, and Bea began to work her fingers through her sister's still-wet and tangled hair. "Now . . . what are we going to do with this?" she asked.

Frieda shook her head.

Bea pulled a comb through Frieda's hair. "Who is it?" she finally asked.

"I thought you would've heard by now."

Bea shrugged. "Yes, I've heard some things. I can't believe it. You of all people."

"What do you mean?"

"You've never liked anyone with money."

"It has nothing to do with his money! How dare you think that of me?" Frieda retorted. "Besides, I've never really known anyone with money before."

Bea sighed. "True enough. But I'm the one who has given even the hill people a chance. Never you."

"I've been wrong. Maybe I've been blind to the fact that rich people can be nice."

"Says you?!" Bea exclaimed. "What kind of gibberish is spewing forth from my cynical sister's mouth?"

Frieda held still and pulled in a ragged breath, closing her eyes. Because the work Frieda did was tawdry, she maintained truthfulness in the other aspects of her life. Maybe it would make up for rumrunning.

"I never expected to like him."

Bea worked out some tangles. "How can you like someone who's running for no reason? Not even getting paid for it. Has it occurred to you that he could be crazy?"

"He isn't."

"Then what?"

Frieda heard the not-so-subtle message. True, Princeton was doing some odd things—including courting her, it seemed. And maybe people doubted his sanity for that reason more than anything else.

"I understand what you're saying, and it does seem crazy . . . On the other hand, I've gotten to know him a bit, and his life is . . . complicated, too. It's not as simple as it seems. But you know me, Bea. You know it has nothing to do with his money."

"Please don't fool yourself. I can't believe I'm saying this, but everything has to do with money."

"Now who's the cynic?"

Bea laughed, slowing her hands on Frieda's hair, as if serious thoughts had overcome her. "I had heard that you and he went to the bars after the runs, but I had no idea it had become so serious."

Frieda tried a smile. "It's not serious. I've simply been invited to join him in the city for the day."

"But he's here temporarily. Don't you think he'll leave and go back to his familiar life?"

Frieda shut her eyes. Bea was making her think of things she didn't want to consider. Was Princeton looking only for some casual summer romance, as everyone was insinuating? She tried to convince herself of that, but she didn't fully believe it. He had more depth than that. He'd told her about his problems; he was a young man burdened with expectations, without any real freedom, and he'd let her inside his heart. She understood him more than anyone else did. No one knew how much they'd already shared. No one else had seen his quick, keen smile when he'd first glimpsed her. And no one had any idea how he'd touched her on the beach the way one touches someone adored. Even if it did turn out to be a summer fling, she wasn't sure she would regret it. With Princeton, feelings were bursting from her that she didn't think she was capable of feeling. She was growing, like a seed becoming a plant. What other people thought didn't matter.

She changed the subject. "Do you think this dress is too formal?"

"No," Bea answered. "It's the best one we've got."

Bea finished combing out Frieda's hair, and then Frieda sat by the open window to dry it in the summer breeze. Bea sat down beside her and convinced Frieda to let her work on her hands. She rubbed oil into them, trimmed calluses, cleaned the nails, and then painted them. Next she tweezed eyebrows and then turned back to Frieda's hair.

"Look how dry and ragged the ends are," Bea said as she snipped with the scissors. "Now let's see if I can put it into one of those sophisticated updos."

She pulled out pins from the dresser drawer and began to fashion the back of Frieda's hair on the crown of her head, leaving some hanging tendrils on the sides. She studied her sister this way and that and then finally pulled out all the pins and let it flow down in long, loose curls. A little wild, completely free.

"This way," Bea said through a sigh. "It's not the latest style, but it's more *you*."

Bea loaned her sister her best pair of shoes, a clutch bag, and stockings, and then insisted that despite the manicure she should wear gloves. Frieda almost always wore long-sleeved work shirts while out in the sun, and so her thin arms were pale, but her hands were tanned to the color of buckskin. Short white gloves solved that problem and covered her bitten nails and callused knuckles as an added benefit. And finally a touch of red lipstick and a dash of rouge on her cheeks.

Princeton picked her up in a new Renault with the top folded back. When he'd offered to come to her house, her first instinct had been to say no. Frieda had only ridden in a motorcar a few times, and of course she wanted to ride with him. But she wasn't sure how he would react to seeing the small run-down house that was her home. In the end she'd decided there was no reason for him not to see the place. There was no shame in the way she lived, though she would not want Princeton to know about her mother. That could be too much. How long before someone in town spilled the beans? Hawkeye would do it in a heartbeat. She hoped he and Princeton never met.

He seemed unfazed by the house. He even came to the door and spoke to Silver, who glared at him suspiciously. Princeton tolerated that, met Bea, and then the two of them were on their way.

"You clean up well," he said to her as he drove, one hand draped casually over the steering wheel. In the bright sunlight he looked and smelled wonderful—a little like oranges, a little like mint. "Nice rags."

"Thank you. It all belongs to my sister."

"She's quite pretty, your sister."

"Yes. I know."

He reached over and touched her hair. "But I like your looks better. Say, I've never seen your hair like this before."

"That's courtesy of Bea, too."

"I like it." He stared ahead at the road. "Yes, she's pretty and blond and bobbed, like so many pretty and blond and bobbed girls. You're different."

She faced ahead and tried not to get swept away. "This is too much. All these compliments. I'll turn pompous."

He laughed. "You? Never."

He explained that he was driving them to the ferry in Atlantic Highlands so she could enjoy riding there in the car, although the ferry service also came to Highlands. On the way he drove as fast as the crowded streets would allow. Streams of tourists were flowing to the shore from the city, the opposite way they were heading, but Princeton took charge of the roads like a holy man who could part waters.

By the time they pulled into the Atlantic Highlands ferry station, she felt at ease. They waited for the *Sea Bird* of the Merchant Steamboat Company to come in, packed with tourists, and he bought her a lemonade from a nearby vendor. She looked down into the glass of lemonade and was surprised to see that the liquid was trembling.

The sun was out, hot and bright, and only a few streaks of cloud tails marred an otherwise vast blue sky. His arm came around her waist, and he found her gloved hand and smiled in a knowing, calming way. He had to see how different this experience was for her—the dress, the gloves, the car, the ferry. She had taken the trolley to Atlantic Highlands a few times with Bea; otherwise, she'd never been outside Highlands. Drawing a breath, she moved closer to him.

Another time she would've laughed at herself. But she was undergoing a magical transformation, and she was letting it happen. With the surging bay before her, the gulls cawing, this handsome man with his hand on the small of her back, the clear arc of the sky above, she let herself savor her first taste of a lovely attraction and a glimpse of the life that she knew others led but had never interested her before. She waved to the tourists, who were gleeful upon their arrival to the shore. He was studying her reactions to everything, but she could only glance at him for a few moments at a time before having to look away.

Before the ferry emptied, she excused herself to use the facilities and almost ran into a man, who stunned her not only with his unexpected presence but also with his appearance. A man perhaps in his forties with white-blond hair and eyes the same color of blue as Bea's. He shoved past her without as much as a glance, but she turned around and followed him with her eyes. Someone called out to him, "Hey, Whitey," and he strode away toward an obvious rumrunning shore boat very similar to Dutch's.

The resemblance went far beyond the coloring. She saw it in the tip of his nose, the angle of his eyes, and even the way he walked. He was Bea's father. She knew this as she knew nothing else, and this knowledge threatened to destroy the magic of the day like someone popping a balloon. It took her right back to poor Della. Obviously this man, Whitey, had frequented the whore of Highlands, perhaps keeping her a safe distance from his place in society. What a bastard. And yet he was another runner, like her. She slowly became aware that the ground was still beneath her feet.

"What's wrong?" Princeton asked when she returned to his side. "You look as though you've seen a ghost."

"Nothing," she said. She had let him see the way she lived, but this was too much.

"Hmm," he murmured. "That's one of the things I like about you, Frieda. You won't let me all the way in, will you? You keep things close to your chest. Most girls I know won't stop gabbing about themselves. Open books that after a little while you want to slam shut. But not you." He hugged her. "My mysterious Frieda."

CHAPTER FOURTEEN

On the way across the bay to New York, she let her anger toward Whitey sail away as the tall buildings and docks of the city came closer into view. Gulls swooped in the sky, waves careened against the hull, and the air was rich with ocean salt, humidity, and perfume. Women wore matching sweater and skirt ensembles, sailor blouses, and ankle-strap button shoes, and men wore slim, unpadded jackets with their baggy trousers and nice new skimmers, boaters, and Panama hats.

She could already feel the pulse of the city before they docked. A feeling of being shaken and then of being consumed as they hailed a taxi, more people and cars and buildings than she'd even imagined. From a distance it looked small and orderly, but once here the city surged chaotic and huge as men in suits rushed about, heads down, as if on important business. Couples walked with their arms linked, and small groups of women pushed baby carriages. In this part of the city at least, many people had the same aristocratic looks and clothing that Princeton had, and she forced herself to hold her head high and pretend as if she belonged. But nothing had prepared her for this onslaught. Only the man beside her kept her centered. He looked after her like a treasured child. His eyes, however, held anything but a parental type of affection.

"How do you like it so far?" he asked her.

"I like it," she said, and then, "sort of."

He laughed. "We've only just begun. By the time the night is over, you're going to love it. I promise. And if not, we don't have to come back. There are plenty of other places I can show you." He told her that most people started out drinking in midtown speakeasies, then as the night wore on headed uptown to the Cotton Club. But he had other places to take her on this, her first day in the city.

They strolled through Central Park and then took a taxi south to Bleecker Street, into the Italian section. Princeton told her of a cozy little hot spot of a restaurant where they could get a bottle of good red wine and a shot of *strega*, all made locally.

Around them in the restaurant, groups of stylishly dressed people shared animated conversations and toasted each other in different languages. The men wore cuffed baggies, close-cut jackets, and unblemished felt hats. A few wore long-tailed tuxedos as if a theater date awaited. Women pulled gold and silver compacts out of their purses and openly applied makeup in public. They pursed their oxblood-red, Clara Bow lips together, checked their thinned eyebrows, and crossed legs clad in patterned silk stockings that coordinated with their outfits. Most of the women were thin with cropped hair and greeted each other with air kisses first on one powdered and rouged cheek, then the other. Occasionally people looked at Princeton and her, as if trying to identify them from memories of past parties.

She and Princeton topped off their dinner of rich Italian food and alcohol with a *caffè espresso*. He told her stories of his exploits at Princeton, and she talked about Bea and Silver and even explained the basics of clamming and how she had lost her boat.

"Better now?" he said, and took her hand.

"Much better."

They went to the section of Greenwich Village near Fifth Avenue where the establishments were more on the Bohemian side, with candles flickering on small intimate tables, the cellar walls painted with colorful murals, and bands playing on small stages. They visited the Pirate's Den, a replica of a pirates' lair entered through a dank and dark basement, and then the Blue Horse, a jazz club restaurant. Drinks were served in tea and coffee cups while people pulled out cigarette cases, ivory cigarette holders, silver lighters, and flasks. Frieda overheard snippets of conversations referring to artists and poets, parties, meetings, and the arrival of this person, the departure of that person. Everyone seemed to flit through the illustrious city as if nothing in the past existed and the future was unimportant, as if only these moments had any power and they must live entire lives in one night in case the future were never to come.

Frieda drank an Orange Blossom; she had never consumed so much alcohol in one night. Soon a flood of warm contentment rushed through her. The tables around them filled up, and occasionally Princeton greeted someone: a handshake for a man, a nod or a gesture for a woman, and then a quick smile before returning to Frieda and their conversation, showing enough disinterest in others that no one attempted to join them. She began to relax. No one had so much as sent anything but a brief appraising glance her way. No one had seen the girl from Highlands out in the city for the first time, and Princeton moved through these waters as if he could float through anything.

He ran into an acquaintance from school and introduced her without hesitation. Toby Hamilton seemed as if cut from the same cloth—smart clothes, blue-blooded looks, an air of sophistication. He was attractive in a way, but his face reminded Frieda of a horse, albeit a thoroughbred. No one was as handsome as Princeton.

Princeton and Toby conversed about politics, the quality of the whiskey in various establishments, the best food in the Village, and reminisced about professors and classmates. There was an easy familiarity and rapport about the men's interaction, and Frieda thought she was witnessing the reunion of dear, old friends.

Toby said to Charles, "What are you doing this summer?" as his eyes floated curiously over Frieda.

"Nothing. Just trying to avoid thinking about school again," Princeton said.

Frieda didn't know how to feel about his answer. So far this summer was the most momentous one of her life. But perhaps he simply didn't want to divulge the truth about the running, or about his involvement with *her*. That part stung. He had introduced her by name but with no qualifiers, such as *"my girlfriend," "my new gal"* . . .

"A whole lot of nothing, huh?" Toby said with obvious doubt on his face.

"I'm having a bit of an escape before my real life has to resume."

"I understand," said Toby, and the men clinked glasses.

After Toby moved on, Frieda asked, "Did you grow up together?"

Princeton downed the rest of his drink. "I barely know the chap."

She was taken aback. "But you seemed so chummy. I thought you were old friends."

He shook his head.

"You must *barely know* a lot of people."

Sitting back, he signaled the waiter for another round. "In fact, that's exactly how I feel. I know lots of people, but not in any meaningful way. It's all so . . . lonely."

Frieda, stunned by his extraordinary honesty, sat still. "I'm sorry you've been lonely."

"I'm less lonely now," he said.

He told her stories of other classmates, those who had gone to Paris to paint or were studying abroad, and he explained that he didn't know them on a deep level. As he spoke of his world, he didn't seem bothered by her lack of knowledge of things outside the borough of Highlands. On the contrary, he asked her about fishing, about the history of the Twin Lights, the Sandy Hook Light, and Bahrs, and he responded as if her experiences were no less valuable than his were. By now she had told him about everything—almost. Not about her mother. She didn't know if she could ever put *that* into words. If he knew, how would he react? Would he judge her, as the town once had? Would that herald the end of them?

A drummer launched into a solo onstage, and it shook the floor. All at once happiness flooded her body. She stood at the center of a new, more complicated world. Before she had always seen things as split in twos: the good and the bad, the poor and the rich, the known and unknown, home and not home—but maybe she'd been wrong to look at the world in such a black-and-white delineation, to place such separations between things, especially people.

She watched people doing the best renditions of the Charleston she'd ever seen, so unlike the jigs and feeble attempts at more modern dances that some of the fishermen's wives jumped into from time to time when they'd been drinking. Talent had always amazed her—people who could sing, play an instrument, dance . . .

"Come on. Let's join them," Princeton said.

She shook her head. "I can't. Really."

"Of course you can."

"I'm not being humble; I don't know how. I've never had a lesson or even practiced with my sister."

"Then practice with me. There's nothing to it. I'll show you the ropes. Dancing happens to be one of my many charms. Even if you were to fall on your face, do you think anyone would notice? That's one of the beautiful things about the city. Everyone blends in. Even you, Frieda. You just don't know it yet."

Why not? She joined him on the dance floor and imitated what she saw others do, laughter flying out of her chest all the while.

"Did I do alright?" she asked him after they got tired and returned to their table.

"You did fine. But do me a favor. I said you could blend in, if that's what you want. But the truth is I don't want you to blend in too much. You're not like the girls in here, mostly frivolous. You're more real than all this."

Blushing—she never blushed!—she said, "Thank you."

"So," he said, leaning forward, "do you agree that dancing is one of my many charms?"

"Yes," she answered.

But his eyes asked for more, and then he said, "What else do you find charming about me?"

Stunned that he was seeking compliments from her, she finally said, "Everything. I find everything about you charming."

"I know you can do better than that. Tell me."

The insecurity she saw in his eyes made him even more charming. Endearing even. And it dawned on her that he was being more open to her than she to him. She must learn to let down her guard. Finally she winked and said, "You're damn handsome, you know."

He shrugged. "Just a shell." And then waited.

"You've seen the world."

He shrugged again.

He had been so free with his feelings, whereas she had been self-protective. She gathered her strength; he deserved no less. "I've never known anyone like you. You've done so much and have so much, and yet I believe you're kind at heart. You're full of goodness. You're soft and tender inside, and I admire you. I think you have a sense of honor." These were difficult words for her to say, as they came straight from her heart, and revealing her feelings had never been easy.

He smiled wryly. "Honor? You don't know me all that well. I haven't always been so nice." He paused. "But maybe you bring out the best in me."

She loved those words. "It has to be in there to begin with. Honor. Goodness. It can't be faked."

Taking her hands in his, he said, "That's one of the nicest things anyone has ever said about me."

CHAPTER FIFTEEN

They had a nightcap on the Lower East Side at The Back of Ratner's, which was entered through a hidden passage. The place was packed. Scents Frieda had never encountered before were worn so heavily on some of the women that they overcame the odor of burning cigarettes and cigars. Teacups holding cocktails came together in clinks and mixed with the sounds of confident laugher and smooth jazz.

Later, looking back, she would think of herself as standing at the edge of the unknown, and slipping . . . yet not caring. Bea and Silver entered her mind, but she pushed them aside. When Princeton produced a key that led into the loveliest brick row house—he called it a townhouse—she'd ever seen, she did nothing to protest. He said it belonged to his parents, who were away in the Hamptons for the summer, and so they would be completely alone.

The place had a rich, dark sophistication. Inside, thick carpets overlaid marble floors and looked as if they'd been transported from the Orient. There were heavy wooden doors, and a massive chandelier in the dining room so lovely, it was as if all the stars in heaven had been captured inside its glinting flares of light.

When he opened his arms, it seemed like the most natural thing in the world to enter that wonderful space. Frieda knew where this was leading. He wanted to make love to her. Even her secret fantasies had never taken her this far. She had never reached the wedding and wedding-night phase. A wedding was supposed to take place before this, wasn't it? She remembered one of the girls at school saying, "Never give it all away without a ring on your finger." That was what other people held as good advice. But when had she ever listened to advice? A sudden memory of her mother flashed unbidden into her mind. Her mother had given it all away, even selling herself in the end, and where had it gotten her? Her mother wouldn't want her to do this. Was she becoming a typical innocent swept away by a hopeless romance, a sad cliché? Was this perhaps the same way her mother had begun to fall? Had impulse triumphed over reason?

She waited for reason, conscience, or fear—something—to speak to her and stop her, but when Princeton kissed her, all that spoke was a drumbeat of previously unknown needs and cravings. It would take an act of God to stop her now. All thoughts and concerns fell away.

He led her to the bedroom, undressed her, and said, "Why, you're lovely, Frieda. Just lovely."

Running his hands through her hair from her brow to the base of her neck, he pulled her to him for her second startling kiss and feel of him and then led her to bed. Was this sin? It didn't feel like it.

She knew nothing of how to proceed, and so she followed where he took her. As he touched her, he told her he loved her skin, and she explored his body as he explored hers, discovering the foreign feeling of a man's contours. He used a rubber, something she'd seen only once before, and that had been a twisted and yellowish thing washed up on the beach. When he realized that she'd never lain with a man before, he seemed momentarily disconcerted. He shifted away from her.

"I thought . . ." Frieda began, "that a man would be happy."

He had been focusing on the ceiling, but he turned back to her. "Of course," he said. "I sometimes forget that you're just a kid really. I'm a fool." Then a few minutes later, with a stroke of his finger across her cheek and down to her chin he said, "A fool for you."

She tucked her head into his neck and breathed in the scent of him, not believing her luck, but also briefly worrying again that perhaps this was all happening too fast—this was her first time, and she was giving her virginity to a man who had yet to say, "I love you." But he kept kissing her and stroking her, and then she didn't care any longer. Outside, the sound of a violin; in here, the smell of rosewater sprinkled on spotless white sheets. He rose above her, and she lived fully in the moment, her arms on his back, tracing the straight bones of his spine, stroking his polished skin, feeling his breath on her face.

When it was over, she said into the darkness as he spooned his body behind her, "I want to call you Charles from now on."

He snuggled closer. "As you wish, my love."

In the morning she awakened with morning light in her eyes; the day had never felt so true, bright, and close. The light was sharp and clear, as if magnified, and the sky beyond the windows was bluer than blue. She rubbed her eyes and realized she had awakened in a different skin. For the first time she felt like a young woman. Not an older sister, a mechanic, or a rumrunner, but plain and simple a woman.

As they readied for the day ahead, uncertainty about the future and the reality of what she had done came crashing over her. In one night her strong facade was all undone. The walls she'd built up had been shattered. She had left her feelings to his mercy, and this was not where she had ever expected to be. Hard to believe that this was her life, that these were her feelings. But Charles was the same as before, taking her to a breakfast place he knew. He read the paper and ate with gusto, then reached over, took her hand and kissed it, and the gesture left her thirsty with optimism.

"So what's your verdict on the city?" he asked her.

"I'm surprised, but I like it. It was a lovely night." She remembered everything. The night on the town had been wonderful, but what came after made it pale in comparison. She remembered the gentleness of how it began, followed by the passion she'd never experienced before. Nothing to shield themselves from each other. She had been so busy absorbing every inch of him that she hadn't given a moment's thought to the emotional aftermath. Even a flash of remembrance of their night together brought on a strange pulling sensation in her pelvis. She could love him that way for the rest of her life.

"No regrets?" he said as he held her hand and raised it to his lips again.

"No regrets."

He went back to his newspaper; then a few minutes later he pointed to an advertisement. "My father invested in this bank."

Frieda thought for a moment and then said, "I don't trust banks."

He let the newspaper fall onto the table. "You don't trust banks? Then where do you keep your money?"

"In the house."

He shook his head once as if jolted. "Frieda dearest, I know you're making a great deal of money these days. It should be in a bank, not under your mattress for God's sake."

Frieda bristled. But truth was that she had at first kept the money under the mattress where Silver slept. Lately, however, she'd moved it to a few old jars she kept in the back of the closet, secreting it away from Silver more than anyone else. If he had the ability, he might throw that dirty money away. "I'll have you know it's not under my mattress. I have a more creative spot than that."

"Do you realize that if you were robbed, all would be lost? Doesn't that concern you? With all those shady characters down by the docks, it's not a place I'd exactly call secure."

A rod shot up Frieda's spine. "There's nothing wrong with where I live. We've never been robbed. Not once."

"Don't take offense, dearest. But that's a lot of money to lose."

"Better than turning it over to a bank and trusting it to someone else."

"Nothing's ever going to happen to the banks."

"Well, you take your chances on the banks; I'll take my chances on a place where I can put my hands on it."

He studied her with curiosity and then picked up the paper again. "Well." He sighed. "I always said I wanted a girl with her own ideas."

They relaxed for a short while longer and then retraced their path back to Highlands. On the ferry ride the swells were silky, the sky pristine and blue, the air fresh. She had to give herself strict silent orders not to choke on joy or break out in smiles and laughter.

When they pulled up in front of the house, Bea was standing on the porch, her arms crossed. Wearing an old dress, she looked angry and unhappy, and an immediate tension hung in the air of the sun-filled, steaming morning, so Charles gave Frieda a quick kiss good-bye and she let herself out of his car.

Bea's face was brooding.

Frieda said, "Where's Silver?" It was almost noon and a beautiful day. He should have been out there on the porch.

"He feels sick."

A sudden fear clenched Frieda's stomach. "Is he ill?" He had taken sick, and she hadn't been here.

Bea narrowed her eyes. "He's sick to his stomach over *you*! When you didn't come back last night, we were sick with worry. I walked all the way to the phone at the drugstore to call the police, but then I thought, what will I tell them? My sister has gone to the city with a man she barely knows and didn't come home? They would've laughed at me. You're an adult, but you're acting like a child. Like an idiot! What have you done?"

She had convinced herself that Bea and Silver wouldn't have worried about her, because she stayed out late on runs all the time. But of course they would've expected her to return at some point last night. They knew she wasn't working, that she had been out with a man they didn't know, so naturally they had been concerned. She hadn't thought it through. Frieda walked softly to the porch steps. She took a step closer, holding the clutch purse that Bea had loaned her in front of her, and a force pulled the words from her gut.

"I think I love him, Bea."

Bea's voice lowered just an iota, but her anger was still burning. "Love—ha! What would you know of love? You've never even been on a date before. You've never had a beau. There are people in this town who think you prefer women, or that you're just incapable of preferring anything except your own sour company. You don't know anything about love. But you've managed to scare me to death and make us worry all night. Did it even occur to you that we would be out of our minds?"

Frieda blinked into the blinding light. "I'm sorry."

"That's all you have to say?"

Frieda shielded her eyes with the flat of her hand. "I'm sorry. I drank—"

"I don't want to hear this!" Bea shouted. She stormed inside. Frieda followed her and glanced at Silver, who sat on the sofa, a small towel in his lap, some bread crumbs on his lips. His eyes sad. So sad. Perhaps after hearing Bea's harsh words and witnessing her anger, he could find only sorrow in his heart for Frieda.

She went to his side and took his good hand. "I'm sorry. I shouldn't have stayed out all night. But I'm fine."

Bea called her name from the bedroom.

As soon as Frieda entered, Bea started up again. "I've thought about this all night, and I've made a decision. I want to go to the city now. Why should I wait until school starts in the fall? I'm doing nothing here but waiting for my life to begin, while you throw yours away. I want to find a place over there and leave as soon as possible."

The floor turned fluid under Frieda's feet. She'd known her sister's disappointment and disapproval before, but not in this way. Before it had been all about her messy appearance or her unsociable ways, but this was a disdain of a different sort. Not from her sister! Who could possibly understand, if not Bea?

"Please, Bea . . . don't punish me."

Bea stared with a stunned look on her face. The room became quiet and still. "What's happening to you? I've never seen you so . . . so passive."

It did seem incomprehensible. Neither Frieda nor anyone else who knew her would've predicted that she would be acting like so many other girls. In her mind she had been too strong for this, but Frieda hadn't learned yet how powerful love could be.

Bea's pose eased, and the earth became solid under Frieda's feet again. They both sat on the edge of the bed.

"I don't want you to go away," Frieda said, forcing herself not to beg. "I especially don't want you to go away mad. I couldn't bear it."

Bea sat without moving for a long time. On her face was a strange sense of wonder mixed with concern. Finally she said, "You must care deeply about him."

Frieda gazed over at her sister and willed all the bad feelings away.

"Does he love you?" Bea asked.

Frieda stared down at her hands, the hands that had only so recently touched his skin. "He hasn't said so."

Bea looked down, too, and her lips pursed as she frowned. Then she glanced up and, as if gathering her own strength, said, "Has he given you any indication?"

"He's very kind to me. He told me I fascinate him, and he once referred to me as 'my love.'"

Bea's face told her she thought that it wasn't much, but it was something. But how much did Bea really know about the matters of the human heart? She had gone to dances at school and had turned away many a suitor. Even with her low beginnings, Bea had been able to attract young men, but she'd never taken anything too seriously, had never stuck to any boy long enough to form attachments. Her future studies had always been her main concern. And Bea had always been such a sweet soul; she wouldn't crush Frieda's hopes even if she didn't believe in them.

Bea touched her sister's cheek. "Just be careful, will you please?"

Frieda couldn't believe it. It was as if for a moment they'd switched roles, and Bea was now taking care of her.

After dinner later they continued the conversation. "Look," Bea said, her eyes softer now. "It makes sense, you know. I can get settled in before school starts and find a job to make some money for the rest of the summer. You've done so much for me; it's time for me to do more for myself. If I have a job, I can take some of the burden off your shoulders."

Bea was no longer angry, so why wouldn't she let this idea go? It was as if once it had been planted, the seed had immediately burst open and there was no way to put it back inside its shell. Frieda had to swallow hard past the lump in her throat before she could speak.

"I don't want you to work. Just concentrate on school. Be the first woman in our family to make something of herself. That means more to me than anything. I have plenty of money put away."

Bea grabbed her sister's hands. "So my wages will be for my run-about money. For clothes and shoes and such. You know how I love all that. I can leave some of my old stuff with you, now that you're in need of it. And I'll get adjusted to city life before my classes begin."

Frieda had never seen such determination in her sister's eyes. It was as if overnight they'd traded roles in personality, too, and Bea was full of resolve, while Frieda was close to defenseless. "You won't know anyone. And it's so big . . . I've been there. I know."

"But I like new things, and I make friends easily. I can't wait to get started. Please, Frieda . . . please . . ." She squeezed harder and then didn't let go.

Bea, leaving now? She looked away and let loss ache throughout her body. She had known it was coming, but she'd believed she had at least two more months. "Silver will miss you. So will I."

Bea said, "You know I can't do it without your blessing."

"If you're sure it's what you want . . ."

"I'm sure."

CHAPTER SIXTEEN

Three days later they went to the ferry dock in Highlands and waited for the steamboat to the city. They had packed Bea's most prized possessions in two borrowed and scarred old suitcases. The cases held her favorite dresses, some skirts and blouses, and her favorite books, along with personal items she couldn't part with.

While they waited, Frieda looked about for Charles. She hadn't seen him since he had dropped her off three mornings before. Not a note or a message. She'd walked the docks and done the required maintenance on Dutch's boat, always listening for the sound of his footsteps coming down the pier, or the lilt of his voice as he called her name. Each time she came up from the engine room and took a glance around, pretending as if she were looking for something else, she was really looking for him, but all she saw were the flat stares of the other runners and fishermen, and the first star fell from her shining new sky.

The days were sunny and warm, the nights cool and damp. It was turning out to be a lovely summer. Along with Bea's leaving, Charles's absence left her aching. She closed her eyes and kept seeing dead fish, a dying dolphin that had washed up on the shore, and piles of empty oyster and clamshells.

The night before at home she had heard heavy footsteps on the porch, and her heart leapt into her throat. But it was only Hicks coming by to say good-bye to Bea and wish her luck.

He gave Bea a perfect sand dollar that he'd kept for years and placed into a little cardboard gift box so that it wouldn't break. Years spent in the sun and salty air were beginning to show on his face; squint lines bloomed from the corners of both eyes.

"Don't forget where you came from," he said to Bea, and then he looked at Frieda as if the message was intended for her instead. But his look contained no anger. His face was the same concerned face she'd always known, and the way he said things with shrugs of his broad shoulders and movements of his eyes was so familiar. She couldn't lose his friendship now. With the pain in her heart, there was no room for anything but fond feelings for others these days.

Frieda wished she could thank him for his friendship and for accepting her the way she was for all these years, but if she spoke anything that came straight from her heart, it would release all the other feelings she was working so hard to contain. Bea's leaving, and Charles . . . There was an awful urge to tell him, her dear old friend, all of it. It was as if Bea had already abandoned her and she had no one else to tell, no one to turn to. Hicks must have realized she was torn up over Bea's leaving, but did he have any idea how she ached over Charles? She couldn't burden Hicks when he obviously still had feelings for her. But his gaze said that he already knew, that he somehow understood.

They stood quietly for a few moments, but the silence was filled with a conversation they could not have.

Word had gotten around that Bea was leaving, and other people had also come by the house with well wishes and little gifts. Bea had friends from school, from the docks, and even the hills. Everyone thought so highly of her sister and so little of Frieda, she realized. Of course she

had known this all along and had done nothing to prevent her isolation before, but it came with a new edge. Who would she turn to now?

The hardest part for Bea was leaving Silver. She had sat with him
for hours during the nights before she left, holding his hand, telling
him her dreams and plans, pulling out her course book, and going over
things with him as any child would do with his or her parent. Once he
smiled on the working side of his face. Frieda tried telling herself she
had done the right thing by releasing her sister. But Bea's absence would
mean leaving Silver more often in the care of Polly and the other nurses
who relieved her from time to time. Silver was fond of Polly, Frieda
could tell, but she wasn't family. Frieda would have no choice, however,
as she couldn't leave him on his own, not even for brief periods of time.
And someone would have to stay the night when Frieda went out on
runs. She'd have to find a second nurse who was willing to work nights.
No problem; she had the money.

Everything was falling into place for Bea. And yet for Frieda every
day passed like the movement of mud in the flats, slow and heavy. Each
hour Charles didn't show up made the dreadful empty ache inside drive
deeper and bloom bigger. Her heart was so heavy that she didn't know
how it could go on beating. Where was he?

She and Bea made the ferry crossing accompanied by rosy-cheeked
tourists with sea-brightened faces. Once in the city, Frieda was immediately lost, as if she'd never come here before. She wore another of Bea's
dresses, but this time she felt uncomfortable. And the rolls of bills she
carried in her handbag, retrieved from her hidden jars, were heavy, precious stones. Bea had even talked her into the lipstick and rouge again,
but Frieda wiped her lips on a handkerchief after the city soot began
to stick to her lips. The girls stood on the sidewalk in a near daze, the
battered, borrowed suitcases a clear giveaway about their humble roots,

despite the decent dresses they wore. Frieda decided then and there that she would buy some new luggage for Bea. Her sister would come home from time to time and deserved to have a nice suitcase when she traveled.

Frieda held her handbag close to her side as some streetwise, Italian-looking boys chased each other down the sidewalk. Cars whizzed past, and Bea coughed on the thick exhaust. They stared up at street signs and asked for directions, bought a newspaper at one passerby's suggestion, and sat in a café until they could get their bearings. The suitcases had become cumbersome and heavy. She and Bea tried to keep them out of others' paths. Their waiter, a man who seemed nice despite his hurried movements, advised them to check for postings in the Village, as summer vacancies could often be found there with immediate occupancy.

Bea had been accepted into the NYU School of Education. Student housing would be available to her in the fall, but she had already expressed a desire for a place of her own, and Frieda had agreed. Bea could live and merge with any of her peers, even bubbly college students dropped off by well-off parents, but having her own place meant that Frieda could visit her sister from time to time. Since Silver would have around-the-clock care now, Frieda might be able to spend some nights in the city with Bea. So an apartment fit their needs best.

After looking around at postings and Bea chatting with some people who seemed local, they were able to find a small apartment in the Village near the campus in an ugly, dark brick, four-story building, but the apartment was rented with solid, basic furnishings, safely tucked up three flights of stairs from the street, and had tall windows and high ceilings that let in the light.

Bea proclaimed, "It's perfect. I'll be happy in this place."

This was so Bea—positive to a fault and already fantasizing about her life in the city. Did she really know what she was getting into? Was she prepared? Frieda said, "Maybe we should look at others."

"No, this feels just right. Besides, I can move in right now. No need to go to a hotel tonight. That'll save some money."

Frieda looked around, tried the windows, and ran the water. She could find no reason to refuse, although she had the strange urge to glom on to her sister and beg her not to leave her just when she needed her so desperately. But instead she said, "If you say so."

Bea pulled her sister into an embrace. "Thank you. You won't be sorry. I'll make you proud."

And so Frieda paid the landlord for the first two months' rent, Bea obtained her key, and they left her bags in the room.

They went into some chic boutiques, where Bea insisted that Frieda pay an exorbitant amount of money for both of them to indulge in a pair of ankle-strapped, Cuban-heeled shoes. Frieda also purchased a long Oriental-style fringed scarf as a going-away gift for her sister, and Bea picked out a new frock for Frieda. As evening was by then coming on, Frieda sought to take Bea to some of the places Charles had taken her on their night on the town. But as people flowed and shoved past them on the streets, she became disoriented. She'd made a wrong turn somewhere, and so she changed direction. But that wasn't it, either. It didn't help that most of the speakeasies had hidden entries.

"I'm sorry. I thought I'd learned my way around somewhat. Silly me."

Bea said, "It's OK. I'm learning the names of the streets."

Relax, Frieda told herself. Bea followed her in the purple light of the city's shadows, while along the avenues the yellow lights of streetlamps attracted insects and brightened the facades of stubborn old buildings, shiny new shops, and cobbled streets that were unknown to her. She shook herself, focused, and changed direction again. She and Bea stumbled around for an hour or so, lost in the maze of streets. What a fine chaperone Frieda had turned out to be.

At last Frieda located the hidden "Garden Door" to Chumley's; she was in the right area. She and Charles had passed by this place, and he had pointed out the location to her, but they hadn't entered, instead going on to another bar. She took Bea by the hand and they entered and found a table. But everything tasted different about this night, as if a sour ingredient had been accidentally baked into something that was supposed to be sweet. The air was stale with smoke, drunken men leered at them, and women looked at them with contempt—or was it pity? The animated conversations, raucous laughter, and clinking of glasses had taken on a sinister tone that Frieda had not heard before. The drinks were weak and expensive, and they couldn't hear each other talk over the sound of the music. There was no one with whom to dance, as the place was filled primarily with couples.

So they simply sat. Bea appeared to bask in the dreams of her life to come and sipped on her drink. But Frieda's mind drifted away on a darker current. Without a partner, the city was a cruel and confusing maze. This and everything else was changing too fast. Even back in Highlands things were changing. Runners were getting edgy and arming themselves. People who seemed more like lifelong criminals, rather than those like herself, were getting in on the action. Lately, in Highlands's hotels one could see automatics and revolvers sitting on the tables during dinner, and the day before on the beach she'd seen some strange men wearing fedora hats, nicely tailored suits with flaring lapels, and polished shoes. From a distance it seemed as if they were having an animated, agitated conversation. The atmosphere in Highlands was changing, and this was her last night with Bea.

Involuntarily, her thoughts drifted to Charles. Frieda relived the night with him—the music, the lights, the dancing, the food, the wine, his touch, the lovemaking—and when she looked around it only then dawned on her that the city and all its offerings had not made the night so wonderful. She had thought she might recreate the magic of that night in a different way with her sister. Now it felt ridiculous. She didn't fit in here; she never had.

She said over the sounds of the crowd, "I can't believe you'll be staying tonight without me. It's just now hitting me. We've always been together."

"You go out on the ocean so many nights without *me*. I've always worried, you know." Bea took another sip of her drink and looked around like someone seeing lovely paintings for the first time. "I'll be fine; in fact, it's going to be wonderful."

As each day had gone by, taking them closer to this night, a knot of fear inside Frieda had been tightening and pushing against her organs. Now it had grown even larger. How would she manage without Bea?

She thought she saw Toby, Charles's thoroughbred friend, in the crowd. Peering around some people waiting for a table, she caught his eye, then instantly regretted it. What if he was here with Charles, and worse yet, they were with other women? But Toby appeared to be alone again, and she gave him a little wave. He hesitated for a moment, then worked his way toward their table.

"Small world. Nice to see you again, Frieda." He gave them a toothy grin, and Frieda introduced Bea. His eyes roamed over her appraisingly, and Frieda wondered what he saw: a pretty young thing who might interest him, or a pretty young thing from the wrong side of the tracks?

Bea perked up at the prospect of spending some time with a new acquaintance. "Would you like to join us?" she asked, although she and Frieda had taken the only chairs at their tiny table.

Toby glanced around. "I doubt I could find a chair."

Frieda sensed that it was a convenient excuse; perhaps he had come over only because it was the polite thing to do. She could see a wariness in his eyes, as if he wouldn't want to get stuck with them.

"It's mobbed in here," Bea stated.

"You think this is a mob?" Toby said. "Just you wait. You won't be able to move in here later."

"I love the energy of the city," said Bea. "I just moved here today all in one day."

His eyebrows rocketed up. "One day?"

Bea beamed. "Yep, found an apartment, dropped off my suitcases, and here I am."

A tiny amused smile. "Congratulations."

Bea said, "Thank you," but uncharacteristically, she had no other comment.

Toby held a drink in one hand and slipped his other hand into his pocket and jingled some change, as if he had found himself at something of a loss. He glanced about furtively and asked Frieda, "Is Charles around?"

After she shook her head, the most awful, desperate urge entered her. "In fact, I don't know where he is. I haven't seen him for a few days."

Toby took a sip of his drink, a bit of discomfort on his face, as if he'd read this situation as clearly as a book: that Charles had spent a night out with a lower-class girl for some fun and then dumped her. He pitied her; Frieda could feel this, and she flooded with shame. She shouldn't have mentioned Charles, much less admitted that she didn't know where he was. She had humiliated herself, but she couldn't take her words back now. The things she was doing baffled her. How had she so quickly slipped out of her familiar self? It was infuriating, this powerlessness, this relinquishment, this falling away of all her old shields, but for the first time ever she could not find a way to build them back up.

Toby said, "I haven't seen him, either." A moment of uncomfortable silence. "He essentially disappeared this summer."

She was struck with a needling of hope that maybe she'd run into Charles in the city. How crazy that she'd stumbled upon Toby, the only person she'd met before in New York. But then again she was on his stomping grounds.

"Do you think he's in the city?" Frieda asked.

"I have no idea. As I said before, he's been out of the picture lately." He took a tiny step back, and Frieda felt the divide between them widen. "Frieda, it was nice to see you again," he said to her, and his look conveyed charm but revealed nothing; then he turned to Bea. "Welcome to New York. I hope you enjoy it."

Frieda managed a smile, and Bea said, "Thank you."

"Well, have a nice evening, ladies." He tipped his hat and wheeled away.

When Frieda turned back to Bea, her sister's face registered a pale new awareness. "You don't know where Charles is?" she gasped. "I had no idea. Obviously he hasn't been around town lately—I haven't seen him—but I thought you knew where he was."

Frieda shook her head.

"My God, Frieda. Why didn't you tell me?"

Wrapping her hands around her tumbler, Frieda stared into it. Then she looked up, letting the pain—finally—show to someone. "I-I didn't want to ruin this for you. This is your time, Bea."

"You're my sister and best friend. I can't believe you kept this inside."

Frieda looked down. How had she come to this?

"So he took you away for a night, ruined your virtue, and then disappeared?" Bea asked with rising anger in her voice.

"He's not like that," Frieda said just loud enough to be heard. "There has to be an explanation. He's not mean. He's not."

"But he simply vanished . . . without a word?"

"Sort of. But he's not a bad man, Bea."

Bea blinked a few times. "O-K," she said. "But I feel terrible leaving you now. I didn't know . . ."

"He's coming back," Frieda said, and gulped.

Bea looked at her with an empathy only a sister could feel, and Frieda had to ward off tears. It had always been the two of them, but now each was heading out alone into uncharted seas. Bea would happily float away, but how would Frieda keep her head above water? Her sister was the one who had always kept her centered and focused, anchored to an old familiar shore.

CHAPTER SEVENTEEN

Keeping occupied was the only relief Frieda could find. She scrubbed the boat while it lifted and lowered on the tides like a big shiny beast, breathing. She worked on the engine even though nothing needed doing. Then she went to Bahrs and poked around for extra work. These things provided a temporary reprieve.

One of Silver's old friends told her that another of his old friends, a man called Dingbat—Frieda never understood why; he seemed perfectly sensible to her—needed some work done on his boat. She found him down the most rickety pier, where many of the old fishing boats gathered together like half-dead insects floating on the sea. These were the boats of the men who'd played it straight through these five years of running.

On the way there she passed gleaming new running boats docked next to old battered fishing craft that needed painting. The haves and have-nots had always existed in Highlands, but now they sat side by side, rubbing shoulders in a harbor crammed to capacity. Today there were more strangers about, and they reminded Frieda of gangsters.

Dingbat, a phlegmatic gaffer, hat pulled down over a bald head compensated by a bushy steel beard, told her he needed a new water pump, a repair that in the past he would have done for himself, but arthritis had made it too difficult. "I'm wondering if you could put this work on credit. Just till I make my next good haul. Then I'll be paying you back."

Dingbat had been one of Silver's favorites, meaning that Silver would spend some time with the man. He had always spoken highly of Dingbat and his wife. But even if Silver hadn't liked the man, Frieda did, and he was just scraping by, while she was storing cash as if she'd live to eternity. Frieda looked around, and a cloak of comfort fell around her. She was home. The docks, this part of the docks, her refuge. She wasn't a wealthy boat owner or a struggling clammer or fisherman, but she breathed to the rhythm of this place.

"No need to pay me," Frieda said.

Dingbat pushed back his stooped shoulders. "I ain't no charity case."

Proud, always proud. "Do as you like, but you're doing me a favor. I'm bored on the days I'm not working. Bored out of my mind in fact. Need to keep busy."

"Bored, huh?" He eyed her warily.

A thought hit her. "You know, if you ever need help out on the water, I'd love to go out with you sometime . . . that is, when I'm not out with Dutch or working on his boat." She paused. "I'm sure you know what I'm doing."

He chewed on something inside his cheek. "Yeah, I know what you're doing." He spat into the water, but his face revealed nothing about his feelings on the matter, and Frieda didn't ask. On the docks people stayed out of other people's business.

"I'd love to go out sometime just to . . . fish and clam." Frieda had often wanted to go out on the water for something other than rumrunning, and Hicks would've been the obvious one to take her. But time around her wasn't good for him, she reasoned, so she had never asked.

Dingbat said with a gleam in his eye, "My wife might get jealous." And he laughed.

Frieda smiled. "I'll promise her to mind myself."

After she fetched her tools and was walking back to Dingbat's slip, she nearly collided with Hawkeye. She smelled his rancid breath before he spoke. "Whatcha doing down here on the wrong side of the tracks?" he asked with a penetrating stare.

She sidestepped him. "Get out of my way."

"I thought you only took to them fancy boats now."

She shoved past him and kept walking. It was a tough day to have to listen to that old bastard. As she strode on, she shook herself, trying to rid herself of him.

Catching a glimpse of the road, she thought she saw Charles's Renault. In the lane across from her, on the other side of the road. She started to wave, but the car sped by without giving her time to see who was driving. Was it Charles? He drove an unusual car, but with all the tourists streaming in and out of town, it wasn't impossible that someone else had driven a car like his down here. But if it was Charles, why hadn't he come down to the docks?

Troubled with questions, Frieda continued walking back to Dingbat's boat. She started working on the engine but was compelled to come up for air and look around for Charles every few minutes.

Dingbat's wife came to sit next to her. Frieda couldn't remember the woman's name. Clara, she thought it was. Silver would never have forgotten.

Her hair was as white as Santa Claus's, and her eyes were red rimmed. She wore a patchy straw hat and an old dress that nearly dragged the ground over her scuffed rubber boots. They exchanged pleasantries while Frieda worked and Clara watched.

Dingbat shouted from the dock, "Don't bother the girl while she's working."

"Can't you see I'm supervising?" Clara retorted, and Frieda laughed.

A few moments passed in comfortable silence. Then Clara said, "What's the matter, honey? You look mighty serious. Like maybe you're lovesick."

Frieda's defenses flew up. She hated that she was so transparent. Pursing her lips, she turned the wrench with more force than was needed. Clara was breaking the unspoken rule about not messing in another person's business. But she knew Clara meant well, and who else did she have to talk to now? Bea was gone.

Frieda kept working, and her movements calmed the spark that so easily rose to flames inside her. "You must be some kind of mind reader."

"Honey, when you get this old, you see things the eyes don't see. You see them with your heart and your mind."

Frieda stopped for a moment. "Sounds witchy."

"No hocus-pocus here. Just lots of living; it lends you some wisdom. Which I'm guessing is a trade-off for lost youth."

Frieda looked out over the harbor toward the bay. A ferry heading to the city belched black smoke from its funnel as it made its way. The day was coming to full brightness; tourists were arriving in droves, while others were going back to their everyday lives. Then she scoured the dock area again; she couldn't help it. If Charles had returned, where was he?

Dingbat's wife tossed a hand-rolled-cigarette butt into the water. Close to shore the water was muddier and floated cigar butts, newspaper pieces, and oil slicks rising and falling on swells slapping against the wooden timbers.

Clara said, "Go on and tell me. Get it off your chest."

Frieda squinted and felt relief even before she spoke. "The truth is I've fallen for a man I don't understand."

Clara sighed. "And he's hurting you."

"No. Not like that. He's not beating me."

"No . . . I mean, hurting your heart."

Frieda kept working, her words flying out of her now as fast as her hands moved. "I never know what he's thinking. Sometimes it's wonderful, like the best thing that's ever happened to me. Other times I'm so unsure. I'm lost. I have no idea where I stand. I think he loves me, but I'm not convinced. I worry all the time."

The woman's face registered something Frieda could not name. Empathy maybe, and she was glad for it. "But that's love, honey child. You always worry about the folks you love."

Frieda couldn't respond. She'd never much pondered the nature of love before, but when she had, she'd never imagined the anguish that accompanied the joy. Of course love involved worry. Worry over Charles had consumed her. She had analyzed his every gesture and expression. When he wasn't close she was miserable, and when he was near she was fearful she was going to lose him.

Why were people drawn to the mysterious, to the far horizon, to something unreachable? What had driven her to the edge, with no promises of what lay beyond it?

She looked at Clara. "Funny, I thought love would be happier."

When she had installed the new water pump, she said good-bye to Dingbat and Clara and then started walking. Out in the sun in the hottest part of the day, through stagnant afternoon air, she had to walk uphill to reach Charles's street. But she needed to know whether he was back or not. Now she had taken a step beyond pitiable. This was ridiculous, and yet the desire to know pulled her as if by an urgent tide.

She had never been to Charles's house, but he had told her what street it was on. If the Renault was parked in front of one of the houses on that street, she would knock on the door. She picked up her pace, almost running, air scorching inside her lungs, flaming in and out, her heart hammering. What if Charles was there and not alone? What if he'd brought another woman? No, he would never be so cruel.

She reached his street, but the car was not there. She didn't know how to feel. Had she wanted to find him doing something she didn't know about? Did she have any reason to be snooping? She didn't even know whether the car she'd seen earlier was his or not. But if he'd been heading home, he would have arrived by now.

Now drenched with sweat, Frieda leaned over her knees to catch her breath. When she stood up, it hit her that even if Charles had been here it didn't necessarily mean he was avoiding her. Maybe he had errands to run. Shopping to do? She remembered how sweet and utterly devoted Charles had been to her in the city, and she admonished herself for having had such crazy thoughts. Something had called him away, but he would be back.

She nearly stumbled. Suddenly she was so tired.

She walked downhill and straightaway to the sand beach, past picnickers and swimmers in their fancy bathing costumes, and into the low surf that barely chuffed against the bar today. In her leather boots she sunk into the wet sand, soaking her shoes, and then she reached down, scooped up seawater, and splashed it on her face. Instantly cooled.

Nothing bad had happened really. Nothing.

CHAPTER EIGHTEEN

The next morning, when she saw Charles walking toward her down the pier on the hottest day of the summer so far, his figure seemed to flutter inside the heat waves, and she thought she might be seeing an apparition or a ghost. Sometimes she felt as if she'd dreamed him into being, that maybe none of it had been real. She had to mentally shake those thoughts away and focus on the man striding toward her.

Charles, her Charles.

Here he was, real and warm and smiling, pushing back his Panama hat, taking her in his arms as soon as she jumped from the boat onto the pier. Ah, the scent of his aftershave, the sleek loveliness of his limbs, and his warm breath in her hair. The sun shone brighter, and the wind came with a new freshness.

"I've missed you," he whispered.

She held him tightly for a moment, afraid that if she let go he would disappear again. Maybe if she held on forever she could keep him here.

He pulled back, his hands gently resting on her arms.

Trying to keep her voice light, she said, "Where have you been?" She was surprised at how weak and relieved she sounded.

But he seemed unfazed. "Family duty," he said as though no further explanation was needed. He didn't seem to grasp how much his absence had affected her. He offered no more excuses. "Can you stop what you're doing, and I'll tell you all about it?"

The joy had come back. He had returned to her.

She had been preparing the *Pauline* for a run. The crew of the *Pauline* was planning to resume its forays into the night. "I can stop for a little while."

"Are we going out on a run tonight?"

"Yes."

He kissed her and took her hand.

"Wait. I'll be just a second." She leapt back onto the boat, scampered down to the engine room, put away her tools, and wiped her hands on a rag. She was dressed in her usual work attire—pants, shirt, hat, and fisherman's boots, her hair tucked up. After taking off her hat, she shook out her hair and wished she had a tube of Bea's lipstick. But she figured that Charles had fallen for her just the way she was, so she joined him on the dock, and he led her down to Bahrs.

"I'm famished," he said as he pulled a chair out for her. "I left early this morning. Traffic was terrible, and the ferries are running late. No time for a bite to eat."

He slid beside her and moved in close, his hands on the tabletop. She stared down at the shape of his hands, the long fingers with downy hair on the knuckles. Glances angled toward them from all directions from fishermen, rumrunners, dockworkers, and the Bahrs family, working to feed a boathouse full of hungry men. The locals were used to Frieda, but although Charles told her it wasn't his first time in the place, he clearly wasn't a regular. Were they wondering how she'd managed to snag a date with a young man like Charles? Although no one mentioned it any longer, they all knew she was the whore's daughter. Did some of them still see her that way? *God, please don't let anyone say something to Charles.* Thankfully, Hawkeye wasn't there. He might tell Charles simply out of meanness.

Charles, however, handled the looks as if they were nothing but bits of dust on his shoulders he could mentally brush away, or perhaps he didn't notice the looks at all. He was dressed in shoes with fringed tongues, front-creased trousers, and a dress shirt, collar open to reveal a tanned chest, and cuffs rolled up to his elbows, showing that the hair on his arms had turned blond. He must have spent the last few days on the beach, and Frieda imagined the striped canvas beach chairs and umbrellas set up by servants, who also brought out drinks in crystal glasses. She tried to imagine his family, and she envisioned the resort types who came on vacations. But she was probably off by a mile. Even the rich who frequented the Highlands area were not cut from the same cloth as Charles was.

They ordered, and as they waited for the food to arrive she said, "Where did you go?"

"I was summoned to the Hamptons. My mother's birthday. Father insisted."

She struggled to form mental images of Charles's family and his life away from here. "Was it a grand party?"

He smiled at her. "Of course it was, but all very stiff, you know. You wouldn't have liked it. Too stuffy for you. The men talk of law, politics, and Wall Street. The women talk of fashion and the latest gossip columns. My father is frantic about the mayoral race coming up in November. All very haughty and long-winded, I'm afraid. But Mother's a dear; her name's Elizabeth, but we've always called her Bitty, among family only of course. She approves of my summer season away more than my father does. She thinks I need it." He blew on his hot coffee.

Frieda's life was so far removed. "Do they have any idea what you're doing?"

He harrumphed. "They know I've taken a residence in this area, but no, they don't know what I'm doing with my nights."

Frieda also assumed they knew nothing of her. She looked at his hands and saw that he'd been biting his nails. She had never before imagined that the wealthy could have the same bad habits as she did.

"Did you see any of your old friends?"

"Hardly," he answered. "Most are abroad." He said this as if it meant nothing special. "Oh, you'll find this interesting. One night we went to the Maidstone Club in East Hampton—very posh place, members only, naturally—where the food and service are excellent, but the main source of entertainment is to watch coast guard boats chasing the local rumrunning boats. It reaches the greatest heights of hypocrisy, you see, because one can order any type of liquor one wants, and the place will never be raided. The members of the club have too many connections. They enjoy watching from the windows as the poor slobs out there risk their lives to bring in the liquor, and then they enjoy the fruits of their labors without any risk to themselves."

Frieda put her hands around her cup of coffee and stared into the dark liquid as if there she might find the solution to the riddle of Charles. "So, that's one of the reasons you do it—as a protest . . ."

He patted her hand, then held it. "Now, Frieda dear, don't assign such glorious and noble aspirations to me. My contribution has little to offer in the grander scheme of things."

Their food arrived.

"I enjoy the sea. I enjoy this town. I like doing things I've never done before . . ." He looked into her eyes. "And I adore you."

She could've sworn the light in the restaurant sparkled, as did the joy in her chest. She sank into the moment. It was as if she had waited her entire life to hear the words "I adore you." Adore was almost like love, maybe one step away?

"I thought I saw your car yesterday. I mean, it was exactly like your car."

He looked stumped for a moment. "I did return yesterday, but I was exhausted. I went straight to bed." He smiled. "I was worn out by the journey."

So Charles had lied when he said he'd come that morning. And his journey from the ferry to the summer house would not have taken him past the docks. And he hadn't gone straight to bed, because his car was not at the summer house. And now he was dressed as if he'd just come from the Hamptons. Again, more questions she couldn't answer. But after a fierce internal battle, she decided to let it go. She couldn't push Charles away just as he'd come back to her. So maybe he had needed a night alone. No harm in that.

She told him about Bea's leaving, about finding the apartment, and their night in New York City, and she loved the way he studied her face. It was enough.

"We saw Toby."

Charles sat back. "Fancy that, meeting him again."

"That's what I thought. Quite a coincidence."

"Did he flirt with you?"

Now it was her turn to be surprised. "Not at all. I don't think he sees me, or Bea, in that way."

"Don't sell yourself short. Besides, that man is a wolf in sheep's clothing."

So he was jealous. Good. That showed he cared. "He was polite, that's all."

"Hmm."

"It wasn't the same without you."

He smiled when she told him about getting lost.

"I should have been with you," he said.

* * *

That afternoon Frieda asked Polly if she could stay all night with Silver, and the kindly middle-aged nurse shook her head. Broad and gray-haired, she was as strong as a mule, and she worked endlessly to clean, cook, and care for Silver. Like all the others in town, she had to know how Frieda was paying her, and obviously she didn't want to bite the proverbial hand that fed her. She also knew that Frieda usually came back from running about two or three in the morning, and that if she was planning to be out the entirety of the night, there was another reason for it. By then everyone in town knew she was seeing Charles. They probably knew about the night they spent together in the city, too. Frieda could imagine what the woman was thinking: running rum was one thing, but carrying on all night unmarried was another. Frieda made a mental note to find another nurse as soon as possible to stay the nights; hopefully one who didn't set up herself as judge and jury.

Crossing herself, Polly said, "I hope Mr. Silver here don't figure out what you're up to." A devout Catholic, she often worked at her tasks to the rhythms of her prayers while holding a rosary. "If he don't get no peace about you, when he dies his soul is destined to wander forever in purgatory."

Frieda started coughing. Polly patted her on the back until Frieda could catch her breath. "For God's sake, Polly, don't even suggest such a thing. Besides, I have no secrets from him."

Polly wrung her hands and looked as if she wanted to say something else, but she simply shook her head and kept quiet.

Frieda was hoping for a smooth run and then to be invited to Charles's summer house for the rest of the night. But that afternoon, as she walked down the pier to where the *Pauline* was docked at the end, ominous gray clouds churned over the water. A summer storm would be coming. The cloud cover would obscure any moonlight, but it could make for a choppy sea.

Rudy and Dutch were already on board. "Glad to see you," said Dutch. "We're heading out early to beat this thing coming in."

"It's light," she said, stating the obvious.

"You think, Frieda?" said Dutch, clearly annoyed. "Where's that damn sap Princeton? I need the strength of his back tonight."

"Damn sap?" Frieda, incensed on his behalf, asked.

"Don't get yourself in a tizzy," Dutch nearly shouted, and then seemed to calm himself. He ran a big, beefy hand through his prematurely silvering hair. "I can't figure that snot-nosed kid. If you had everything in the world, a rich mama and papa, and law school to come, would you be out here doing this?"

"Come now, Dutch. You love it."

"I love it, but someday it'll be over, and then it'll be back to toiling endless hours on the sea, scratching out a living. Don't fool yourself. You'd take the easy life if it got handed to you." He cocked his head to one side and squinted at her, seeming to consider his words carefully. "You don't think it's being handed to you, do you? You don't think that boy is going to take you away from all this, do you?"

She didn't answer. Instead, Frieda went down below to start the engines and smiled when she heard Charles's voice above her on the boat. He was explaining to Dutch that he could see the harbor with binoculars from his summer house and saw that Dutch was preparing to head out early, so he'd come straightaway.

It was barely three o'clock, and yet Frieda counted thirteen other boats of all rigs and sizes also heading out. Dutch cut a course out toward Rum Row, slapping the boat over waves and sending up sheets of spray on either side. The clouds still hung out at sea, denying the rain and cover a storm might have provided. And yet many boat captains had become so confident that they regularly ran during the daylight hours anyway. The guard didn't have near the numbers to match them all, and many runners had decided their chances of getting caught were the same during the day as during the night.

Out in open water they bounced through the chop and slid over swells while Rudy kept watch on the bow for guard boats, hijackers, and the weather. The cradle of the sea was rocking rough today, but they stayed the course. Frieda didn't mind rocky runs, but rain was always disconcerting, because it cut down on visibility. She was having more nightmares than ever, and in the most common one the boat was heading broadside into a larger craft; she always awakened with a start a split second before they hit. Frieda shook her head, as if she could rid herself of the memory by scattering it over the water.

Dutch located the rum boat he lately preferred, the steamer *Dolphin*, and had to wait his turn while other small boats were loading. On the large vessel the men were too busy to exchange money. Instead every available crew member was occupied with handing down cases to all the smaller craft and also keeping a lookout for trouble. But that payment plan took a lot of faith in the shore boats' captains, because any of them could later claim to have been hijacked or caught by the guard and then never come back to pay.

The boats in front of Dutch pushed off, and he was able to pull in alongside the *Dolphin* and begin shouting his order while Rudy threw over the fenders and lines. Dutch ordered both Rudy and Charles to help load quickly, as the bigger boat had men on watch and visibility remained excellent, the storm still hovering a few miles farther out at sea.

Frieda stayed below to keep the engines running and ready to take off on a moment's notice. The boat sank lower into the water as the cases were loaded, and she figured they were about half-full when she heard the officer on watch aboard the *Dolphin* shout, "Cutter coming from the northeast!"

Frieda scrambled up out of the engine room and took a look. There was a dark bloom of smoke on the horizon and the easily recognizable white hull of one of the coast guard's seventy-five-foot cutters coming their way. American boats with liquor on board could be seized by US authorities anywhere in the world; no limit of jurisdiction protected them.

"Get out of here!" shouted the lead man from the *Dolphin*. As they all knew, the contact boats' best option was to get a head start and outrun the guard.

The smaller boats cast off, but Dutch and some of the other captains who ran bigger, swifter boats decided to stick around and wait to see what developed. Confidence was catching.

Dutch said, "Fuck that cutter. He only makes fourteen knots, and I can go faster than that even when heavy." He ordered Rudy to stop loading and keep watch on the cutter's progress while he and Charles continued to pull cases on board.

"Frieda, down below deck," he shouted at her.

There was never any doubt who was in charge on the *Pauline*. Dutch went about packing the boat just as coolly as before. Before she went down, Frieda glanced at Charles, whose brow had broken out in a sweat, though his face gleamed with excitement. He was probably happy the cutter was in the area—he'd have better stories to tell—and for a moment Dutch's questions to her from earlier, the ones she'd never answered, rang in her ears.

Rudy took up binoculars in the bow, the tiniest of trembling in his hands, and she ducked down under as ordered and waited for the moment Dutch would tell them to flee. When the cutter was within about four miles of the steamer, however, the guardsmen must have changed their minds. The cutter turned around and went back the way she had come. Inexplicably changing plans. Maybe they had received a distress call, and by policy their first duty was rescue at sea, or maybe they'd spied so many bigger, faster boats they'd figured it was pointless to give chase.

No one knew for certain, but the lead man on board the steamer said, "Well, you fellers, that there is a right kind gentleman, leaving us to conduct our business in peace."

Dutch turned in the cutter's direction and shouted into the wind, "Bon voyage, you fuckers!"

As soon as the cutter disappeared into the haze of the horizon, all the smaller boats reappeared as if pulled out of a magician's hat, and they waited their turn in line. Dutch finished loading and ordered them to push off and begin the journey home. With the engines running like the well-oiled machines they were, Frieda came up on deck for fresh air and to help look out for other boats. Charles sat by himself at the stern, and her first thought was to sit next to him as she usually did. Instead, Dutch's insistent questions haunted her, and she didn't want to add fuel to the fire by appearing to cling too closely to Charles. Dutch's questions only reminded her of her own.

You don't think that boy is going to take you away from all this, do you?

She'd never wanted to escape from all this, and she still didn't. But she did want Charles as she'd never wanted anything before. And he wanted her, at least for now. What about when the summer was over, though? She watched him as he cupped his hands around a cigarette, struggling to light it in the wind. Finally he got the thing lit and sat back on his elbows smoking casually, as if this were all he'd ever wanted. He turned his face up to the sky and closed his eyes. The elegance of him was so intriguing, so compelling.

For an hour or so there was no further sign of the cutter. Frieda silenced her inner fears, settled in next to Charles for the remainder of the ride, and watched his body fully relax as the sea moved underneath them. It was that way for her, too; they were kindred spirits when it came to the sea. Over these depths she could almost forget everything and simply drink in the windswept afternoon that was quickly turning to evening. They bounced and thudded into a glorious setting sun.

. But when the bay was in sight—it was about seven o'clock—this time it was Rudy who shouted, "Cutter!"

The amount of smoke from her funnel meant she was coming on at full speed. Inshore from the *Pauline* and most of the other boats, she was obviously planning on cutting off the entrance to the bay where all of them needed to pass, setting herself up to intercept the chosen boat, and so the race began. Dutch hollered that they had nothing to worry about. They were in one of the fastest boats in these waters. The slowest boats veered off to nearby beaches, where they could slide into shoals too shallow for the cutter and dump their loads someplace where they could return.

The crew of the *Pauline* watched several of the smaller craft evade capture that way. But the cutter got on the tail of a twenty-five-footer so loaded down with cargo that barely nine inches of freeboard was showing on her hull. They signaled for her to heave to and she obeyed. There were guns in the bow and stern of the cutter, which the coast guard crew were now authorized to use if a boat didn't respond to signals. The newly sanctioned use of force had made any guard boat feel more menacing.

The guardsmen were boarding the doomed vessel as Dutch swept the *Pauline* past them in utter defiance. *Foolish,* Frieda thought. They had never been so close to a cutter, close enough for the guardsmen on board to remember their faces. What was Dutch thinking? A trigger-happy guardsman could have taken one or all of them out. The guard wasn't authorized to fire if unprovoked, but the sense of lawlessness and recklessness about this business was expanding. The guard could claim they'd been shot upon first, and if something like that happened, who would believe a runner?

Even Charles seemed momentarily flummoxed. This life was over-coming Dutch, a man for whom she used to hold a great deal of respect for his cautiousness and attention to detail, but now openly brusque and impulsive, flaunting his success in front of the big white cutter with her gleaming brass fittings. As they made the sweep, the cutter was near enough that Frieda could see she had a crew of about forty or fifty men, all in spotless uniforms, the officers draped with gold braids. Strangely, she admired what they did. They were honestly going about the business of enforcing a law. However unpopular, it was a law, and they were charged with an impossible task.

The storm finally thundered in with lashing rain and wind that churned the bay into a froth. It was a miserable trip for the rest of the way. Charles turned up his collar and pulled a cap down well over his eyes, while Frieda went back below deck. Now the chop was rocking the boat from side to side, and the wind came with a howl. She found herself uncharacteristically nauseated, slithering eels in her stomach. Normally she had great sea legs and a cast-iron stomach. The boat pitched and surged against a rising swell, but Dutch never blinked an eye. Frieda held close to the engines for warmth.

Maybe it was best to go out with a captain who was fearless after all.

They got the load dropped, then eased the boat back into her slip just as the storm clouds curdled away. They had time for a late dinner. Frieda also had time to go home, clean up, and dress in one of the frocks that Bea had left with her, this one a cream-colored, crepe-y dress with a V-neck and a dropped waistline marked by a wide black band. She ran into town to the dress shop to buy stockings—in Rose Morn or Teatime shade, as Bea always preferred—sniffed the colognes on display, then made her purchases and ran outside to rush home and finish getting ready. As she rounded the corner onto her street, she stopped short.

Hicks was sitting on the porch with Silver, but once he caught sight of Frieda he lifted himself slowly from his chair. Even from a distance she caught the look in his eyes. He'd never seen her dressed for a date, dressed up for a man. He had to have heard about Charles and her, but his look was that of disbelief, disappointment, and perhaps pain. An old pain from long ago, never forgotten, always swirling deep in his eyes. Seeing her dressed to go out had probably made it all too real for Hicks. She lifted her hand in greeting and started walking again, but Hicks took the porch steps down, turned away from her, and started walking slowly in the opposite direction.

"Hicks!" she called out. There was too much pain in this world; she wanted to cause no more of it. But what was she to say to him? Still, she wanted to see his face up close and try in some way to make him understand.

He turned halfway around but kept moving farther from her. "Didn't recognize you," he shouted behind him, "with all the new scraps."

"Wait," she called, but she couldn't very well run in those shoes, and Hicks kept striding away.

"Hicks!" she called out again.

But he continued to walk away.

A strange urge rose in her throat to shout something else, but she stopped. What did she want to say to him? Another urge made her want to run after him, hold him, feel his warmth, comfort him, and let him comfort her; she had to turn away to suppress it. What was this feeling? What, what?

She joined Charles for the short drive to the Cedar Grove Hotel for dinner in the Water Witch section of town. She'd never been to the resort to enjoy its simple elegance and soft lighting, fine linen tablecloths, real silverware, and crystal wine and water goblets. While waiters hovered nearby to cater to their every need, Charles educated her about the proper use of cutlery while simultaneously smirking at the absurdity of such rules.

He seemed elated by the events of the night. They had foiled a coast guard cutter so close that they could've spit on it. "That was something, wasn't it?"

Frieda touched the napkin to her lips the way the other women in this restaurant were doing. "Rudy says the guard is getting better."

"Didn't look too outstanding today."

"They've put more boats into service, like that cutter."

"Lots of laid-up old destroyers from the navy, reconditioned for the guard."

"Still, there are more boats and more men—five thousand, I heard."

He sighed. "We have a good captain and a good boat."

"It was foolish to taunt them."

"Yeah," he said, and smiled, although a faint shadow crossed his face. "That might not have been such a good idea. But it was exciting, wasn't it?"

She managed to return his smile, but the sight of the cutter in the area and Rudy's warnings gave her an uneasy feeling. Maybe she *would* get out after this summer. Maybe she would go somewhere with Charles, or better yet he would stay here so she could stay with Silver. Or maybe he would walk away from all of it, including her, as Dutch had insinuated.

The next night Dutch said he needed a few days off.

So Charles took Frieda out again. They went to the outdoor summer theater at Highland Beach on Sandy Hook, as by then the evening air was fresh and cool, and the scum seemed washed from everything they were doing. There they could watch a motion picture outdoors and get dinner in the Bamboo Room. She loved being seen with him, especially out among the tourists, who didn't know her. They looked like any other couple out for a summer's evening. They looked right together; they fit.

Charles scanned the crowd, drew her near, and whispered, "Interesting lot here."

At first, all Frieda saw were the typical tourists, with a few locals mixed in. And then she saw some shifty-eyed, well-dressed gangster types. What were they doing here?

"See the man over there with the blond?"

Frieda followed his gaze.

"They both wear wedding rings, only they aren't married to each other."

Frieda's eyebrows rose. "How do you know?"

"I can read people. Look at the way he defers to her. He listens to her, breathes her in. Men don't treat their wives that way."

"In your world," Frieda shot back. "I happen to know several men who treat their wives well."

"Name one."

It was an easy answer. "Rudy."

"Ah, well, I wouldn't know about that. I'd have to see them together."

He locked on to another couple. "Those two, definitely married. Look how stiff they are. Probably arguing."

Frieda wished he'd focus more on her. But she said, "Probably need to roll around in the hay more often."

"Ha!" Charles laughed. "No doubt."

He picked out the newlyweds, some other cheaters, and predicted the breakup of another couple that very evening. He pointed out a man who needed money and another one who had too much. Then spinsters and widows.

Frieda said, "Maybe you can kidnap a few and take them home for further study."

Laughing aloud, Charles hugged her. "Jealous of my attentions, are you?"

Warmth flushed her face. "How sure you are of yourself."

He pulled her closer. "You couldn't be more wrong about that."

CHAPTER NINETEEN

That night he took her to his summer house, a colonial-style home in the hills, which, although it was one of the smaller ones on the street, still seemed like a mansion to Frieda. What did he do with all the space and furnishings? His bed was unmade, and he turned on only one small lamp. And yet she could see that the house was decorated in a nautical theme with the colors of the sea—greens, blues, and grays. It had a soft, comfortable lightness. The floor was solid under her feet and didn't creak, and the windows were spotless. The bathroom and kitchen held every modern convenience, and the smell of the house was of freshly laundered cotton mixed with the scents of the ocean wafting through the windows, which offered a sweeping view beyond.

He made sweet love to Frieda on top of fine linens while he left the French doors open to the veranda and sea breezes hummed over them. Afterward, she tried to sleep but found her mind jumbled. Frieda turned the subject of Charles over and over in her mind. She worried about the most insane possibilities and dreamed of equally impossible ones. Terror seized her when she thought about the end of summer and the start of the fall semester at Harvard taking Charles away, and she was sure this love affair couldn't last. Nothing in her life had ever promised a happy ending. She wasn't even sure that she deserved a happy ending. And yet hope was like a strong drink, soaking her brain with happy thoughts and possibilities.

Charles, not sleeping either and wearing only his underwear, took cigarettes and a gold lighter out to the veranda facing the bay and lit up a smoke, offering her one, which she declined. He stretched out in a wicker chair and seemed pensive, quiet.

Wrapped in his luxurious robe, Frieda followed him and found the veranda filled with flowerpots and vines climbing trellises at both ends. She sat beside him. After gazing over the water for what felt like a long time, she asked him, "What will you do after this?"

He took a long, slow drag on the cigarette. "I try not to think about it."

"It's already the end of June. The Fourth of July is coming. I always feel that after Independence Day passes, summer goes by so fast. July passes quickly, and after that August and the beginning of fall."

He smiled wryly. "That's generally the way it goes, Frieda. July, August, September . . ."

"Of course—"

"That's precisely why I try not to think about it." He stood. "Maybe I don't understand what I'm doing. Must I? Must you? Must everyone?"

Frieda wondered at his irritation. "I guess not. I guess there are many inexplicable things. But if we believe in something, maybe it helps." She wanted to say if we believe in *someone* . . .

"You're beginning to sound sentimental now. Don't get soft on me," he said with a delicious smile that stung. Suddenly she was so cold, as if winter had just blown in.

She kept her face still. He had no clue.

"Give me a back rub, will you?" he said.

Frieda positioned herself behind his chair and began to knead and massage his lovely, smooth, tanned skin. His muscles relaxed as she worked them, but his sudden dismissive statement had stiffened her every bone. *Don't get soft on me.* How was she to interpret that?

He sighed. "This life out in the elements suits me. Doing things, physical things. Being out of doors, breathing hard, the sun on my face, and the wind in my hair."

She told herself that what he'd said before didn't amount to anything; he was just joking with her, being himself. Talking, talking, talking. She gave his back a playful tap. "You're beginning to sound poetic."

"Ha! Me, a poet? I doubt it."

She returned to his beautiful back. "Have you seen the way people look after years of hard labor out in the sun and wind?"

He chuffed out a laugh. "There you go again. Drawing a line in the sand between us. But you're right. Don't trust anyone or anything."

"I never said anything like that!"

"You don't have to. We're more alike than you know. We don't completely fit where we're supposed to, and we can't escape it, either."

His mood had shifted like a curtain falling over a candle. She continued the massage, softening and stretching out the tight areas up near his neck, hoping to work out this inexplicable melancholy that had overcome him. She should've kept her mouth shut, but questions had a way of seeping out of her. Maybe she was seeking assurance that his depressed mood had nothing to do with her. "Do you really hate the idea of law school?"

He sat up straighter, his new position revealing that anger was beginning to overcome sadness. "I can't wait to pore over old books in musty old libraries, memorizing cases."

She said nothing. If he went, that was exactly the way she would want to picture him: studying, learning, making a future, and remembering her.

With barbs of irritation shooting at her, he said over his shoulder, "Don't you see that's why I'm here? So I can put it out of my mind?"

She stopped massaging and walked around to face him. "Couldn't you do something else instead? If you like the sea, couldn't you stay, maybe open a business? You have the means."

He laughed. "That would not be up to the standards my father has set for me."

"A successful businessman?"

Staring out to sea, he stubbed out the cigarette. "Now, this is where we differ. You have no idea."

That stung, too, even though it was probably the truth.

He looked up at her. "What will you do after the summer's over?"

She shrugged. "I don't know. More of the same, or maybe I'll quit running. I think I have enough put away for Bea. Eventually maybe I'll get my own boat."

"And it's your choice, right?"

She nodded.

He faced away, and the wind lifted his hair. Frieda brushed hers away from her face.

"This is what I'm struggling with. You get to make your choices. I don't. I know you'll find this hard to believe, but I envy you people down here."

A hot bloom of anger. *"You people?"* she shrieked, astonished.

"You know what I mean. No one is telling you what to do with your lives."

"We're limited by so many things!"

He gazed out to sea again. "I was afraid it would come to this. We have much in common, but it's not enough. You don't understand me, and I don't understand you. You envy me; I envy you."

"Be careful what you wish for. You've romanticized a simple life by the sea. It's harder than it looks. People are making money *now*, but it hasn't always been this way, and how long will it last? We have worries you cannot even comprehend. There's nothing original about a hardscrabble living."

With a chilly focus in his eyes, he tipped an imaginary hat. "Fine response, Frieda, and I do so enjoy our verbal battles. Money is to be made everywhere in this country. Opportunities abound; one has only to be bold. Look around you; that's what has happened here. Running for rum, even though it's illegal, is the kind of thing Americans do. Take the bull by the horns so to speak; tackle a new problem and create a way to best it. Come up with new ideas, new solutions. I'm part of a cursed class that doesn't have that option. We must do as we're told." He paused and raked a hand through his hair, and that sadness which Frieda had always seen barely concealed in his eyes bloomed to life. He lowered his head and grasped it in his hands as if he could exorcise the demons roaming around in there. "Perhaps I did come here looking for something . . . But more than anything I want to be understood." He lifted his gaze and squinted at her. "And now I see that I won't find that here."

His words tore into her like the ragged edge of a blade. She wanted to understand him and to know him more than any other person in the world. Perhaps . . . perhaps Charles's life *had* been empty. Perhaps he *had* been alone. Perhaps wealth and all its trappings really *weren't* things to always yearn for. She let those thoughts seep into her, a realization about a way of life in a world beyond her reach, and apparently beyond her understanding. She shook her head without meaning to. Then why did so many people desire to be wealthy? But her prying and continuing in this way would only push him away. "I understand you more than you know. I'm trying, at least. But no more talk of the future."

He reached out, put his arm around her waist, and sighed. "Yes, please."

Frieda went back to the massage and intently listened as Charles resumed talking.

Under her touch, Charles's mood seemed to lift, whereas a strange heaviness entered her. With the rubble of responsibilities on her shoulders, how she longed for the ability to put questions and uncertainty aside, to live only in the current day, the current moment. Charles, despite his self-pitying, could live for the present a lot better than she could. Perhaps the differences in their backgrounds were in fact impossible to brush away.

CHAPTER TWENTY

"I have a favor to ask," Frieda said to Charles a week later.

She had spent the previous night at his summer house, and they were sharing steaming cups of coffee on the veranda in the morning that had dawned only an hour earlier, warm and yellow. The *Pauline* was on hiatus because of a big moon, and Charles and Frieda were planning to return for another night in the city, to take Bea with them to paint the town red.

Frieda stood at the rail without looking at him, while he lounged behind her in a chair. "I'd like to arrive in Atlantic Highlands an hour or so early, before the ferry comes."

"Sure," he said. "What for?"

Frieda chewed on a nail. "Someone I need to talk to."

"Why, love, that's kind of mysterious. Do you want to tell me about it?"

She glanced back at him and said, "Not yet," then gazed over the bay and gauged the conditions of the water.

* * *

When they arrived at the ferry station later that afternoon, Charles went in search of lunch, having expressed no further curiosity about Frieda's favor, leaving her to her own devices. She wore Bea's dress again, topped by a wide-brimmed hat, and as soon as Charles was out of sight she asked around for Whitey and was promptly directed to his boat.

The marina in Atlantic Highlands was similar to the one in Highlands. As she came upon Whitey's boat, down near the end of one of the piers lined with boat slips, those slips filled with everything from crude fishing boats to new luxury yachts, she was momentarily taken aback by its similarities to Dutch's. Named *Sally*, she was fifty feet long, another Jersey sea skiff built for running. The sun reflected off Whitey's near-colorless hair, gleaming in the brightness of day. He sat on the transom, a cigar in one hand, the other one pointed at a teenaged boy, whose face was hidden under a hat. It looked as though Whitey was giving the younger man a good talking-to. But as she approached, he stopped, looked up, and straightened his back.

A skinny, bearded old codger stepped up from the engine compartment. All three of them stared at her suspiciously, as if there were cause for immediate concern about a nicely dressed young woman coming near them.

She walked to the end of the slip, where the boat was backed stern in, and looked at Whitey, into eyes that were so much like her sister's. She tried to contain herself, to not let her rage boil over. She had waited for a moment like this for a long time and didn't want to spoil it with hysterics. "Might I have a moment of your time?"

He spat a bit of tobacco from his mouth over the side of the boat. Then he set an unwavering gaze on her face. "What's your business?"

"Personal."

A man on a boat in the next slip whooped. He was the size of a bear and just as grizzled. "Personal, you say? Why old Whitey here? Why not me?"

She gazed around. Other men on other boats were paying attention now, too. One of them wolf-whistled. She turned her attention back to the matter at hand as Whitey sat still, appraising her. Slowly he lifted himself and said, "Sure."

She hadn't remembered him as being so tall and ruggedly built. When she'd first seen him, her impression had been that he was of average size. But this man was more Viking warrior than Dutch was. She'd imagined slapping him, but her hand would probably just bounce off this monster.

He walked behind her up the pier as many sets of eyes openly followed them. She led him to the gravel-covered parking area, where a few cars were beginning to arrive for the next ferry and people were going about their business, not paying them or their little drama any attention.

"What's this about?" Whitey said as he stood before her, the cigar clamped between his teeth, his hands at his sides.

Frieda worked hard to keep her voice steady. "Do you remember Della Hope? The whore from Highlands? She was my mother."

Slowly he reached up and took the cigar out of his mouth. Its acrid smell wafted over to her, but his eyes had filled with instant realization. A bit of fear, a bit of interest, a bit of caution in them, too. Good. She wanted him to be nervous. "I remember her. I heard she passed on a long time ago. Sorry for your loss."

"I have a sister who looks just like you. Bea, Beatrice Hope."

He simply stood there, as if a hundred little gears were cranking to life inside his head. His gaze was softer but not shamed. Finally he said, "I figured this day would come."

"So you knew?"

He gestured around and shuffled his feet a bit. "This area ain't nothing but a bunch of small towns. People told me there was a girl, one of Della's daughters, who could be mine."

"And yet you did nothing about it."

"Wasn't much for me to do. I didn't know nothing for sure, and I was about nineteen when I went to see Della. Bachelor night, you know? I got married the next day."

"How does someone do that? What kind of person can do that? You knew you had a daughter and yet you kept away."

"By the time I found out it was likely, I was married with kids. And I knew you girls was being taken care of. What was I supposed to do? Based only on looks, I was supposed to come and claim her?"

Frieda pulled in a ragged breath, not sure what she was feeling or how to react. She had imagined lashing out at him, calling him names, and even shaming him in front of others. But now with Bea's absence, Silver's condition, and the mystery of Charles, it seemed much of the fight had been taken out of her, and her desire to strike out at him was waning. Her heart, which had been racing, slowed, and she found herself at a loss.

He said, "What do you want?"

Frieda shifted her purse from one hand to the other. The sun was near blinding, and it hurt her eyes. She shielded her face with the flat of her hand. "I-I'm not sure."

"Well, if you're aiming to ruin a man's life, go on ahead. I'll march you right up those streets and take you to see my wife. She's a good, God-fearing, churchgoing woman, and it'd break her heart. But tell her all of it, if that's what you're aiming to do. I'd rather that than waiting around for it to happen."

"That's not why I came."

"Then what?"

She thought about the tiny rooms where she had lived for the first five years of her life. Though she could barely remember it now, thoughts of that place still brought only sorrow and hopelessness. "Did you care anything about my mother?"

"She was a sweet woman. But I hardly knew her, to tell you the truth. I went to her that one time. I was a kid doing a foolish wild thing right before getting married. You weren't there, and I had no idea Della would be getting in the family way. I only heard about you two girls years later. Guess when people began to see your sister out and about they put two and two together."

Nodding, Frieda dropped her hand from her eyes.

"Why aren't you looking for your own father?"

She snapped back. "I have one. His name is Silver. He never knew my mother, at least not in the biblical sense, but he raised Bea and me. He has been our father." But the truth was she hadn't looked for her own father, because it was easier to hate a nameless, faceless person than a real one. Today had shown her that for certain. If her natural father turned out to be decent, what would she do? She would be lost. Besides, she had Silver. She had no need for another father.

He glanced away, then stared into her face, still flushed with outrage. He spoke with more gentleness than she imagined such a big man would possess. "I know Silver. A fine man. I heard he's took sick."

This nearly rocked Frieda off her heels. He knew Silver? If these two men knew each other, then Silver had to know that Whitey was Bea's father. She stuttered out, "He . . . he's doing fine."

They stood in silence, the minutes ticking by as brilliant sunlight poured down.

"If it's money you're after, I've been doing well for myself lately. I can send some for Beatrice."

"No, no, it's not money I'm looking for. I have plenty for her. Did you know your daughter is very bright, very kind, too, and that she was accepted into NYU? She's in the city now. I'm going to be seeing her tonight, in fact."

A new expression entered his eyes, what seemed to be a mix of sadness and pride. "I'm glad to hear that."

"You'd be proud of her."

He said softly. "I am. From what you're telling me, I already am."

She was having a hard time gathering up her emotions and sorting through them. She had expected him to be a monster, but he wasn't. Just a regular man who had "sinned" once and nothing more.

"What else?" he asked.

Finally she centered herself. "Nothing else. I just thought you should know. But apparently you already did."

"I'm sorry if I've gone and disappointed you. Do you aim to tell Miss Beatrice?"

She shrugged. "I don't know yet. She's never expressed much interest in her natural parentage. I'm not sure I'd do that to her."

"What's your name?"

"Frieda."

"Well, Frieda, I'm pleased to've met you, despite what you may be thinking. And I want to thank you for not saying anything in front of my boy. That young man on the boat back there, he's my oldest son. At a turning point in his life. Stuck in that place between boy and man. Don't think it would have set well with him if he found out about this."

"What will you say when you go back?" she asked, and gestured in the direction of the piers.

"I'll think of something. Maybe I'll say that you're sweet on me." He smiled but not in a leering way, more like an apology.

She could find no more to say to this man. All her imagined recriminations had gotten up and walked away. All the elation she had imagined feeling from this confrontation had disappeared. It had been easier to hate him.

Finally she asked, "Why *Sally*?"

"That's my daughter's name. My oldest daughter."

"How many kids do you have?"

"Four—two girls and two boys." He stared down at his feet. "Guess if Beatrice is mine, that means I have five."

"Well . . ." She drew in a long breath, prepared to end this.

He looked at her pleadingly, but he was not the kind of man who'd ever beg. "Frieda, let me know about Beatrice from time to time. Come and see me, will you?"

She nodded and felt tears about to bloom, but she buried them down.

Once the ferry began to surge over the bay waters, Frieda finally experienced a bit of the elation she'd expected to feel while confronting Whitey, but it had little to do with him. She realized anew that she didn't want or need to know her natural father. Would she ever see Whitey again? Would Bea want to know? Would she in time tell her?

She didn't know.

The strength of the ferry's engines jolted through her, and its groaning filled her ears. The ferry pitched forward against the chop in the bay, and the movement gave her a sensation of solid forward momentum, of change.

Once in the city they headed straight to Bea's apartment, and Frieda was relieved she remembered the way. At the door, just as she was prepared to knock her eyes landed on a note slipped between the bottom of the door and the threshold. It read:

> *Sorry I won't be able to make it tonight. I've joined a fan club for people who are intrigued by Mrs Dalloway. Couldn't miss it. I'm having so much fun and learning so much. Hope you have a swell night. Love, Bea.*

Frieda swallowed before speaking, and as she folded the note she said to Charles, "She can't make it. A previous commitment."

Charles knew she had written to her sister and had planned the evening over a succession of letters. He knew how excitedly she had been looking forward to it.

"Perhaps baby sister doesn't like the idea of you and me," Charles said.

Frieda shook her head. "She's not like that." She couldn't imagine what had gone wrong. Despite the geographical separation from her sister, Frieda had still sensed an invisible filament connecting her with Bea across space and time. But now it felt missing. She couldn't imagine that Bea had felt her fan club more important than her sister. Then again, Bea was exactly the kind of girl to be swept away by the city. She'd probably been whizzed into a circle of people who were very like her: smart and visionary, maybe a little flighty. People who wouldn't think that much about missing a prearranged meeting.

She whispered, "How could a book be so important?"

"Have you read it?"

She shook her head.

"I'll give you my copy."

"I-I don't really read."

His face fell. "You don't know how to read?"

Insulted, she looked up. "Of course I know *how* to read. I finished high school. I just don't read for pleasure."

He gently rubbed her upper arms. "You're upset about your sister, but I think it's actually good news. She's met a group of friends. She's not sitting around waiting for us. Didn't you want that for her? Plus that means that tonight I have you all to myself."

"But I have money for her. She might need it for her tuition; I'm not sure when it's due."

"Slip the money under the door."

"Is that smart?"

Charles said, "What else are you going to do?"

So she took the cash, which she had already secured in an ᴠ lope, from her clutch bag and slipped it under Bea's door. She almost knocked again before leaving, as if her sister's note had been some sort of mistake and Bea was lounging inside. Her sister's absence prickled keenly—Frieda missed her endless chatter, smart remarks, and little idiosyncrasies. The clothes strewn about, books everywhere, and her mannerisms; the way she laughed and the way she stood in the kitchen with one hand on the small of her back while she stirred something in a pot on the stove with the other. And now the city had swallowed her whole.

Everything about the evening had changed because of worries about Bea, but as they had dinner at Voisin, supped on the famous French cuisine, and then went out for dancing at the equally famous Cotton Club in Harlem, Frieda's worries worked themselves away. It helped that Charles had purchased a bottle of good scotch, which they passed between them and swigged. The gin served at the Cotton Club was known to have a volcanic effect on the brain.

All around Frieda were women wearing embroidered silks, chemises in flesh and soft pastel colors, feathered and sequined headbands, long pearl necklaces, numerous bangles, and bracelets clamped on their upper arms, the air around them filled with the scents of Chanel and Guerlain. The men wore tailored double-breasted suits or the occasional tuxedo. It was completely beyond her existence, but she was struck by an intense new realization.

She had expected so little of others, especially others of a different social stratum. Perhaps she had been the closed-minded one, inhibited by her own narrow ideas and prejudices, burdened with so many internal scars. She had imposed her ignorance onto others; she was the one who had needed to learn more. She pulled in a few deep breaths and felt as if her belief in humanity was broadening. She thought of all the lights out there in the city, blinking alive bits of wisdom inside her. From the outside the city had looked almost as if it were carved in miniature, but once here it was a place that could make them all bigger people.

Their last stop was an underground speakeasy. Inside, Charles ran into the same young man Frieda had seen with him that very first night in the bar down on the docks. As she and Charles were sitting at the crowded bar, the man clapped a hand on Charles's shoulder. She recognized his horn-rimmed glasses and remembered that he and Charles had first sought to rent a fishing boat and try running by themselves and how foolish she'd thought them. She had no idea what this other young man was doing with his summer. He was dressed more formally than they were, with a silk tie, finely tailored jacket, perfectly pressed shirt, and wing tip shoes. He had a slight frame but held himself as only aristocrats did—tall, straight, proud—and he had that ease Frieda had come to envy. She hadn't noticed before how the extreme thickness of his eyebrows contrasted with his small features, but still his face came together in an interesting mix.

Charles introduced the man as Will Reuben, and his eyes lit when he recognized Frieda. "I remember you. The feisty girl in the bar in Highlands." He glanced at Charles as if seeing his friend in a new light. Maybe even a new respect.

Frieda said, "I don't make such a good first impression."

Will smiled and looked from his friend's face back into hers. "On the contrary, you must have made quite a good first impression."

Her cheeks burned. She rested her hands in her lap—they might begin to tremble. So she had the approval of one of Charles's friends, and it was much more than she had hoped for.

"How've you been?" Charles asked Will.

"I'd be better if I could get a drink."

Frieda worked to get the bartender's attention, while Charles and Will caught up. She could hear snippets of the conversation over the drone of the crowd, bursts of laughter, and music played by the house band. Charles told Will little about his summer, but Will got the gist of it. Will, on the other hand, said that he'd been in the Hamptons and was preparing for law school in the fall; Frieda was surprised to hear that the rest of the conversation centered on Harvard and their plans for the upcoming fall semester. Charles gave no indication that he wasn't going to comply with his father's expectations, and she didn't know if his ambiguity was simply because he didn't want to delve into this tonight or if he was truly going. An unexpected heaviness reached across the bar, the people, and the tabletops and came to rest on her shoulders.

Will asked, "Where are you going to live?"

"I have no idea," answered Charles.

"You better make some arrangements soon, or you'll end up in a dormitory."

Charles scoffed at that. "Not a chance."

"I've rented a house near the campus. You could stay there with me if you want."

"Thanks for the offer, but—"

Shouts came. Men on the lookout yelled that the police were coming and beamed flashlights down the front stairwell. A contained rush ensued. Bartenders immediately put bottles of wine and liquor into under-the-counter storage, and patrons downed what was left in their glasses. Some women laughed, as if this were all some great joke, and poked another cigarette into their long holders. Waiters began to steer customers toward the back exit and narrow stairway leading to an alley.

Charles said, "Don't worry. The police are primarily after the owners, rarely the patrons. But it's still time to get out of the way. You never know . . ."

They got caught up in the frenzy of those wishing to escape, the crowd moving as one mob of humanity, some people still holding bottles and glasses in the air, others shoving to get out first, and for a moment Frieda lost hold of Charles's hand. She was unused to crowds like this and wasn't comfortable pushing her way through, but Charles waited, took her arm, and navigated through. They climbed a stairway to ground level, then burst out into a stinking alley, where women wearing fine leather or silk shoes tiptoed, tripping and laughing through the damp muck, and men deposited bottles on the ground and led those ladies away.

Frieda was surprised to find that they had lost Will on the way out, but Charles whispered, "Good. Too much talk of sore subjects," as he took her hand to his chest and ferried them down the alley toward the lights of the city streets.

Later that night, after a long session of lovemaking and new, previously unexplored sensations, Frieda propped herself up on one elbow in the bed next to Charles. "Tell me more about Will."

Charles, lying on his back and gazing toward the ceiling, pushed the hair from his forehead. "What about him?"

"Well . . . he's a friend of yours, right? A closer friend than, say . . . Toby."

He sighed. "I don't pry into your friendships."

She smirked. "You know them already."

"Dutch and Rudy?"

"That's about it."

Charles pulled her close. "Alright . . . Ah, Will Reuben. Pleasant chap. Smart. He has a friend of the female persuasion. Bess Templeton. Pretty girl. Appears tall, but I think it's an illusion caused by the way she holds her nose high in the air. She and Will argue all the time. They even quarrel in letters."

"Maybe it's love," said Frieda.

"Ha! You amuse me."

Frieda smiled and snuggled in, relishing the scent of him after sex.

He pulled in a breath. "Quite right. Maybe it is love."

"Or lust."

"Ha again!" Charles exclaimed. "But that would be impossible. Bess Templeton wouldn't lower her knickers for the Prince of Wales unless she first had an enormous ring on her finger and an outlandish engagement party in the works."

"Maybe I should've thought of that."

He laughed again and rolled over to face her. He touched her hair, then gently brushed it away from her face, his eyes filled with what Frieda could only interpret as love. And then words that moved her in her core: "You—never. You're unspoiled. Fresh as a daisy."

"Most of the time I smell of Eau de Fish."

Another burst of laughter. "Stop it. You're slaying me."

That night she watched Charles as he slept. His eyes flitted underneath his lids, and his limbs twitched from time to time. He slept fitfully, and she wished she could rest her hands on him in a way that would help. What could she do? And what was there to do to make him stay in a place he loved and with a person who loved him?

When she returned home the next morning, Bea's absence the night before hit Frieda like a jolt through her chest. Silver was already settled on the front porch, and Polly appeared behind the screen door. "Thank the Lord you're back," she muttered.

"Why? Is something wrong?" Frieda asked as she sat down beside Silver. Under his eyes were sunken purplish crescents, but he looked much as he always did.

"I have a family, you know. I can't stay here all day and all night," Polly yelled from inside as Frieda heard the woman gathering her things to leave.

"I'm going to stay home for a few days," Frieda said loud enough for Polly to hear, but she was really speaking to Silver.

Later, as they sat and watched the water, the comings and goings of boats, and the sun crossing the sky, she said, "I met Whitey. You never told me you knew who Bea's father was."

His eyes registered surprise. A silence ensued, soon filled by a trill of tourist voices nearby—people taking a walk, she presumed—and after they passed she could hear the clangs and hums of boats entering the bay from the river. She looked out over the bay, which had gone flat to the smeared blue horizon.

"He's not all that far away. It was bound to be discovered because of his pale hair and eyes. But don't worry; I didn't make a scene. Amazingly, he seems like a decent man."

Silver pointed to himself with his good hand, and his eyes became insistent, animated. He pointed to himself so vehemently that he was almost striking himself.

Frieda took both of his hands in hers and searched his eyes. "Of course you—you are our real father."

His eyes asked, *Then why?*

"I don't know why. Just curious, I guess." She waited while a mounting sense of apprehension stirred within her, but she had to ask. "Do you know who fathered me, too?"

He shook his head, and she didn't know whether or not she felt relief. She was stunned to see tears in Silver's eyes. He wrenched his good hand away from her and pointed to himself again. How horrible it must be for him not to be able to speak. She had hoped for a long time that his ability to articulate words would return. It was obvious that he was concerned for her, and often as she lay awake at night she imagined what he would say to her about Charles if he could. Silver had always seemed like a man untouched by the pull of romantic love, so would he understand? Would he tell her she was crazy, that she was only going to be hurt in the end? Would he fight her on this, too?

She said, "I know that. Of course you've been my father in every way except for that one way, and Bea and I haven't thanked you enough. I don't know what would have happened to us if it weren't for you." She would never again mention *fathers* to him. She waited another moment, then repeated, "Thank you. Thank you."

She should've said more. She should have recalled sweet memories and relived them with him. She should've spoken of his sacrifice and care that had kept them safe and in school, his focus always on their well-being. She should have conjured up old stories that would amuse him and let him know how much he'd done. She should've talked of how he'd given up his bedroom for them, his earnings, and his life. She should've spoken of love. She had thought she had years—at least months—more to do so.

Instead, she said no more, and he set that sad, solid gaze on her, and she let it hold her still.

CHAPTER
TWENTY-ONE

July flowed by like a river. Sometimes, when they weren't running, it was slow, hot, and lazy, and other times, when they were working, it was a wild rush. The borough of Highlands celebrated the Fourth of July and ushered in the height of the tourist season. Hotels and beach resorts were packed with visitors from the city and inland people with the means to take seaside vacations. Women wore the new stretched, ribbed jersey Jantzen swimsuits that fell inches above the knee over stockings and beach boots, and carried Oriental parasols while near the water. Men drove new Chrysler B-70s and the new men's swimwear of a wool tank over shorts while they smoked and discussed the latest movies.

Rumrunners were taking advantage of excellent ocean conditions. The crew of the *Pauline* began to make more runs during the day, under the scorching sun, with huge beach flies from Sandy Hook biting them on any exposed skin. Charles went along on every run, did his fair share of the work, and never complained. Dutch was more afraid of the go-through men running at night with their speedboats than he was of a coast guard boat that could see him during the daylight hours. They saw the cutter often, but the boat didn't chase them, as if the guardsmen were all too aware that the *Pauline* would outrun them and it wasn't worth their time to pursue.

But newer, faster guard boats were showing up, and once a guardsman fired warning shots across the bow of a boat under chase and accidentally hit a man on board. Although the crew of the chased boat made an urgent landing and tried to get the man to a hospital, he bled to death on the floorboards of one of their delivery trucks. And no one knew or trusted all the shifty-looking newcomers in town. Why were they here?

People were getting jittery.

Frieda received weekly letters from Bea that contained effusive descriptions of her activities in the city. The letters arrived on the same day each week, as if Bea had set herself up on a mandatory writing schedule, but Frieda was so relieved she didn't care. In the letters Bea apologized for missing the evening with Frieda and Charles, explaining that the city was so all-encompassing, and she felt she might have been a third wheel on the date anyway. She asked them to visit again and assured her that she wouldn't miss it the next time. Bea had secured a job in a drugstore and had learned to use a cash register. Frieda sent money double-wrapped in a thick envelope anyway, and at night, with the lights of the city blinking over the water, she had a hard time imagining that her little sister was over there, obviously happy, fitting in and creating a life of her own. It was what Frieda had always wanted, but she hadn't expected the change to be so sudden.

* * *

One day Hicks showed up at her house driving an old Ford Model T Runabout.

Frieda flew down the steps. "Is it yours?" she asked.

Hicks gave her one of his rare smiles, and relief was like a salve. She hadn't spoken to him since he'd walked away from the porch and from her. Occasionally they had passed by each other and waved, but that was all. Hicks was clearly no longer cross, and his forgiving nature stunned her yet again. He seemed to be able to get past hard feelings like flipping a switch. She didn't know if it was because of the soft spot in his heart he held for her, or if he was that way with everyone. All she knew was that he was here, and it was like walking into the arms of an old friend. In fact, he had spruced up for the occasion. He wore a clean pair of dungarees, had combed his hair off his face, and held an old felt hat in his hands in front of himself. His face was tanned smoothly by the sun on the lower part of his face, whereas his forehead was baby white, and the contrast made Hicks look as constant as the sun and the moon. "Of course it's mine. A little rusty. Needs some paint." And yet she could see Hicks's pride over this purchase. Maybe he was in an awkward way saying, *See, I can make something of myself, too.*

"It's great. It's yours."

"Come out for a ride?"

She looked back at Silver, who sat on the porch. She had recently purchased him a new battery-powered receiver radio, which he listened to voraciously. Frieda figured it kept him company.

"Could we take him, too?" she asked Hicks.

"I don't see why not."

With Hicks's help, she got Silver into the seat, while Polly, who had come over to cook, watched disapprovingly. Frieda squeezed in beside Silver and shut the door as Hicks jumped in behind the wheel. The motorcar was a beat-up rattletrap, but Silver seemed to enjoy the ride around town, even smiling from time to time on the good side of his face.

Hicks appeared to think it was a grand adventure. He waved at people they knew in the lower Highlands and stopped to talk with local men, who looked over the vehicle. Then they took to the hills and drove past summer "cottages," churches, and the school. By accident they passed Charles's summer house, and Frieda saw the Renault parked outside. He was home. But she said nothing about it to Hicks.

"How did you get this?" Frieda asked. Hicks had still not participated in any illegal activities and continued to make his living legally, from the sea, scraping clams off the shoals and doing some engine work from time to time. He finally replaced the hat on his head, shading most of his face, but a soft light glowed on his chin and lips.

"I've been saving," he answered, and a rare note of pride entered his voice. "And I got a good deal on her. She wasn't running, so I rebuilt the engine myself."

"So she's a woman, just like a boat?" Frieda asked, grinning, as the wind whipped through her hair and the engine made satisfying sounds as Hicks accelerated.

"A woman, yes. Finicky and needing lots of attention."

She laughed.

"And she runs either hot or cold, rarely in between."

Frieda laughed again.

After their ride they settled Silver back on the porch, and Hicks offered to teach Frieda how to drive the old car. She eagerly let him show her the laborious steps of cranking the engine to a start and how to work pedals and a clutch. After some instruction she took the wheel and nearly veered off the road on her first attempt to follow a straight line, but then she fell into the rhythm of it.

As she drove, Hicks said, "When this is all over . . ." and gestured toward the sea. "The running, I mean. It'd be smart for you to know how to work on car engines."

"What makes you think it's going to be over?"

"Everything ends, Frieda." He tipped his hat back on his head to catch some air on his forehead, a familiar move she'd seen so many times back when he was teaching her to become a mechanic, and he draped an elbow out the window. "Someday they'll get rid of this damn fool law, and you'll have to go back to making a legal living. Car engine's about the same as a boat engine, and cars are more popular than boats. Pretty soon everybody is going to own one, even poor folks."

"You think so?"

"Sure."

He told her to brake before the road curved, and she followed his instructions. She drove through the town and also many memories. Two years she'd worked alongside this man, learning the ropes of being a mechanic. And he'd asked for nothing in return. At the next intersection she braked and made a turn. "So, what are you naming this contraption?"

Gazing straight ahead, he turned quiet, his hands on his knees fidgeting slightly. "I was thinking of calling her Della . . . after your mama. I didn't know her of course, but I do know how much she meant to you."

Frieda's mouth dried. "How do you know that?"

"You wouldn't visit her grave if you hadn't loved her."

Frieda could only nod. Hicks was almost too perceptive for comfort.

"Besides, I like the name. So that's what I'm calling this baby—that is, if you don't mind."

She smiled at him, even though thoughts of her mother always made her a touch sad. "That's really nice of you, Hicks."

She drove on. "Do you mind if we stop at her grave?"

"Whatever you want," he said softly.

She tilted her head from one side to the other, working out the kinks.

"Never mind," she said. "It's too nice a day for graveyards."

Again he said, "Whatever you want."

Focusing on the road, she tightened her grip on the wheel. "Someone puts flowers on her grave every now and then. A long time ago I used to think it was Silver, but even before he had the stroke I figured out it wasn't him. Do you know who it is?"

He sat quiet, unmoving, facing ahead. "No."

"Do you have any idea . . . ?"

"None. Sorry. Has to be someone roughly twice your age for him to have known her."

"How do you know it's a man?"

"I don't. I guess I just imagine it that way. Maybe I'm a romantic type, only you never saw it."

She looked over and saw yearning in his eyes. He still had feelings for her—unbelievable. For a moment she was overcome with conflict. She and Hicks shared something like love, didn't they? Maybe the finer parts of it, at least. They had the love of understanding, compassion, commonalities, and despite the differences in their lines of work, they shared community and passion about the same things. But it went beyond that. She respected Hicks, because he possessed something far-seeing about life.

But her heart belonged to someone else. Her life was with Charles now, and she was too consumed by his kisses and loveliness. She filled with a deep ache at the thought of their nights together, which lifted her above anything she'd ever imagined before.

He shook his head and said, "I'm not a man for graveyards myself. Don't ever go into one unless I have to for a family burial."

"Do you believe they're haunted?"

"No," he said as if quite sure of himself. "I don't believe in ghosts, don't believe in heaven or hell. Don't believe in any of that stuff."

"So, if you don't believe in ghosts or an afterlife, what do you believe in?" she asked, and couldn't quite believe how the conversation had turned.

"I believe in the here and now. I believe in people."

"What does that mean?"

He sighed. "That people show you who they are in the here and now."

Frieda smirked and made a chuffing sound. "You must not think very much of me in the here and now."

"Hardly true." He sat still and never took his eyes from the road ahead. "You're the fish that got away."

When she saw Charles that night, right away she could see there was something different about him. He had suddenly sealed himself off again. He made polite talk, but when it came to anything else it was as if he'd built a seawall between them. They were staying in for a quiet night at the summer house and had steamed clams on the stove for dinner. Now they sat on the veranda with a bottle of what Charles said was exceptionally good scotch, poured into crystal tumblers over ice, and the setting sunlight was peach and orange and lit his lovely face with the most luminous color.

He could've been a movie star. He could've lit up the screen and broken the hearts of many a young woman. The deep tan he was acquiring set his teeth off like a row of shining, straight tiles. Moments such as this, full of his disarming loveliness, sent Frieda spinning. It was hard to fathom that Charles was spending his time with her, that she was *with* him. But what was wrong now?

"You're quiet today," she finally said. But he wasn't exactly quiet. The distance between them, however, was hard to admit and even harder to describe. It was only a feeling, but a strong one nevertheless.

He smiled, but there was no joy in it. "Many devious thoughts roam inside this mind." He tapped his temple.

"Devious?"

"I saw you out today," he said. "I saw you out in an old motorcar with another guy."

She turned more fully toward him, not knowing yet if his comment amounted to an observation or some kind of accusation.

"You mean Hicks? He's not *another guy*. I've known him my entire life."

He asked flatly, "Who is he to you?"

"A family friend. He's a clammer. He's the one who bought Silver's boat, the boat I wanted to be mine."

Charles rubbed his chin. "Why don't you buy her back? Or better yet, get yourself a nice boat."

"It was—it is—a nice boat. Simple but solid. Silver built her himself. Maybe I will try to buy it back someday."

When Charles stayed quiet, she said, "Anyway, Hicks is just a friend. Well, more than a friend. He also trained me to be a mechanic. He gave me a skill I can always use."

Shrugging as if it meant nothing to him, Charles said, "I'm not the jealous type."

She reached over and playfully punched him in the arm. "And why not? If I saw you with another woman, I'd be jealous."

"Jealousy is a vile emotion," he said, and took a swig of the scotch.

"Oh really?"

He nodded once. "It's beneath me."

She almost laughed but thought better of it. "Why did you mention him, then?"

After that a leaden silence fell over them, and his body tensed. His lips formed a straight, thin line, and his eyes were like blue ice. A chill filtered through the planks beneath her feet and traveled up her spine.

His tone was devoid of emotion when he said, "Don't flatter yourself, Frieda."

It was like a blow to the chest.

He gave her a look as dark as coal, then stood up and went inside.

Don't flatter yourself, Frieda. She sat without moving as darkness came out of the earth and the lights across the water began to wink awake. She slowly drew her arms around her and hugged herself tightly. She'd never been one to flatter herself, but Charles had been doing plenty of that. What did he want from her, anyway? She could go in after him and demand to know the meaning of his slight. She should have at least told him how his comment hurt. The old Frieda wouldn't have hesitated, but she had to be careful with Charles now. She shuddered against the incoming night breezes. She didn't know what was in Charles's heart; she didn't understand him, and maybe she never would.

The telephone rang and she heard Charles answer. Of course she had known there was a telephone in the house, but she hadn't heard it ring before. Though curious as to who was calling, she stayed out on the veranda. She wouldn't eavesdrop. For now she had to go on playing the part of someone whose world had not been shaken to its core. Charles hated any pressure; that much she knew, and she had to be sure not to apply any more weight to what he saw as his burdens.

When he came back outside, any ill feelings toward her seemed to have been swept away by other concerns.

"Dear old Dad," he said as a way of explanation.

"Oh? What did he want?"

"To talk some sense into me."

"About what?" She was pulling teeth.

"You don't want to hear about it."

"Yes, I do. I want to know everything about you."

He shot a guarded look her way. "I thought we had an agreement. No talk of the future."

"I'm not talking about the future. I'm talking about the here and now." Hicks's words were coming out of her mouth.

He settled back into the chair with his scotch and lit a
"It's not important."

The pale light and smoke masked his features, veiling the face that
she thought she had been learning to read so well. But tonight she
found him indecipherable, and a sense of retreat came up in the air.

Maybe that was the first night she felt Charles slipping away. Or
maybe it had started earlier, on her first night here at the house. Or
maybe he had never been anywhere near her grasp from the very beginning. So it was no surprise that during the night, in her dream she tried
to cup water in her hands, but as hard as she attempted to contain it,
the liquid slowly but surely fell through her fingers.

She awakened before dawn the next morning. Charles was still sleeping,
oblivious to the anguish he had caused, and she slipped into her clothes
and let herself out of the house without a sound. She didn't want to
see him in the harsh morning sunlight. Did she want to see him at all?
Don't flatter yourself, Frieda. She walked back to Silver's house, her
body as flimsy and her bones as fragile as a fallen bird's, and she wondered how long the sheets beside Charles would stay warm.

Why did the tides always turn?

When she arrived home, the sun was up, and slanted beams of light
made their way inside the house, illuminating floating dust particles
in the air. Polly quickly left, although Silver hadn't been fed or readied
for the day. Frieda did the morning chores, dressed Silver, and fed him
eggs she scrambled soft in the frying pan. He was weaker today, or had
he been growing weaker each and every day, only she hadn't noticed it?
She had been too consumed with her own life to recognize the facts.
Silver, too, was slipping away from her.

CHAPTER TWENTY-TWO

August came to the shore with a heat wave, dazzling white sunlight, and cloudless skies, along with hordes of tourists escaping the city. Frieda hadn't stepped but a few feet away from the house, and that was only to take a short walk and stretch her legs while Silver was sleeping. She'd sent word to Dutch that she had to stay with Silver and for the time being couldn't work on the boat or go on runs. Each day she saw more weakness in Silver's body and a duller light in his eyes. He barely ate, and even getting water in him had become a chore. She'd called the doctor, who, after examining Silver, pulled Frieda aside and told her to "prepare for the worst."

She had written to Bea twice, informing her of Silver's decline and asking her to come visit before it was too late, but so far she hadn't received a letter in return. If Bea had had a phone, Frieda would've been calling her sister daily. She moved through the days alternating between a sense of panic and a strange sense of calm. Panic when she wondered what Bea was doing to keep herself so busy in the city; calm when she sat with Silver and held his good hand and let the happy memories he had provided for her sink into her soul. Hicks visited, sat with Silver, and told him fishing stories. Seeing those two men together brought on such choking emotion, Frieda thought she might have to step outside to breathe. Both men had wanted only the best for her. She almost suggested that Hicks go to the city to get Bea, but in the end she couldn't ask for any more from him.

A full week and two days had passed since the morning she'd let herself out of Charles's summer house without a word. Of course her mind drifted to him, especially as she sat during the quiet hours between household chores and looking after Silver. Each night, when the sun finally sank behind the hills, it struck her particularly hard that he hadn't sought her out. She'd seen with the binoculars that he was still going out on runs with Dutch and Rudy, along with another person, whom she assumed was the mechanic Dutch had hired in her absence. So Charles was around; he simply hadn't come to her. At night, if not overcome with worry about Silver, Charles's treatment of her—his words and his distance the last time she'd seen him—ran through her thoughts like a swift and dark current.

When Silver slept, she stepped out on the porch and turned toward the bay. The view was the same—the Hook, the lighthouse, ferries crossing, gulls flying—but she had changed. She had lost herself somehow with Charles. His happiness had become more important than hers. His moods had to be danced around. His vagueness had to be tolerated. But she had let him get away with it. Silver had allowed her to grow up independent and strong. He would hate to know how she had subjugated herself.

She had just begun to feel a slow return to something resembling normalcy when she looked up one day from the porch and saw him walking down her street. The sight of him brought with it an unbearable aching hope; she hadn't begun to heal after all. She had to grab hold of a chair and sink down into it as Charles approached. She curled herself into Silver's favorite spot. This morning Silver had been too weak to get up; his eyes had pleaded with her to let him be, in the bed.

Charles was soon standing before her, and still she couldn't make herself meet his gaze. Instead, she studied his fine leather loafers, now water ruined and salt encrusted from spending his summer down here.

He pulled in a couple of breaths and let them out with a heavy sigh. "I heard about Silver," he said slowly. "I'm sorry."

He came up the porch steps and took a seat beside her. "I didn't know whether to leave you alone or come keep you company."

She looked away.

"Did I do the right thing by coming here?"

Finally she made herself turn his way and look at him, really look at him. His eyes were misty and pleading. This was the side of Charles that weakened her, body and spirit. He was more beautiful, inside and out, when he allowed himself to be vulnerable. She wanted to touch his cheek, where she saw the very slightest quivering. She wanted to claim the pain she saw in his eyes and then do everything in her power to wash it away. She wanted to rush into his arms and simply hold still in that wonderful space. When it was wonderful . . .

"I don't know," she finally said. "Did you?"

"I hope so," he said, and squinted into the sunlight. "Look, I know I hurt you. I suffer from foul moods; it's been a lifelong challenge at times. I didn't want to show that ugly side of me, and so I did my best to conceal it from you. But it was never a realistic ploy; you were bound to see me for what I am."

The hope in her chest bloomed bigger. "I do see you for what you are, and I lo—" She stopped herself. "I care for you. I told you once I wanted to know everything about you, and I meant it."

"I know," he finally said, holding his hands between his knees and studying them with seeming intensity. Then he turned to her, and the sunlight brightened him and her world. Oh, to be the subject of those marvelous adoring eyes again. Was this the way it was going to be? Their relationship like a bellows: times of closeness alternating with times of distance?

"I never expected to find such a jewel as you in a place like this. I never expected to find such a jewel anywhere. Perhaps I don't know what to do with the discovery. Perhaps I don't know what to do with you."

She pulled in a stunned breath. "I want to help you figure it out."

"You push, Frieda. You expect so much."

"I won't—I'll try not to."

He set that lovely gaze on her, and he smiled wryly. She extended a hand and he grasped it.

"I'm sorry."

Nodding, she was about to say she was sorry, too, when he straightened up, as if gathering strength and digging himself up out of some deeper place.

His voice rose in a small show of determination. "But this is not a time to be thinking and talking about someone as worthless as me. You have your father to think about now."

"You're not worthless."

"Let's not go on about that—"

"You're not worthless," she said again. "How could you say that?"

He passed a hand through the air. "Enough about me. You have no idea how silly my little concerns feel to me at this moment. I want to help you. What can I do?"

She fought off tears and instead let a smile open her face. "You're already doing it."

From then on, whenever Dutch wasn't making a night run Charles came over and brought food, spirits, and cigarettes and seemed perfectly content to let the hours slip away in Frieda's company, and occasionally

Silver's, as the sun went down. He told her that Dutch's interim engineer wasn't pulling his weight on the boat, and Dutch was all too eager for Frieda to return to the business. But he also told her that everyone understood and reassured her that she was doing the right thing to stay at home for now.

Silver was slipping away slowly but steadily, like seawater sinks into the sand. Every day he appeared more gaunt and pale, and bones were pushing out the fragile skin in his face. Several times a day he fell into a coughing spell that exhausted him so much that he had to sleep for a few hours afterward. He had no appetite and had lost interest in sitting on the porch, only doing so when Frieda and Charles insisted that he needed to get fresher, more cooling air. Surprisingly, Charles didn't shy away from illness and what Frieda had been told was impending death. If anything, he seemed at his best, and Frieda wondered if perhaps medicine was his true calling rather than law. But she saved that suggestion for later, better times. The important thing now was that he wasn't abandoning her. When she thought of Bea, a powerful sense of disbelief dawned on her, and she didn't know how she would've made it through without Charles.

On a dark night, when Charles was away on a run, Frieda saw a marked turn for the worse in Silver and sent for the doctor. Silver's breaths were coming in gasps, then pausing for moments before resuming, and she considered having him taken to the hospital. She didn't know if she could do that, however, because she knew that Silver preferred to spend what were probably his last moments of life in his own home and not in a hospital bed.

He looked at the ceiling and moved his lips on the good side of his face, as if trying to speak. Yet he wasn't trying to speak to Frieda. Instead, he was either trying to talk to himself or to some spirit that had appeared to him as he approached the end. Then he stopped trying to form words and lay still without moving. The peace in his eyes told

Frieda he was not in unbearable pain, maybe no pain at all. Th
fluttered on his good hand, and she took the hand in hers.

Frieda stared at the floor and then back at his face. He closed his
eyes and appeared to sleep peacefully for a few moments. Then his
eyes flew open and sought out Frieda. He took his hand from hers,
reached up, and rubbed his chin, the same mannerism Frieda had seen
thousands of times, the gesture he made when he was about to say
something funny or clever or share a memory. It was a movement that
indicated pleasure and anticipation, and his eyes again found the ceiling
or perhaps what he believed or hoped might be beyond it. He laid his
arm at his side, and the sheets over his chest stopped moving. Frieda
went to take his good hand again and found it still warm but without a
reciprocating squeeze. She stayed there in the stillness, listening to the
sounds of boats coming and going, a ship's horn, some distant fleeting
music from a resort, then a hush as the tide flowed out to sea.

She thought of better days, of Silver in his boat, squinting in the
sunlight, showing her how to bait a hook, teaching her how to stand in
the boat without falling when swells rolled under them, pointing out
constellations at night, telling her and Bea that all over the world people
were gazing at the same stars, joining everyone together in this strange
state he called humanity.

Frieda had no idea who her blood father was, and yet this man
had given her a loving home. She pressed her lips to his hand, already
blanching of color, and laid it back beside him on the bed. Moments
later she walked from the house to where she would stay until the doctor arrived: under the stars in the middle of the street.

Hicks took the ferry to the city to fetch Bea while Frieda made funeral
arrangements. Silver wouldn't have liked what he called a "fuss" made
over him, and he wasn't a religious, churchgoing man, so she decided
to bury him without a lot of ceremony. At least she didn't have to worry

over the cost of things, and she purchased the nicest understated casket at the local funeral home, then let the funeral director put Silver in a room for viewing for just one day.

In a rare moment of clarity, she decided to bury Silver next to her mother. He'd never purchased a plot, and now she was left to make decisions. Her mother and father, never lovers, laid to rest side by side . . . It gave her a small comfort.

After the simple burial, she chose to hold a small service outside the house that Silver had loved, under the scorching sun in full view of the sea. Silver didn't like to let anything wait that could be done soon, so she planned the funeral for the day after the burial. Hicks had found a kindly Methodist minister to conduct a simple ceremony in the front yard of the house, using the front porch that Silver had so loved as a pulpit.

The day was still, bright, and hot. An eerie silence spilled over everything; not even sounds from the beaches drifted near. Silver would have liked the sounds of beachgoers' merrymaking, but Frieda didn't know if she'd be able to take it.

People began gathering, and there was still no sign of Bea. Finally, just moments before the minister was to begin, Hicks drove up in his old Runabout, with Bea and another man beside her. All three slipped silently out of the car and went to the back of the gathering. Hicks wore what Frieda knew to be his only suit. Bea was dressed in a new black, sleeveless frock, a straw hat adorned with a black ribbon sitting smartly on her head, as calm, poised, and pretty as a photograph. The other man held close to Bea, his hand at her back, indicating that they were together, and Bea made no move to join Frieda at the front of the crowd. Frieda took in the man in one long glance. He looked to be nearing thirty and wore shiny wire-framed glasses and a waxed moustache that curled up on both sides. Slight in build and dressed in a brown suit, he looked like a teacher—or a snake charmer masquerading as a teacher.

Frieda turned toward the minister and did not look back throughout the ceremony. Hicks stayed with Bea and the unknown man, while Charles stood next to Frieda, keeping a respectful distance from her and listening to the minister. He had his feet planted, holding so still that Frieda once glanced his way to see how he was handling all this. She had no idea what experiences he'd had with death before.

Frieda was gratified by all the people who'd come to pay their respects to Silver, including almost all the fishermen he'd once worked alongside, Dutch and Rudy, Polly and her family, the Bahrs family, and some of Bea's former teachers and classmates. A few bar owners, shopkeepers, some kind churchwomen. And Hawkeye. She was surprised Hawkeye would have the nerve to come, but today all of her anger had stood up and walked out of the door. The minister kept it simple and didn't preach but also managed to paint the hope of a better life beyond as a final message to those who stood in the sweltering sun. When he finished and said a final prayer, the wind picked up and blew the heat away.

The women set out casserole dishes, cakes, and pies in the cluttered kitchen Frieda had yet to clean well enough for visitors, and they made coffee and tea. Frieda glanced out the window. Bea was sitting on the porch with the man she'd brought, but Frieda was too busy to join them. There would be time to catch up after the others left. Too late she realized that she didn't have enough plates, silverware, and cups for the group, and so Charles drove quickly to his summer house and returned with enough for everyone.

"A fine fisherman," "A fine man," "We've missed him," "God rest his soul," and "May he find his eternal peace now" were some of the comments that the well-wishers made. People conversed in small groups, but no one made mention of the rumrunning that was likely on many of their minds, as if out of respect for Silver, who'd never made an illegal dime in his life. They all knew what Frieda did of course, but since many were in one way or another participating, too, no one needed reminding.

The house and yard were full of people, and yet an emptiness inside the place made Frieda's body feel hollow. Silver was the only man she was sure had really loved her. The one man who was most needed here was gone. Gone, she had to keep telling herself when she gazed at the places he liked to sit, when she thought she heard his old voice, when she caught the scent of him in the air. Soon even that would be gone.

Behind her, the murmur of voices, the clink of dishes, the distant sounds of a piano. Before her, the sea shimmered in the setting sun, the tide coming in, the currents tracing their ever-eternal paths to and fro. *The sea was a landscape of longing,* she thought, *a landscape of ceaseless change.* No matter how peaceful, it would not last. Change could be only seconds away.

After all was said and done, people started filtering away, and Frieda realized, almost too late, that Hicks was leaving with the rest of them. She followed him down the shell-strung street, the sun lowering into the hills in front of her, nearly blinding her. "Hicks!" she called out, shading her face with the flat of her hand.

He kept walking, and at first Frieda thought he meant to ignore her. But slowly he stopped in his tracks. He turned and came toward her.

A moment alone with someone who'd known Silver as she had. She was able to take her deepest breath of the day, and a tiny sad smile might even have formed on her lips. "Thanks for going for Bea. Thanks for everything."

His gaze traveled beyond her, to where Charles was waiting on the porch for her return. In his eyes was more pain than the world should be able to hold, and Frieda didn't know if it was for Silver or because he was having to witness Charles and her together, so obviously together now. She would've liked to believe that his suffering came from the loss of Silver, but Hicks had clearly not let go of his weakness for her, as was

evident in the way he looked at her, his mouth softening, his eyes fu.
with a longing she did not feel in return.

"Anything for you," he finally said.

"Thank you," she repeated helplessly.

"If there's anything else you need, you know where to find me."

She wanted to say something else, something about his steadfast-
ness and his faith in her despite it all. Regardless of all the undercur-
rents between them and surrounding them, Hicks had stayed on course,
unswerving. He had that quality that made one want to join hands
with him and go along. She wished she could express that, but she
could form no further words. Did he love her even now? And if so,
with what kind of love? Funny how death made one reexamine all the
things about life. The biggest questions in life. The question of love had
never haunted her so.

Her throat was paralyzed, her mind swimming. What was love of
any kind, for that matter? Was it the unbridled passion and longing of
the sea during a storm? Was it what she felt for Charles? That thrill, that
risk? The push and pull of power? Or was it the quiet, soft caress of the
sea during a calm? Was it a solid and secure fondness and affection? Was
it what she felt for Hicks, his centeredness that held her still?

She opened her mouth to say something, but no sound emerged.
Charles was waiting. Hicks flicked his eyes in his direction, and the
moment was lost. Hicks tipped his hat, backed up a few steps, turned,
and walked away.

CHAPTER
TWENTY-THREE

After all the townspeople had gone, Frieda began to wash dishes, and Charles stood beside her to dry and stack the plates.

Bea appeared in the kitchen. She stood with her feet together, holding her hat in front of her, her eyes enhanced with a rimming of kohl but wavering with want of crying, her mouth stained cherry red, wisps of her bob framing her brave face. After glancing at her sister, Frieda turned back to the dishes.

Excusing himself, Charles left the two women alone.

Bea exhaled. "I'm sorry I didn't come sooner," she said softly to Frieda's back.

Frieda wanted to be angry, but her sister's presence made her realize how much she'd missed Bea, and all she wanted to do in that moment was hug her. She turned away from the sink and took Bea into her arms.

Bea silently cried into Frieda's shoulder. "At the end . . . was he in pain?" she asked, swiping at tears on her face as she finally stepped back.

"I don't think so," said Frieda.

"I'm sorry you had to go through it alone."

Frieda looked away. "I wasn't completely alone. Charles has been wonderful."

"I'm so happy for you, Frieda. And I'm sorry, truly sorry."

"Did you get my letters?"

"Yes, but I had been away on a holiday. When I returned and read them, I immediately made plans to come. Then Hicks showed up, and I realized I was too late. I'm so, so sorry, Frieda."

Everyone was so, so sorry for everything. Charles was sorry for hurting her, Bea was sorry for abandoning her, and the townspeople were sorry that Silver was dead. Finally she said, "I suppose it was just bad timing."

Bea hugged her sister again.

"Where were you?" Frieda asked.

"Oh, here and there. I've been to so many places I can't wait to tell you about."

"Because of the man you brought?"

"Yes," Bea said firmly. "I'm happy for you and Charles. And so . . . I hope you'll be equally happy for me. I have wonderful news." Bea produced her left hand, where a diamond glinted on her ring finger. "I'm engaged."

Frieda couldn't squelch the gasp that escaped from her lips.

"That's right," Bea said, and smiled brilliantly. "His name is August Freeman. I met him at the fan club for *Mrs Dalloway*, and you won't believe this part of the story: he's a professor at NYU. An English professor. Isn't that amazing? We started to date, and it soon became evident that we were meant for each other. We love the same books and authors, we love the city, and we want to travel the world together. He's madly in love with me, I assure you. Oh Frieda, I never imagined being this happy. Please say you're happy for me. Once you get to know him, you will be."

Frieda tried to control a rising sense of panic that tasted of acid in her throat. She became aware of every bone and muscle in her body and the way Bea expertly carried herself, a young woman in love. Bea was radiant, transcendent.

"You scarcely know him."

Bea's face lit up with a natural glowing charm. "I knew you would say that, but I've seen him almost daily since we met. He's on break from the university, and after I finish my day at the drugstore he takes me out. We've been all over the city and up to Long Island and out to Nantucket. We peruse used-book stores and frequent little coffeehouses, reading alongside each other. It's so perfect, Frieda. Fate brought us together. If I hadn't met him this summer, I probably would've been enrolled in one of his classes during the school year. I might have been just any other student, although he assures me I would've stood out"—she smiled coyly—"but I think fate intervened and allowed us to meet before the school year began."

Frieda tried to interpret what Bea was saying. "You can date your professor. No law against that."

Bea's face fell. "I'm not going to date my professor, Frieda. I'm going to marry him in just a matter of weeks. I'm going to be his wife, not his student."

"Wait a minute. What are you saying?"

"I'm saying that I'm not going to enroll in classes. I'm going to be a wife . . . and maybe a mother, too."

Bea's words yanked Frieda's heart out of her chest. "You can't mean that. You're giving up school? You can get married, although I think this is much too fast of an engagement, but even if you insist on getting married, surely you can still go to school."

"I no longer want to go to college."

Frieda's body opened up, and all its contents blew away. "Bea, no school? It's what you've always wanted. What Silver and I both have worked toward for so long."

"I knew you would say that." Bea took in a huge breath and let it out slowly. "I didn't know what it was like to fall in love. I didn't know how it would change me."

"You always wanted to be a teacher! Always!"

Bea lifted her arms to her sides and then let them fall. "I've changed my mind."

"Has he talked you into giving up on your dreams?"

"Please don't do this. Please don't paint him as some sort of villain. He loves me; I love him. That's all there is to it. We want to go forward together, as man and wife. I hope that someday I'll have a house full of children to teach—my own children. You know I've always been more traditional in my wishes than you."

"Yes, I figured you'd eventually get married and have children, but not now. You're eighteen, for Christ sakes."

Bea held still, and eyes that had been misty became sharp with determination. "I've made my decision. I would love it if you could be happy for me, but I've made my decision. Look on the bright side—I don't need all that money you've been socking away for school. And with Silver gone, it's all yours."

"I don't want the money for me. It was always for you! So you could better yourself, so you could always take care of yourself. I wanted you to be a new breed of woman, a woman who can stand up on her own."

"I'm sorry to disappoint, but this is me now. This is what I want. And no one is going to talk me out of it. Please don't try." Bea was the picture of promise and purpose, and Frieda wondered if her sister had rehearsed this moment, whereas Frieda was caught completely off guard. But why hadn't she imagined such a possibility? Bea was exactly the kind of girl who could be swept off her feet by a whirlwind romance. Even Frieda herself had succumbed to one. And still Frieda was stunned. She couldn't help restating her words of protest.

"I have to! I've known you my entire life. I've listened to all your dreams and plans. Never once did you say you wanted to get married right out of high school and settle down. What about all your dreams?"

"Well, I have August now." She waited while Frieda tried to sort this through in her mind. Not Bea. She couldn't lose her plans for

Bea, on top of losing Silver. Bea said softly, "And apparently you have Charles."

Frieda raked her hands through her hair. Of course Bea would've been lonely in the city. Pretty as she was, of course she would meet men. But Frieda couldn't grasp this no matter how hard she tried. "This is not the way everything was supposed to happen."

Bea stepped forward and took her sister's hand. "I didn't expect it, either. But this is what I want. It's my life, you know. Please be happy for me. I want you to be at the wedding. It will be a simple affair in the city. Please let me introduce you to August. You'll like him; you'll understand once you get to know him."

Frieda doubted that, and all her protestations had changed nothing.

True to Bea's word, August Freeman was indeed a likable sort. After Frieda and Charles had spent the rest of the evening with the newly engaged couple, saying useless things, surrounded by Silver's ghostly presence, Frieda could see how much August was trying. He was intelligent and well educated but didn't flaunt it. He was soft-spoken and deferential to others. He didn't seem shocked by the conditions in which Bea had been raised, and he did truly seem to adore Bea. He had snared a beautiful, young, blue-eyed bird just set free from her cage—why wouldn't he adore her? Bea was her usual polite self, but it wasn't long until she seemed anxious to go, as if she didn't like the taste of the air there any longer.

Frieda, try as she might, couldn't find anything specific to oppose about the man Bea had chosen to marry, only that he had snatched the buds of her sister's dreams and crushed them in his hands.

CHAPTER
TWENTY-FOUR

After Bea and August left, Charles took Frieda back to his summer house, freeing her from the brutal bevy of her memories, both of Silver and Bea, which held her in their grip inside the house where the three of them had lived for so long. And there she would stay with him for almost two weeks until rumrunning duty would call them back to business. There above the town and the sea he cooked for her, surprising her with big breakfasts of eggs and ham, and dinners of sautéed fish, roast beef, salads, and fresh vegetables. He walked to the market daily for groceries and also brought bottles of wine, for which he'd developed a taste while in Europe and about which he sought to educate her over nightly candlelit dinners on the veranda.

Overcome by his kindness, Frieda allowed herself to be babied. How sweet it was to escape from the rest of the world within the walls and crystal-knobbed, heavy doors of this house. Inside she listened to the sighing of silk draperies, walked the solid, polished plank flooring in bare feet, and experienced nights of love.

Each morning the passion of the previous night cooling, Frieda returned—at least in part—to the outside world, her thoughts invariably drifting to her sister.

"I'm afraid that with Silver gone, there's no cord that binds Bea and me together anymore." The day was crystalline with blinding early sunlight shearing off the far ocean. Still in underclothes, they had wandered onto the veranda to watch the sun rise. Fishing boats and runners streamed flat scars across the bay and headed out for a day's work.

Charles sighed. "She's in the early throes of love. And in my experience, love is the grand excuse so many people employ for absurd behavior. It may pass. Give her time," he said as he donned his robe and sashed it around his waist.

Frieda turned to him. "So you agree she should go to school?"

"Of course. What do you know of this new chap of hers? It might not last, after all, and then where would your dear sister be?"

"What a cynic you are when it comes to love, to matters of the heart."

He waved a hand through the air. "Quite. Love is a shabby subject."

Love a shabby subject? Love had changed her life. Her uncertain future rushed toward her, made ever the shakier because of Charles's refusal to discuss it. She envied Bea her clear plans and dreams, her engagement and belief that life now unrolled before her like a shimmering carpet.

"Once Bea sets her mind to something, she won't let go without a fight, and now all she wants is to be a wife."

"Write to her. Keep in touch. Force yourself upon her if you have to."

"I doubt she wants to hear from me. I wasn't very gracious."

"Do it anyway. Write her today."

"Today?"

"Why not? What else is there pressing for you to do?"

The corners of her lips lifted in a soft smile. "Nothing. You ... care of everything. Who would've thought you'd turn out to be such a fine nursemaid?"

He shrugged. "I have my good moments. But back to you. Write your sister today. And if we must talk of love, then here's what I think: She thinks she's in love with the professor, but the person who means the most to her is you. I saw it in her face. She loves you; she loves her family."

Frieda's mouth dried. It was time to ask. "And you, Charles; who and what do you love?"

He gave her a devilish smile and patted his stomach. "At the moment I love the idea of breakfast."

A slow smile crept across her face despite herself, despite him successfully dodging the question.

Frieda walked to the railing. "I'll think about it."

"Today."

She spun around. "But she's gone; I know it."

He reached for her hands and cradled them in his. His had become reddened and chapped by work on the boat and domestic chores, much like hers. Dried by salt water, baked by relentless sun, scoured and scrubbed with strong soap too often, they mirrored life here. He smelled of smoke and sea, of the salt in the air, of this house, of domestic bliss and sex, of everything she loved. He had been here for her when she'd most needed him, and she would never forget it. She had to tamp down the urge to hold him, to wrap her arms around him and make him stay with her.

As if he'd read her mind he said, "Abandonment is a common theme for you, isn't it?"

A tiny gasp escaped her lips. Frieda shook her head, but what he'd just said was far too close for comfort, too true. How could Charles be both brilliant and intuitive at times and then at other times so oblivious? "That's not the point."

Now Charles was the one shaking his head. "You're both so headstrong."

"We are not."

"Of course you are," Charles said, and stroked her cheek before turning back toward the sea.

They were washing and drying the breakfast dishes side by side when the outside world came calling. Urgent pounding on the front door startled them. Quickly glancing at each other, they left their chore. Charles grabbed a hand towel and headed toward the door, with Frieda close on his heels, snatching up a sweater to cover herself. No one had bothered them during their time of respite, and a band of tension wrapped around Frieda's chest.

Dutch, smelling of sweat and gasoline, stood on the front porch. Though Charles invited him inside, he declined.

Skipping all niceties, Dutch said, "A boat from Atlantic Highlands has gone missing. No sign of the crew. Must have been bumped off."

It was the first time something like that had happened in their area.

"While you two have been up here, things have happened. Haven't you talked to anyone?" Without waiting for an answer, Dutch continued: "The boat went out during the day three days ago. Hasn't been seen since. And it was a fierce boat, too, almost the same as ours." Dutch scratched his white-blond thatch.

Charles said, "You mean a running boat?"

Clearly irritated, Dutch shifted his weight. "Of course I mean a running boat. What do you think I'm here for? Sorry to intrude on your love nest, but you ought to know what's happening outside these nice walls."

"Is anyone looking for the crew?"

"Other runners from the area been looking, coast guard, too, but there ain't no sign of hide nor hair. They been asking at the big boats; seems they never made it out there to deal that day. Probably got ambushed on their way out when they were holding all the cash on board. The crew are surely stiffs by now, probably shot down in the deep by the devil go-throughs, who then surely stole the boat or burnt it to leave no evidence behind."

Charles carried on with more questions, while something tugged at Frieda's memories, a feeling she couldn't describe. She almost knew what was coming. And yet she hoped . . .

Charles said, "Did you know them?"

"I knew them. Not well, though. Big fella by the name of Whitey ran the boat. His crew were Atlantic Highlands locals, too—though not as well-known. Whitey was a lifelong boatman, had a wife and a bunch of kids. Even went to church."

Frieda's heart fell into her stomach. The sounds of the town waking up and working fell away, and the floor heaved so much that Frieda had to fight for balance. A moment earlier her problems had seemed huge; now they curled small compared to this.

Big fella by the name of Whitey ran the boat.

Frieda's hand flew to her pale face, the words sinking in, and she wrapped her arms about herself while Charles and Dutch conversed, unaware of how the news had pummeled her. She had only spoken to Whitey that one time, wanting to hate him but coming away liking him more than she'd thought possible. He was Bea's blood father, and in that way he seemed almost a blood relation of hers. It was an odd connection, but blood linked them to the same person, a person Frieda dearly loved and one whom Whitey might have been allowed to love in another lifetime. And what of all those white-headed children? She shuddered.

Sights and sounds returned in a rush, and she asked, "Was his oldest son on the boat, too?"

Dutch peered at her appraisingly, one eyebrow lowering. "No. Didn't know you were acquainted with Whitey, Frieda." He clearly had also figured out Bea's parentage.

She didn't care. "I met him once."

"Nice guy, huh?"

She didn't answer, just waited.

"That's the only good luck. Whitey's boy usually runs with them, but he'd taken the day off."

At least Whitey's wife hadn't lost one of her children, too. Small consolation, she guessed, but something.

"That's why I'm here," Dutch said, bringing her back to the present. "No more time off. I understand you been needing to pay some respects to Silver, but we have to get back to work. Boat's just sitting in the water, and I got bills to pay. It's obvious what we're up against now—bastards out to steal and to kill rumrunners with no price to pay after. They got away with it clean. Some runners are putting armor plating on the hulls, but that ain't going to work; it's going to slow them down. We got to find ways to move the boat faster, Frieda. I need you back. That other engine man wasn't worth a damn. Our only chance is to outrun them. I need you to make us the fastest boat on the water."

"We're already fast—"

"Are you with me or not? You coming back or not?"

She and Charles glanced at each other. Frieda said, "To tell you the truth, I don't think I'm doing myself much good lying around and thinking about Silver. I want to come back."

"That's great news." He pointed a thick, chapped finger right at her face. "But if you come back, it's your job to make the boat impossible to catch. We have to be able to escape them, because if they get near us, they gonna kill us, you hear?" He waited for a response. She could still picture Whitey so clearly in her mind.

"Frieda, you hear me? Find out some way for us to power out on even more speed. Do it." He turned his glare on Charles. "Are you weaseling out now, Princeton?"

Charles stuck his hands into his robe pockets. "No, I never said that."

"I gotta know who I can count on and who I can't."

"Tell us what to do."

"All you have to do is show up and do what you've always done. Frieda here—well, she's got some extra fiddling to do. Do what you have to do, Frieda, and I don't care how much it costs. See you on the docks?" he asked.

Frieda nodded glumly.

Dutch looked around the empty porch and front lawn. "And by the way, no more day runs. Only at night, with no moon. Maybe we'll get lucky, and they won't never find us."

It took a couple of hours before Frieda could shake images of death out of her mind and chills out of her body, but recent events had wiped away the kind of restraint she usually imposed on herself. She managed to tell Charles about Whitey, so suddenly and brutally *gone*, to explain that he had fathered Bea, and along the way to reveal that their mother had been the town whore. It was time to find out if Charles could accept it.

"Did you know?" she asked.

"That detail was never mentioned to me," Charles answered, and looked her straight in the eyes, his beautiful face showing no distaste. An early-afternoon rainstorm had blown in, and wind lashed against the windows. She and Charles were seated in the parlor, a room they rarely used. Even with its nautically themed decor, the room felt stiff and formal. Quite the odd place to hold a conversation such as this one.

Frieda hadn't realized how high she'd been holding her shoulders until she let them fall. Amazing that no one had told Charles about her mother. Perhaps she had judged the townspeople too harshly. She stared down at her hands. "I-I thought at least one person would be unable to resist telling you such a juicy piece of gossip."

"It *is* quite the story, Frieda. Pretty serious stuff."

"Sorry. My life is serious."

"I mean no offense."

"I'm not offended." She looked up. "But are you offended by my past?"

"You had no choice in it."

"You aren't answering."

He glanced away for a moment, pensive, as if his mind hadn't fully registered all the pictures forming in his mind. Slowly he looked back. "I'm not as flimsy as you think."

"I'd never call you flimsy."

He ran a hand through his tousled hair. Neither one of them had yet groomed themselves for the day ahead. Dutch's news and demands had set the day on a very different course. Before he'd shown up, they'd planned to picnic on the Hook. Now, in response to Dutch's demands, Frieda had turned her thoughts instead to going down to the docks and working on the boat. But the weather had interfered with that, too.

Charles grimaced, then his face went flat. "Maybe we should stop going out with Dutch."

Frieda blinked. "That's not what you just said to him. You said you were still going."

"A man has a right to change his mind."

"A woman, too?"

"Of course. You don't owe Dutch anything. And now with your sister getting married and Silver . . ."

"Passed, I know," Frieda finished for him. "I guess I don't have to make all this money anymore, but . . ." She clasped her hands together and gazed up at Charles. "I'm still hoping Bea changes her mind and goes to school."

"Then her husband should pay for her classes."

"She might change her mind about getting married, too."

"It's possible, but she gave away her shot at your money in my opinion," Charles said.

"I was there when Silver had his stroke. I know that life can change in an instant. The only safety net I have is the money. No family besides Silver and Bea. No one with money. No connections. How much is enough? It's hard for you to . . . understand."

"What good is that money if you're dead at the bottom of the sea?"

Frieda gulped. Whitey's demise had made that all too real. And so close by . . . Bea might have had a chance to know her father, but now it was too late. Should Frieda have told Bea about him? Would Bea have been interested? There would be no point in ever telling her now. Why tell someone their blood father had been decent and then died in a horrible way?

Charles took her hand and led her onto the veranda. They stood under the roof and stared out at the rain. Raindrops bounced on the hard summer soil and roofs and ran in rivulets down the town streets. Clouds hung around them like an impenetrable curtain, but in between passing mists they could briefly see the chop of high seas in the bay.

"Pay no attention to me," Charles finally breathed out as he squeezed her hand. "Just a moment of doubt. But we'll be going out on dark nights. And you have a homework assignment to make the boat faster."

But his doubt had already infected her. "Maybe I shouldn't. Maybe we should all quit. Dutch and Rudy have kids, and Rudy already told me he's thinking about getting out when summer's over. Maybe it's not right for me to enable them to go on risking their lives."

ing her hand, Charles lowered his brow and looked
take this for a moral issue. Either you want to continue
and find better ways to do so or you don't."

"But it *is* a moral issue."

Charles smiled in a sad way. "I don't see it that way. I don't see
things as black and white, wrong or right. But then again I've always
lacked much of a moral compass. I couldn't kill another person, but
that's about it for me. I can't help you make any decisions, Frieda. It's
your call."

Frieda smiled weakly in vague assent, then gazed into the falling
sky. She had never sought guidance from him, only love and the will-
ingness to let her love him. But it would be nice to really discuss things
and come to mutual conclusions. She found it more interesting than
off-putting that they differed so much in the way they saw things, but
for the boat to keep being successful they all had to be in agreement.
Silently he stepped away and went back into the house, leaving her
alone with a tangle of thoughts. Bea. The boat. The lost men. Whitey.
Dutch's demands.

But there was never much doubt about what she would do. Dutch
had given her a job. He trusted her with his boat, and she'd made a lot
of money because of him. She felt as if she owed him.

And lastly, Charles. Loving him was perhaps like peering into the
rain—a sort of sightlessness, akin to stumbling about in a storm, grabbing the things you want to find, and letting the others wash away.

CHAPTER
TWENTY-FIVE

The next morning she readied herself for a day of work on the docks. She had been away with Silver and then Charles for too long. Now she was ready to shake herself free of burdens of the heart and focus on the boat instead. Besides, she had orders.

She went to see the man who knew more about boat engines than anyone else in the area: Hicks. A day of solid rain had temporarily masked the scents of sea, and it smelled of wet earth. The streets were littered with leaves, branches, and bits of soggy newspaper. She found the *Wren* in its usual slip along the dock, but there was no sign of her owner. Frieda almost boarded the boat to wait for Hicks at the helm, but the boat brought back memories of Silver. It was a glorious summer day, the kind that Silver would've loved—sun bouncing white off the water and a blue sky crossed by gulls cawing and swooping. Water sloshing against the piers, revealing barnacles that glistened in the light, and an easy wind on her face.

She walked away and went to look in the dockside bar for him, the same one where she'd first been acknowledged by Charles. That night now seemed a lifetime ago as she opened the door to the smoky, cavernous place. A few of the regular drunks sat inside, but there were also some men she'd never seen before. Hardened types. Criminal looking. What were they up to?

No sight of Hicks, she walked toward Bahrs; along the way she ran into a man she knew was a friend of both Dutch and Hicks. A rail-thin, rheumy-eyed man with a limp by the name of Hector. Also a good mechanic, one who had formerly worked for Dutch, and she greeted him, but before she could start talking, Hector pulled her down a small alley.

"What's wrong?"

"Lots a strangers around lately."

She really had been out of touch for a long time. She had never seen people act so suspiciously, as if a wave of paranoia had swept in during her absence. "I saw them. Who are they?"

"I don't know, but steer clear, and don't let anyone overhear your conversations."

When she finally raised the subject of the boat, he told her to replace the carburetors with new ones and consider adding naphtha to the fuel to boost octane. But new carburetors were expensive and naphtha was highly flammable. He advised her to consider the changes carefully and warned her a final time about the strangers in town.

She went to discuss the ideas of naphtha with Dutch. He was captain and owner and should make the decisions. She found Rudy at the pier washing the boat, and he told her Dutch had gone for a meeting with some new buyers at the Highland House Hotel. Frieda wouldn't dare interrupt his meeting, but she decided to head over there in hopes of catching Dutch on his way out.

The hotel, built in 1898 in the old Victorian style, stood on Navesink Avenue near the bridge, one of four grand hotels in the borough. Frieda sat on the steps leading up to the ornate portico fronting the building and waited while the sun poured down and the air turned stagnant and still.

Dutch finally emerged. After she told him they needed to talk about the boat, he nudged her farther down the steps toward the street.

"What's going on?" she asked.

"Some runners have quit and gone to work for the government. I don't want any one of them leaning in on my conversations no more."

"Who?"

He rattled off some familiar names. It was shocking.

Knowing that these men had been as eager about running as Dutch himself, Frieda shook her head. "Why would they go work for the government?"

"They can get a nice little salary and then blackmail all their old friends for a portion of the take, so they're still making money, but with nearly no risk. Bloodsucking sons of whores, double-crossing crooks. Don't trust anyone now." Frieda blinked once, hard. Compounding this news, she recalled seeing other strange and unknown men down at the docks—the innocuous, quiet, shifty-eyed sorts. Were they government guys? She would have to advise Charles to be careful about talking in public now, even down at the docks and in Bahrs. She blinked again and then stared at Dutch. His hair was now a mix of blond and white, his skin aged and ruddy, and he looked more the Viking warrior than ever.

She told him what she'd learned about the carburetors and naphtha, the pros and the cons. And then finished with, "The new carburetors are expensive."

He didn't hesitate. "How much money is it worth to stay alive?"

Frieda gazed out at the view, so beautiful from these heights. The tide was still, a momentary calm before it swept back to the sea.

She spun her gaze to Dutch. "Are you saying you want me to do it?"

"Hell yeah, I'm saying I want you to do it. So I have to lay out some cash. The money we're pulling in from the booze will make up for it. 'Specially if we don't have to worry about them bastards chasing us down, we can go out more often. It'll be better than ever."

Frieda glanced away again, toward the water. "The naphtha is risky."

"Everything we do is risky."

"I think we should give it more thought."

"Bullshit. This is the best news I've had in weeks. Get on it right away, will you?"

She hesitated. "O-K. I guess."

"That's an order, girl. Remember you said you'd always follow my orders?"

"Of course, but—"

"No buts. Time's a wasting."

"I'm going to do it *right*, Dutch. Not in a hurry."

"I didn't say not to do it right. But you can be right and fast at the same time, cain't you?"

"No pressure."

"I'm under pressure. Don't talk to me about pressure. No money coming in: that's pressure."

"I know, I know."

He reached over and patted her on the shoulder. "Atta girl."

She shook her head and smiled grimly at the same time.

When she returned to the docks, more fishermen and clammers had come in for the day, and some of them looked at her strangely. At first she thought it was because of Silver's death and the fact that she'd been away for a while. But then she remembered what Dutch and Hector had told her about locals and runners who had turned informant, and it occurred to her: maybe they were worried that with Silver gone, she'd stop running and turn against them. Trust was hard to come by these days.

Hicks was on board the *Wren*. Wearing his fishing gear, but with his hair combed back with pomade, he was coiling the mooring lines. She followed him on board, where he told her he'd spent his morning at the funeral service for Whitey and the other men lost on his boat.

"But there are no . . . bodies," Frieda said solemnly, tears threatening to fall at that brutal realization. She sat next to Hicks and stared down at her hands, curled into a knot.

"I guess the wives wanted to have some kind of service anyway."

"How was it?"

"Lots of weeping."

"That makes sense." She peered upward. "But I'm surprised you went. I didn't know you knew Whitey all that well."

"I didn't know him well."

"So . . . why did you go?"

He looked away, and she could tell that Hicks didn't want to answer. Frieda decided it wasn't worth prying and changed the subject. There was nothing more to be said about Whitey and his men anyway. They were gone; their story had ended, and in such a vile way, no one wanted to fixate on it. She told him what she planned to do with Dutch's boat, and he cautioned her against adding naphtha, saying the dangers were too great. "You can carry five-gallon containers of naphtha on board in case you want to add it as a booster, but the stuff could blow up like a bomb. It's like liquid dynamite."

Frieda frowned, her chest tightening.

"Find ways to lighten the boat instead—take only what's necessary and nothing more—but don't use the naphtha."

She listened intently to what Hicks said, but in the end she told him she was doing it anyway. "Will you help me with the carburetors?"

"Not a chance."

"I'm under Dutch's orders, and I'm going to do it. If you help me, I know it'll be done right."

Hicks looked tormented, as if the decision was tearing him apart. Finally he breathed out, "I can't. I just can't . . ."

She felt strongly that Hicks wanted to say more, and she knew what it was. She could've finished his sentence for him: ". . . spend that much time around you anymore."

Frieda closed her eyes for a moment. "Understood."

"I'll look in on you as you replace the carburetors, but I've never used naphtha. You're on your own there."

"Understood," Frieda said again.

The next few days were spent below deck on the *Pauline*, replacing the carburetors and making adjustments for a new fuel mixture. She worked all through the daylight hours and then at night by a light Hicks had rigged up. Despite what he'd said, Hicks didn't exactly leave her on her own. He wouldn't help directly with the work, but he stayed nearby. He brought her mugs of steaming coffee, handed her tools, went in search of anything she needed, and even advised her on a few of the adjustments. He was helping with something that he didn't think was right, and all because of her.

The night she completed the work, he suggested they take the boat out for a short test run. Frieda glanced toward the hills and the house where Charles awaited her return. She would've rather headed back to him, but it was difficult to turn down Hicks's offer. So they started the engine and slid away from the docks on that sickle-moon night. They rode free of other boats, then opened up the throttle out in the bay. The boat was loaded with only Frieda's tools and gear, and she flew over the surface as if it were made of slick oil instead of heaving salt seas.

They throttled down to a crawl, turned around, and let her drift for a few minutes. Frieda looked around, always searching the seas, always on the alert for danger. Which made her think of Whitey again, despite her desire to push his memory away.

"Did you figure out that Whitey was Bea's father?" she asked Hicks while staring into the night.

Slowly he said, "Yes."

A simple answer, but one that left her longing for more. Normally around Hicks she felt comfortable and serene, but something was nagging at her tonight. What he wouldn't say to her. The killers out there. The boat. The naphtha. Charles. Hicks's one-word reply felt incomplete, and it seemed everyone was withholding something from her.

Hicks was too kind to suffer one of her snarky comments, so she simply asked, "How long ago?"

"Does it matter?"

Frieda let loose a sigh. "Probably not. I'm just curious."

"Not sure when I guessed it, but it was a long time ago. Probably the first time I ever laid eyes on Whitey. The resemblance, their coloring, it was too close to be coincidence. Right off I was pretty sure."

Frieda nodded. "Is that why you went to the service?"

He fixed his soft gaze on her. "I figured Bea doesn't know."

"You're right."

"And you—you figure out everything. But I guessed you wouldn't go, so I went for you."

Why did he always do that? Things that made her feel as if she owed him? But she had never managed to stay angry or annoyed with Hicks. He was too kind, and she knew he could tell that she was unhappy. She was sure he also knew that he couldn't fix her unhappiness. Part of her despair came from what she had let herself become: a woman consumed by a man. And how could Hicks help her with that?

In another few days the moon had waned to the slimmest of scratches, and Dutch decided they were back in business. On the first night they were to go out, both he and Charles were late for the cast-off time.

With everything ready to go, Frieda and Rudy waited for them in the boat.

Frieda glanced around as the town began to fall silent behind them and lights clicked off in houses settling down for the night. "I'm surprised Dutch would be late."

Rudy took off his glasses, brushed off some dust, then replaced them, curling the ends around the back of his ears. "A palm reader's been in town telling people's fortunes. Making the rounds of all the speakeasies. I saw Dutch with her."

Astounded, Frieda turned to Rudy. "He's getting his palm read?"

He nodded knowingly. "Dutch is a strange man. Superstitious as hell. Behind all that bravado there's a lot of restlessness rattling around."

Frieda could scarcely imagine Dutch succumbing to the hype of a palm reader. "How long have you known him?"

"Long time. He was a friend of my uncle's, so I always knew who he was, and when I first started fishing he showed me some tricks. He always had better luck than me."

"And he's ended up a captain."

"I don't envy him. I think he's made too much money. The more material things you have, the more you have to lose. And hell, I'm a good first mate."

Frieda thought about Dutch for a minute longer. He was as unpredictable as a teenage girl at times, but solid as Ulysses on the water.

"Did you go to the palm reader?"

"Not me," Rudy said. "I don't want to know what's around the next corner. I like my life mysterious." He winked. "I'd rather wait and see."

Frieda relaxed in the glow of Rudy's company. She always felt a tinge of wonder when he talked. She hated to bring up a serious subject but was curious. "Have you made a decision about quitting yet?"

"Nah. Just waiting and seeing."

Frieda nodded.

"Besides, I haven't got that sailboat yet."

* * *

First Dutch and then Charles appeared, ready to go out, and when the *Pauline* finally cast off, the seas were flat and black and the wind puffed only a few salty, steamy gusts from time to time. They headed out to the rum boats just before ten, easily cutting through the water, and once beyond the Hook, Dutch ran at full speed to test the changes Frieda had made and to make certain that if anyone was out there they'd have a hard time catching up to the *Pauline.* They skimmed the surface as if they were airborne.

Dutch whooped. "Love it! Great job, Frieda!"

The most dangerous part of the journey was now, when they had all the cash on board to buy the contraband. The go-through men preferred hijacking boats when they were loaded with money rather than booze. Even with the increase in speed, the crew of the *Pauline* held at rapt attention, and the air was thick with apprehension. A fear of the unknown, a dread of something appearing out of the darkness, driving closer, overtaking them. Over the sound of the engines the night seemed still—too quiet, too shadowy.

But the run was uneventful and ended up being highly profitable. When they had cleared the drop zone and were heading into the docks for the night, Charles whispered to Frieda, "It's all going to be OK now."

She reached for his hand, and he took it.

All night long they'd had no contact, Frieda spending most of her time below deck and Charles on deck near the helm. Rudy, in the bow position, had leaned down and spoken to Frieda a few times, once saying, "Good work," complimenting her skills with the engines. He'd smiled, and for the first time in a long while she felt a burst of pride, or at least satisfaction in her work. Pleasing Dutch was one thing—he was her boss—but pleasing kindhearted, cautious Rudy was another thing altogether. She smiled back at him, and he gave her a thumbs-up.

Frieda had been staying every night at Charles's house, and so after that night's run they headed home without stopping at the bar to celebrate. Charles had seemed preoccupied all night and only wanted to fall into bed when they entered the still, dark house. Frieda had a hard time going to sleep; Charles was breathing deeply and twitching a bit in his sleep as he dreamed restlessly beside her. She was perplexed by her insomnia. The engine adjustments had worked, the boat was faster, they were making money again, and everything had gone well. So why was her mind a mess of thoughts and feelings she couldn't decipher?

It was the tiny chill in the predawn air, an indication that summer was nearing a close, a sign of change to come. She felt it on her arms—not a breeze but a shift in the air. The long sultry nights were over. Every sunrise and sunset was another little slip toward September, a month that loomed as desolate and unwelcome as sleet. Each day that went by with no words of assurance from Charles, another star fell from her sky. Summer was seeping away, but Frieda still believed they had time. Charles still had time to make a decision, to turn his life around, to trust in what they had. She had hope, though she already knew that hope could sometimes be a sad mistake.

In the morning Charles was still asleep when Frieda awakened. She slipped out of bed and bathed, then wrapped herself in his robe and padded about the house in her bare feet, her hair dripping down her back. As she puttered about the kitchen making coffee, a short stack of mail on the kitchen table caught her attention. She had seen few pieces of mail arrive here for Charles, so she was curious. Sipping on steaming coffee, she crept closer. Two envelopes, both of which had been opened. The first had come from Harvard University, and the other had a return name of Bitty Wallace, Charles's mother. She stared at the envelopes for a while, blowing on her coffee to cool it and listening for any sounds indicating that Charles was up and about.

Her hands landed on the top envelope. But she was less interested in the letter from Harvard than the letter from Charles's mother. Had he ever mentioned her to his mother? Would there be any clues inside? Or any clues as to Charles's plans for the future?

She slid the second envelope out from under the top one and set down her coffee cup. With both hands shaking, she slipped her fingers inside the envelope, her heart pounding. It had been opened already, and he would never know. She had not sought to pry into Charles's private affairs before, although when she thought about it now, almost living here had afforded her many opportunities to go snooping. She had never fallen so low, but . . .

"What are you doing?"

Charles. Standing in the passageway to the kitchen, wearing only his underclothes, a look of infuriated disbelief on his face.

Suddenly lightheaded, Frieda dropped the envelope on the table. "I-I . . ." What had she been doing? She had no idea what to say.

"Were you going to read my letter?" Charles demanded as he took a step closer. "From my *mother*?"

A cold sweat broke out on her forehead. "No, not really. I only picked it up."

"Come now," he said with a disgusted laugh. "You were only picking it up?"

"I don't know what I was doing!" Frieda searched his face, hoping to find some compassion there.

He stood with both feet planted, like a soldier. "Come now," he said again. "Excuses don't become you, Frieda. Just tell the truth. What are you looking for?"

Frieda licked her lips nervously. She gazed into his eyes and let her guard melt away. "I'm having a hard time of it, don't you see? I-I don't know where I stand with you. I don't know what you're planning to do, and summer's almost over. I don't know anything. Maybe I was drawn to the letter to see if I could find any hints of what's to come. You tell me nothing."

"What do you want to know? I'll tell you, Frieda. You have only to ask. You don't have to go snooping in my mail!"

Frieda stammered, searching for words, sputtering.

"What? What do you really want to know? Am I leaving here? Most likely. Is that it? Good enough for you?"

She hadn't prepared herself for this answer. Knowing that she should have did nothing to alleviate the wretched confirmation that he was leaving. But his leaving didn't necessarily mean an end to them together. She couldn't bear not knowing any longer. "What I really want to know is . . . where I stand, how you feel about me . . . Even if you leave we can still carry on . . ."

"Carry on?"

"You know, see each other, belong to each other . . ."

"Fall in love?" Charles asked. "Marry? Sail into the sunset and live happily ever after?"

She blinked back tears.

His face softened a bit, but his eyes bored into hers. "Do you want me to tell you I love you? Do you want to go down that road of dramatics and misery? Is that what you really want?"

Frieda tried to gather herself. He'd said "I love you," but couched in a most disagreeable, cruel question. She couldn't even begin to dissect that now. Instead she half yelled, "It doesn't have to be dramatic and miserable!"

"Oh, really? Look at us now!"

"Of course I don't want it to be like *this*!" She lifted her hands, then let them fall. "But do I want to be free to love you? Yes! Of course I do."

His face set like stone, he said softly, "This is what love does to people."

Tears flooded her eyes, but she blinked them away. "What happened to you? I thought I was thorny, but you make me seem like some kind of *optimist*."

"Nothing happened to me. I was born a pessimist, and a pessimist is never disappointed. I'm loyal to pessimism. It always delivers. And I'm a realist as well. About myself, about you, about everything. There are no happy endings."

She wanted to beg and plead with him. *Why not?* she cried inside, but instead she said, "Once I got close, you began to hold yourself out of reach." Her voice trailed off in despair. Saying it, showing her own weakness and need, was freeing in a way. Just let him see how much she needed him.

He stared at her coldly, and for the first time she saw that Charles was an awful man to love, an awful man to want. How had it come to this? She felt dizzy and hot. Her body damp, she opened her robe to let in some air. A trickle of sweat swam down her spine.

Charles's gaze drifted to where the robe opened. She wore nothing underneath, and he was also near naked.

He heaved out a sigh. "Why can't what I've given you be enough? I have very special feelings for you. You're the only woman who has ever stayed with me."

Special feelings. Another slap in the face. "That brings me little comfort. People have special feelings for their dogs. And they let strangers stay in their houses. Perhaps I'm nothing but your *whore*."

He leaned back as if stricken. "And this is how you think of me. To say such a thing."

She went to him then, each step slow and cautious as she closed the distance between them. Charles had never looked so lovely, nor vulnerable; her need had never been so great, and she knew that somewhere deep inside he needed her, too. She kissed him. He pulled her in closer and kissed her for a long time as she went through several layers of emotion: affection, want, desire, and then beyond where they could stop and where Frieda abandoned free will.

Charles cupped the back of her head in his hand and whispered, rasping in her ear, "Is this what you want?"

Even if she had been able to speak, there was as much a "Hell, no" inside her as there was a "God, yes," but she was too lost in the touching, the passion, the ardent kisses, his hands all over her, them rolling on the floor, even as there was something dark and cold about it. He had given her nothing. She had not gained even a glint of further insight into his complicated soul. Her surrender under the circumstances was shocking and abhorrent, and when it was over she was left with a trembling fear that she had been snared for the rest of her days in a web, caught inside the trap that was him.

CHAPTER
TWENTY-SIX

There would be no moon that night; it was perfect for a run. Frieda spent the day alone at her house, pacing the moaning wood-plank floor and fighting off a sickness that twisted her stomach and dried her mouth, illness over what was happening with Charles, and to her. What were they, after all? What did they do for each other that made them better people, happier people?

After nightfall the crew gathered at the *Pauline* and readied for the run. Charles was last to arrive, and Frieda found she couldn't look into his face. Nothing felt right, everything seemed sluggish and slovenly, and she had tried desperately not to succumb to an obsession that was swirling her down.

Dutch as usual was worked up about something. "Coast guard intel raided ZA today," he said to Rudy and Frieda.

She and Rudy exchanged knowing looks, and Charles said, "What's that?"

"Radio station."

Frieda was finally able to look at Charles, but only briefly.

Working on the dock lines, Rudy said through gritted teeth, "Three-letter codes are too easy. We should've expected this."

From the helm, Dutch harrumphed. "That don't make it any easier to find the station. Must have been a rat somewhere along this shore. Probably old Raleigh."

Raleigh was a stolid, wheezy sort, one of those who'd gone from rumrunner to government informant. "So the station's out of business?" Frieda asked.

After shooting her an incredulous look, Dutch said, "You think, Frieda?"

She gave him back a mock grin and helped Rudy with the fenders.

"Makes no sense," Dutch went on. "If you were guard intel, what would you rather do—shut down a radio station, when you're getting intel from it and you know it's just going to set up someplace else, or keep it running so you can monitor what's going on?" He spat over the side of the boat. "Probably some officer needed something big to report to his superiors. Even if he's shooting his own damn self in the foot in the process."

"What does that mean for us?" asked Charles, who had perked up.

"Not a fucking thing," Dutch, red in the face, snapped at Charles. "We don't need the radio. Started out just fine without it. I got Cobra on alert for the drop, and we'll just use a light signal like we did in the good old days. No need to get yourself spooked."

Dutch was in a fine humor tonight. He whispered to Frieda, "Someday that boyfriend of yours is going to say something smart."

Ignoring him, Frieda went below and checked the engines.

They glided out of port under a star-clear night. The ride out was black and still, the sea moving in heavy, sheet-like swells they slashed through and barely bounced over. Frieda gazed off unseeingly, her usual adrenaline surge absent as she recalled with revulsion how she'd succumbed to Charles in an act that wasn't exactly cruel but wasn't loving, either. Their disparities had bedeviled the both of them. The way they saw things differently had fueled the passion, that want of true understanding, which neither would get. Was the very hopelessness of ever being together permanently what made them so hungry?

They reached the offshore boat *Temiscouda* first, and Dutch decided to do business with her instead of his usual suppliers. Not quite in harmony with the crew of that unfamiliar boat, the *Pauline*'s crew took a bit longer to load but finally got their rhythm established and filled the boat to capacity with the contraband. She had barely ten inches of freeboard above the waterline. The water was mercury heavy and undulating. As the men worked, Charles glanced up at Frieda from time to time and finally gave her a smile when the loading was completed.

She couldn't help herself; she smiled back.

And when he came to sit beside her as they plowed through the midnight seas on the way back in, she sat still, only wanting to be near him, nothing more. Everything seemed too quiet, too serene, and a sense of awful foreboding came over her. Her time together with Charles was coming to an end. Charles had perhaps known this for a long time, but he remained silent, too, looking out at black sea and black sky. He reached for her hand and she let him take it.

An hour of silence, and then Rudy announced from the bow, "Boat in pursuit, sir."

"Damn," breathed Dutch with more frustration than fear. The crew of the *Pauline* was used to evading the guard, and now that they were on the way in, that's all it figured to be. "And we're heavy tonight."

"Probably a cutter, sir, yet to identify."

Dutch went to full throttle and swiped through the troughs. The triple engines, even with a heavy load, lifted the boat out of the water and sent her soaring. Only a few minutes more and they should be leaving the annoying boat behind. At that point in time that's all she was: an annoyance.

And yet it soon became obvious that the inky shadow against the sea and sky behind them kept coming and, surprisingly, was gaining on them. Even heavy, Dutch could outrun the coast guard, and lately the guard boats didn't try to catch him, instead going after easier prey.

Dutch kept looking over his shoulder. "Guard should've identified itself by now." Coast guard boats could run dark for a while but by law had to identify themselves at some point while in pursuit. The crew all knew this. A bony, cold hand reached inside Frieda's stomach and clamped on. Maybe this was no guard boat; maybe this was a go-through boat.

The dark boat kept coming.

Dutch kept his eyes focused ahead, but Frieda could see that he was firing on all cylinders now. He had to be considering what their plan should be, if indeed it was a go-through boat. They'd been chased by go-through men only once before a long time ago and had managed to escape them with one of Rudy's booby traps tossed behind them to entangle itself in the offensive boat's prop. Frieda told herself they could do it again, but a tightening sensation crept over her scalp. She glanced at Charles, who was looking back at the pursuing boat as if he could make it vanish simply by the intensity of his stare.

Any doubt about what they faced vanished when the dark boat suddenly shined a spotlight on them for a long moment. It was their way of marking the *Pauline* so they could keep her in sight and follow behind her dead astern.

"Guard wouldn't have done that, right?" Charles shouted to Dutch over the thrumming engine noise. His hat blew away in the wind they were creating.

Rudy, who had moved to the stern now, studied the sea behind them with his binoculars. After what seemed like an eternity, he said, "Private boat. Nothing to identify her. And she's getting closer."

Dutch said nothing, simply watching as the twinkling lights along the shore came into view. At first he followed the course straight ahead and then apparently thought better of it. "Change of course," he yelled. "Got to follow the coast south. Can't get trapped in the bay." He told them to hold on and then made a wide, veering, but steady turn so he wouldn't have to slow down. Frieda had to clamp on to the deck rail as the boat heeled powerfully to port, and sea spray showered her face and stung her eyes.

After the turn the *Pauline* leveled out and began slicing again. Sounds of the other engine had all but disappeared, but then Rudy announced, "Dark boat changed course, too, sir."

Frieda gulped down an escalating sense of panic. It could only be one thing. Bloodthirsty hijackers who might not only steal but also kill. They were hardened, probably lifelong criminals, and they were coming for the *Pauline*.

Their pursuers shined the spotlight again, apparently to make sure the *Pauline* had noticed their matched change of course. Those flashes of light now so eerie and ghastly.

"Why are they chasing us now?" Frieda asked. The hijackers preferred to take the cash from boats on the way out rather than the liquor they had on board coming in.

Dutch yelled, "Fuckers want the damn boat. Knew we'd get targeted someday. They'd love to get their hands on the *Pauline*."

Frieda remembered the strange men she'd seen lately dockside. She'd feared they were government men scouting them out, but maybe they'd been the hijackers instead.

"Shouldn't we dump the liquor?" asked Charles with a shrillness to his voice.

"Simmer down," Dutch said. "I'm going to get us a little closer in before we dump. Maybe we can come back for it."

"Screw the liquor," Charles shouted.

"Easy for you to say, Princeton."

Waving away Dutch's words, Charles paced the deck, his near-to-perfect balance and agility cranked to life by anxiety.

Dutch steered the boat closer to shore and then gave the order to dump. "We'll outrun them once we're light," he said.

Frieda, Rudy, and Charles began to pull out of the holds bags they'd just purchased, tossing them on the deck. Rudy quickly tied some floats to a few of them, and they tossed the contraband directly behind them in hopes that the dark boat would hit something or that its propeller would get tangled in the twine. Even if that failed, the *Pauline*, without her load, would be able to fly.

To Frieda it felt as if it took hours to dump the liquor, but with every few tosses the boat lifted a bit out of the water and ran faster. The night was muggy and warm, and the physical labor was taking its toll; she had to remove her slicker. Sweat was creeping down her neck and back. She, Rudy, and Charles were tired and probably distracted by fear, but they lifted and tossed and lifted and tossed their way through an endless cargo. After the contraband was finally gone, Rudy picked up his binoculars, studied the heavy seas beyond their wake, and finally said, "Don't see them now."

Frieda breathed, and Charles whooped.

"Shame to have lost that load," Dutch said, and swiped the seawater from his face with the back of his hand. But instead of changing course to the mouth of the bay, Dutch held a steady course south along the shore. He was making sure, Frieda thought, but the cold clamp on her stomach started to release its fierce hold, if but a little.

The sea seemed to flatten out, along with their nerves. Dutch stood at the helm, Rudy took his post back on the bow, and Charles pulled Frieda down beside him, facing the shore.

He cupped the back of his head in his hands and stretched out his panther body. That same pang, the one that always returned to Frieda's pelvis when he did this, flared again, as if organically. What was the meaning of such a pull? Would it ever go away? Frieda took off her hat and sat as still as stone. If only getting rid of this longing could be as easy as heaving over the liquor. Charles would leave, and she would go back to her old life. And that would be that. Would he ever think of her in years to come?

"That was a little more excitement than I bargained for."

Frieda simply nodded as millions of stars seemed to dim. She didn't trust her voice against this rising choking sensation.

"Why aren't we going in?" he asked.

She recovered herself well enough. Charles clearly hadn't even noticed what had besieged her, but her voice sounded as if it came from someone else, not her. "Give him a minute. Dutch wants to be certain we lost them. If we turn around too soon, we could plow right back into a trap."

"It's going to be a long night," Charles said, and sighed.

"Yes," Frieda said, and so they simply sat, each lost in a place where the other could not go. She and Charles believed in different things. She could not have him, but releasing him was near to impossible, too.

I'll miss him. I'll miss the inexplicable, and I'll miss those moments of magic.

A bright light landed on the stern and flooded the deck. It sucked the air out of Frieda and put her on the edge of collapse.

"Goddammit!" yelled Dutch.

Rudy hustled to the stern and raised the binoculars. "She's back."

Charles looked ill, and Frieda raked her fingernails against her arms.

Apparently the dark boat had slowed to avoid hitting the cases, but now she was in pursuit again. They were being trailed and stalked, and no one needed to say this. The most evil of forces on these waters had planned an ambush of the *Pauline*, and despite their efforts to evade it, now it was executing a plan to perfection.

She left Charles's side. The *Pauline* must not be overtaken; they could not let the hijackers get within range of a machine gun. The go-through men would not hesitate to kill, and with their preference for the Thompson submachine gun, they could fire five or six hundred shots a minute. Her thoughts flew to Whitey. Was this the way his demise had begun?

She looked up. The darkness was not dark enough to bury them. The stars were bright, and Frieda saw the Big Dipper outlined as clear as white chalk dots on a schoolhouse blackboard. She listened to the thundering engines; they should be able to outrun the other boat now that the *Pauline* was running light. So why weren't they?

Frieda went below to do a check. The engines were hot but running smoothly. Below deck the rumble of the hull thrumming across the current and waves crashing behind in their wake made her intestines twine, and she had to come up for air.

Rudy reported that the other boat seemed to be slowly gaining on them. Dutch's boat was fast, but shockingly, the other boat appeared to be faster. "What the hell?" Dutch shouted to no one in particular. "I thought no one could outrun us."

Now, a fast and frantic flight. Rudy went below, and Frieda helped him rig together some booby traps made of old ropes, floats, wire, and wood he kept on board. The same thing had worked once before to thwart their followers, but why hadn't they constructed these contraptions in advance? They'd been too cocky, thinking themselves and their boat almost invincible. They'd naively thought they had the fastest boat around. *Surprise, surprise.*

Frieda's hands trembled as she worked, but Rudy was solid, and with both of them focused they had three traps put together in short order. They dragged the traps onto the deck, and Rudy said to Frieda and Charles, "Let's toss them all at once. If there's several in the water, it'll better our chances that damn boat hits one of them."

They balanced their traps and themselves in the stern and waited for Rudy to give the signal to throw. Just before he did so, he caught Frieda's eye and his look said it all.

This has to work.

"Now!" Rudy shouted, and they heaved the booby traps into the wake behind them.

They held their breaths, waiting. Moments stretched out like the longest of sleepless hours. Rudy lifted the binoculars to his face.

"Might have done the trick," he said, a little nervous smile playing on his lips.

They waited. And waited. And finally began to hope.

Dutch looked over his shoulder and eased up a bit on the throttle. "Looks like we missed our date with the devil. So long, you motherfuckers!"

Then the light shined on them again. As before, their ploy had only temporarily slowed the dark boat, which had probably made a sharp turn to avoid a hit but was now back on course. She kept coming, slowly gaining on them, and no one said anything after that. Behind them, she was a powerful black shark tracking her prey methodically, determinedly, purposely.

Each time the dark boat flashed the spotlight on the *Pauline*, it seemed that the light was sharper and brighter. Frieda thought through their options, as she knew Dutch and Rudy were also doing. The *Pauline* was too big to hide in an inlet and probably needed as much draft or more than the dark boat did, so going shallow and hoping the other boat would run aground first was not a good option.

Charles stepped up beside Dutch. "Can't we radio for help?"

Over the sound of whining engines, Rudy shouted, "Station's out, remember?"

Dutch finally answered in an amazingly calm voice, "Wouldn't've made a damn bit of difference anyways. It would take too long, and no one's going to come out and risk getting kilt, too."

Dutch was wired for this kind of thing, and Frieda made herself try to believe the salty sea captain in him would get them out of this.

When Dutch told Rudy to go below and fetch the Colt pistol he kept on board, Frieda wondered what the point was, though she didn't say that to Dutch. The other boat had machine guns; what good would a pistol do? Were they going to end up in a hopeless gunfight to the death?

They held course, the boat running hard across black water swells, her bow held high out of the sea, slicing through the troughs and spewing silvery panes of water on both sides. They flew past the occasional pleasure boat anchored for the night, and Charles said, "Can't we ask them for help?"

Dutch laughed and leaned forward at the helm as if he could push the boat faster by the sheer power of his resolve. He looked like a man who could tear through a tugboat line with his bare hands. "What are they supposed to do? These guys are probably Mafia, and we'd just end up getting some poor guy and his family shot dead."

Charles went pallid.

A few staggeringly quiet moments later, Dutch barked, "Frieda, check the fuel."

She did as ordered and reported back. "One tank's empty. I switched over to the second tank on the way in, but it's still over half-full." She had also ascertained that the engines were still running hot but not hissing or steaming. Doing what they were supposed to do.

"Good," Dutch said, and she knew what he was thinking: maybe the other boat would run out of fuel first. It would be the only way to evade them now.

They flew past the distant red and green lights of channel buoys, the running lights of legitimate boats, and the blinking lights that lined the

shore. Safety so close and yet so very far away. Their situation c
have been direr. Where was the guard now?

Frieda suppressed weak cries that were building in her throat a.
fought against the swell of tears blurring her vision. Rudy came an
put his arm around her, while they continued sliding over the bleak
ocean, and overhead the constellations continued to eternally rotate.
Now the sea was rolling more, too. Still hours before dawn. And they
would run out of fuel before that. Sickness was beginning to congeal in
her stomach and crawl up Frieda's throat. She managed to keep a clot
of something sour from spurting out of her mouth.

Rudy began to whisper prayers, while Charles sat huddled against
the sea spray and wrapped his arms around himself.

He sprung up and approached Dutch again. "Why don't we get in
close, jump over, and swim to shore?"

Dutch glanced over his shoulder and then turned back to face the
sea ahead.

"I'm not leaving my boat. Besides, you think you'd make it? It's a lot
longer swim than you think, Princeton. What with riptides, jellies, and
breakers, I'd guess your chances ain't good. But if you want to go, go."

Charles seemed to be considering Dutch's words. He looked at
Frieda, and she shook her head.

"Besides, they see you in the water, they might just go find you
and shoot you for the fun of it," Dutch said, his eyes fixed on the water
ahead. "We're better off in the boat. At least we got a fighting chance."

"What chance?"

"Maybe she'll run empty before we do."

Charles shouted, "She probably came out just a while ago. We've
been out for hours. She could be close to full."

"Well, what do you suggest, Princeton? Got any better ideas, then
fire away!"

"Why not beach the boat and make a run for it on shore?"

goddamn night. Who's gonna help you? And
en, too, on the lookout for us. They want

e just give it to them and then pledge not to go to

Dutch laughed bitterly. "They don't have to take pledges. They make sure no one goes to the law by killing everyone."

Charles was soaked; either with seawater or sweat, Frieda didn't know.

And the dark boat kept coming, slowly but surely gaining on them. Charles finally sat down, hands clenched together, and hung his head low.

Dutch looked over at him. "Probably don't need to hide your head. They could probably hit us with a Thompson by now, but they don't want to sink this baby, so they're not shooting, not yet."

Rudy said, "Waiting until they can be sure of accuracy."

Dutch nodded.

An hour or more passed, or maybe it was less. Farther down the Jersey shore, lights were becoming sparse. Behind them the dark boat kept hunting, drawing closer.

There was nothing to say. Each person lost in his or her thoughts, there was nothing to do but keep on and hope, pray . . . for a miracle.

Haunted thoughts enter the mind when loss of life is imminent. Frieda thought of the afterlife and hoped it existed. If so, maybe she would see her mother and Silver again. And Whitey, too. But thoughts of her life haunted her more brutally. All the things done wrong, all the anger and bitterness she'd held inside for so long, things she'd said to people, her fights with Silver, disappointing him—how she'd maybe driven Bea away from her, too. Her shabby treatment of Hicks, her fury at Hawkeye. If only she could have one more day to make amends with the living before passing on. In one day she could apologize and go to her grave with perhaps less regret. She clamped her eyes shut. *Just one more day . . .*

Dutch shouted something about the fuel, and Frieda instantly jarred back to the present. She went below and checked the sight glasses on the fuel tanks, knowing what she would find. She came up, clutching the handrails to the companionway. "Second tank's almost empty."

Dutch shouted, "Then do something, goddammit. Use the naphtha."

They had five-gallon tanks of naphtha on board.

Frieda yelled, "Engines are too hot."

"Do it!" Dutch fired. "We're sitting ducks if we don't. It's our only chance!"

She glanced from Rudy's frightened face to Charles's desperate one and back to Dutch's doggedly determined one. Rudy's redheaded children flashed in her mind. The boat thumped over a swell, and sickness spurted into the back of Frieda's throat and burned her tongue. Her balance failed, and she smacked face-first into the transom. Pain erupted high up her nose, and her teeth went numb.

She heard Dutch yell, "Do it now!"

She tasted blood streaming from her nostrils. Retching, she reached for the transom and heaved over the stern of the boat. Her guts emptied, and then a ferocious knowing cracked inside her brain. *Rudy.* Horror-struck, she whipped around.

Rudy was hanging on to the port-side gunwale with one hand and holding the naphtha can in the other, pouring naphtha into the fuel fill.

"No!" she screamed.

Soundlessly Rudy's silhouette lit up with flames, then the white-hot explosion knocked her down to the deck, forced choking black smoke into her lungs, sprayed flaming splinters on her body and hair, and a split second later the sea began to rush in.

So fast.

Immersed now in a black, cold silence.

Sinking, drowning.

Flashes of memories: skimming over the water into darkness, salt on her lips, big boats lingering on the horizon, crates of liquor luring them out, rolls of bills in her hands, lawmen on the take, and funerals. Desire and kisses. New York City on the arm of a man. A nice dress. Racing over the ocean. Whiskey bottles. Fear and exultation.

Just let it all go . . .

But the pulse of blood coursing through her veins and arteries walloped in her head, and her heart was still beating fiercely and would not surrender easily. She couldn't see her floating hair or the bubbles that escaped from her mouth, or the way her body drifted downward. But even as the water took her lower, she was heavy, her regret immense, and it was that very thing that saved her: the weight of her, the weight of her life. She had so much to make right.

A red light glowed above her, and a sudden burst of determination sparked her limbs to life. She aimed for the darkness beside the light. She frog-legged upward again and again, until with long strokes of her arms and legs she broke the surface, gulping life-giving oxygen. It all came back. *Rudy.* While hateful spits of sea and embers nailed her face, she thrashed about and swept her eyes around the waters surrounding her. Not far away the burning remnants of the boat. The water dancing with wild flames lighting the swells with burning oil and naphtha. She swam crab-like through the fiery debris field. *Dutch, Charles, Rudy.* Rudy, who had been closest to the tank.

She found him facedown in the sea, grabbed him by what remained of his shredded, burnt clothing, and turned him over. He looked and felt lifeless. "Rudy! Rudy!" she yelled.

The skin hung off his face in lacy strings, but she thought he might be breathing. She put an arm under his shoulders so that his face stayed above water, and she treaded water with her other arm and her legs. Putting her cheek over Rudy's mouth and nose, she felt the movement of air. He was alive.

Dutch appeared, treading silently in the dark waters around her. He whispered urgently, "Keep quiet, damn you. Let's get him away from the flames so they can't see us. If we're lucky, they'll think we're dead."

One on either side of Rudy, they towed him farther out into blacker water. But where was Charles? Where was he?

Dutch said, "At least the fuckers didn't get my *Pauline*."

They held still, keeping Rudy afloat, as the go-through boat made a sweep around the debris, missing them by mere yards in the water, the heads of the crew all turned in the other direction, toward the burning wreckage. Their three dim heads in the midst of dark seas had not been spotted.

As Frieda stared after the other boat, a faint splashing sound floated into her ears. Charles. Her heart thwacking against her ribs, she lifted her head to find him. There he was; she caught the arc of his arms as he swam toward the shore, an inky shadow plowing through the heft of the ocean, the spray from his desperate flight rising ghostlike into the blackness. The roar of a distant engine told them that the hunters were leaving. The hijackers had lost what they had wanted most: the boat. And so the four of them at least had a fighting chance to make it to shore and get Rudy to a hospital. But somehow Frieda already knew that Charles, taking his flawed humanity with him, would not come back to help.

Indeed, where was love now?

Time held its breath as she and Dutch slowly battled the sea, keeping Rudy afloat, towing him between them, stopping when they had to in order to float and rest a minute, then treading and swimming again. Over and over again: *tow, float, tread, swim. Tow, float, rest, swim.*

As they battled currents and swells and began to shiver with cold in this black sea for what felt like many hours but was probably only one or two, fatigue set in. Swells slapped her in the face, and she had to spit out seawater and fight the currents, all the while not letting Rudy out of her grasp. She kept checking; he wasn't speaking, but his mouth once fluttered open, and he was still breathing. Still alive. Frieda's feet cramped, and there were long trembling moments when she thought she could not go on. But Dutch breathlessly whispered encouragement, and she ignored the pain. He would not give up until they all went down together. Frieda realized she would rather die, too, than leave Rudy out here. The three of them would make it or none of them would.

Slowly they made progress. The few lights they could see when they peered over swells were getting brighter, and they rammed on until Frieda heard the hiss of waves making contact with shore.

Dutch said, "Breakers coming."

Then white foam and rushing bubbles all around, a sucking undertow, and yet they held on, rode in on top of a big crasher, and finally crawled and dug up the sand like men lost at sea for months, gasping for air, heaving, coughing, spitting, and pulling Rudy to safety.

Dutch had been the faithful captain after all.

CHAPTER
TWENTY-SEVEN

The newspapers reported that an organized crime boat had chased a rumrunning boat until the latter's crew attempted to fuel their boat with naphtha, causing an explosion and destroying the rum boat. All four crew members had survived—three with only minor burns and injuries, but one seriously burned and blinded for life. The pursuing boat had never been found.

Every day Frieda visited Rudy at the hospital in Long Branch, where he'd been transferred after receiving emergency care at Fort Hancock's army hospital. He was receiving burn treatment, and each morning she took the trolley and then the bus to Long Branch. She went through the motions of living, but she was like a pale version of herself. She had never felt so flimsy and worthless.

Two weeks after the accident, as she stepped off the trolley back from her trip, she looked up into a satin-blue sky. The sun was warm, birds flitted in the trees and skimmed the shallows, and yet it was joyless. The earth had continued to rotate on its axis, oblivious to the agony on its surface. She knew she would live through it only because she'd lived through her mother's death and Silver's death. And somehow survived. But each day her body felt heavier yet less substantial, like stone turning to dust. This event was the most wretched, piled on top of all the other things in her life she'd done wrong, and her only escape was found in short spells of restless slumber, only to awaken and be struck with remembrance.

Rudy was blind, and it was her fault.

Rudy, the sweetest of them all, with his wife who'd given up everything to be with him, and his children. Those three redheaded cherubs.

Her feet made contact with the ground; amazing she could still move. She hadn't been able to eat, and she drank only when the primal urge to survive drove her to the faucet. She walked because when she sat still, the bony fingers of self-loathing and remorse curled in and crushed her. Mostly she walked with no destination in mind and dreamed of walking backward, wishing that she could turn back time. On that particular day, however, she found herself walking up the low rise that overlooked Silver's and her mother's graves, as if propelled by some otherworldly phantom.

She staggered and stopped. A man was there, standing before her mother's grave. She instantly recognized the shape of him, the stoop of his shoulders, and his dull shade of gray hair.

Hawkeye. The man she'd always hated. It looked as though he whispered something, genuflected, and then backed away.

It seemed hardly possible that still more sadness could rush into her shattered soul. She had thought herself already too damaged to feel anything more, but as she watched, memories flooded her. She had cursed him, belittled him, and directed the full force of her anger at him. And she remembered how this man had once angrily told her how he hoped she would one day love someone she couldn't have.

Hawkeye's wish had come true. She had not seen Charles since the explosion. His summer house stood empty, with no sign he'd ever lived there. She knew he had made it, both by the fresh tracks she and Dutch had seen that night in the sand, and because the newspapers had reported that all four crew members had survived. But no information had come from Charles. He had simply vanished. Obviously he couldn't face what he had been a part of. And what he had done to her, to Dutch, and to Rudy. He had left them in the water; he left them altogether.

But no anger existed inside her now; agony took up too much space, leaving no room for anything else. And Hawkeye . . . her mother had seen something in him. She had let him sit at their table. Was he the only one she had allowed to do that? Then a new realization: Hawkeye had no flowers with him. A small new hope unfurled; maybe someone else had felt something for her mother. The mystery would endure.

If only she could endure along with it.

She watched as Hawkeye slowly strode away in the opposite direction, down the incline, and back toward town.

No, no anger left now.

She found Hicks working on the *Wren* in port, readying to go out over the shoals for his second time that day. As she walked the pier, apparitions of long-dead sailors rose and hovered over the water, then quickly dissipated, as if swallowed whole by the traitorous sea. The waters seemed malevolent now, filled with skeletons of boats and creatures, the surface a layer of silvery deception over a black pit.

Slowly walking up to Hicks, she found that her mouth would not work. She didn't even know why she was here, why she was seeking him out. She'd talked to no one except Rudy and his family since her last night on the boat . . . and no one could help her now.

Hicks squinted up at her, and his gaze held all the sadness of this tragedy. He didn't even attempt to brighten his voice, just said flatly, "About to go out. Want to come with me?"

She shook her head, gazed out at the water, and searched out her voice. All she could see in the water now was that dreadful last scene . . . It would always be seared in her mind. Rudy's body lit up with flames. Skin peeling off his face. His eyes destroyed. And this water, this sea, was nothing now but the scene of her crimes. "I'm never going out there again."

After a moment, as if considering what she had said, Hicks stepped up onto the pier and took her arm ever so gently. "Then sit with me for a bit."

She let him settle her on the weathered wood pier, and they sat side by side with their legs dangling over the water, just as they had on that fateful day when he'd first told her about rumrunning. Only four years had passed, but everything had changed. She had lost Silver, Bea, and Charles. And she would never stop seeing Rudy's sightless eyes.

Hicks breathed steadily—in and out, in and out.

She finally gulped, trembling, and said, "I messed up real bad, Hicks."

Hicks looked down at his hands, looked over at her, then back at his hands.

Swallowing, she fought against a suffocating sensation. "And it won't ever be over."

Hicks followed her gaze over the bay. "I know you won't believe this right now, and it may not ever be *over*, but it will get more bearable."

"I don't know how to live with this regret."

He looked at her now with the eyes of one who saw everything. All along he had seen the possible, far-reaching consequences of rumrunning and had kept himself out of it. He had been one of the true adults.

How she wished she had taken his course. "If you didn't regret what happened, you wouldn't be human. Seems to be a universal condition." He glanced away. "I'll sell you the boat if you want. Maybe that will help."

Frieda shook her head. "I gave all the money I'd saved to Rudy's wife so she can take care of him and the boys. And everything I can possibly spare from now on is going to him, too. Besides, I don't want the boat."

His voice gentle, he said slowly, "But you love it."

Shaking her head again, she wrapped her arms around herself, even though the day was warm, the air still.

Hicks said, "You're just lost right now. Give it time. Time really does heal, at least somewhat."

Heal? Rudy would never heal; he would never see again. He would never get the sailboat he dreamed of. He wouldn't see his boys grow up, watch them graduate, marry, or see his grandchildren. "I don't think so."

She looked north up the shoreline where Silver's house—now her house—sat. That was the place where her life had truly begun; how had she managed to muck it up so badly in the years since? She had to turn away from the house and face the water. Sunlight shimmered on little whitecaps out in the blue beyond. Boats bobbed against the blinding horizon. *Blinding.*

"Things happen, Frieda. Bad things happen. And sometimes they happen to good people."

Frieda remembered the day Rudy had told her Charles actually *wasn't* too good for her. Voice trembling, she breathed out, "The best person."

Hicks nodded and stayed quiet.

Minutes passed, then Hicks broke the silence with the kindest of voices. "It wasn't your fault."

Up the shore a wave washed in and slipped away. "It was my job to take care of the engines. Instead, I was sick over my personal life and sick with fear. I didn't do my job. He did it for me, and now he's . . ." She hadn't said the word *blind* yet and couldn't make herself say it now.

Hicks just sat, listening, waiting.

Blind. Blind.

Hicks said again—ever so softly, barely above a whisper—"It wasn't your fault."

He scooted closer, curved his arm around her, the same way Rudy had done on the boat that night, and Frieda finally let the fear, anger, and self-loathing pour out of her body. Not caring who saw or heard, she sobbed wretchedly into her hands.

CHAPTER
TWENTY-EIGHT

On the day she was to see Bea, Frieda dressed well. She slipped into one of the sheath dresses Bea had left behind and put her hair up under a hat. She didn't want to embarrass her sister by her appearance, and she didn't want to stick out today. She had important things to do.

They met at a café near the university and sat outside at a tiny table on even tinier round chairs. The last heat wave of the Indian summer had rolled in, and Bea was dressed in summery perfection. She was still a daisy, with her plum cheeks, perpetual smile, and waves of styled blond hair. But the expression in her eyes was not one Frieda recognized. She couldn't put a finger on exactly what it was, but perhaps Bea had matured. She seemed older. She had grown up.

Bea ordered coffee and then, with shimmering concern in her eyes, asked, "So, how are you? Please tell me the truth."

Frieda folded her hands on the tabletop. "I'm not here to talk about me. I'm here to ask for your forgiveness."

Bea waved a hand in the air. "You'll do nothing of the sort."

"Listen to me, please," Frieda pleaded, pulling in a ragged breath. "I tried to tell you what to do with your life, and I shouldn't have. Your decisions are yours alone. I was angry; I no longer am. If you're happy, then I'm happy."

Bea looked at her sister skeptically. "You haven't answered my question, not that you need to. I can see it written all over you. You're in anguish."

Frieda fought the swell of tears. Since she'd cried with Hicks, all the pent-up tears of a lifetime had kept pouring out of her. She had watered the ground with them, drenched her clothes, and dropped them into the sea. She had never known that tear ducts could produce so much. "All I want is your forgiveness."

Clearly moved by Frieda's emotion, Bea took her sister's hand. "You'll always have that." Bea squeezed Frieda's hand and continued to study her sister. "What happened with Charles?"

The oxygen drained from the sun-filled day. "Nothing," Frieda answered with a hard-fought breath. "Absolutely nothing, except that I went a little crazy."

"Lots of people went a little crazy. All that excitement, all that money. It wasn't just you."

"I went a little crazy long before that. I wish . . ."

"What?"

Despite the purity of her thought, Frieda had to squeeze out the words. "I wish I'd been more like you."

Bea sighed through a sad smile. "We'll always be sisters, you know."

Frieda said chokingly, "Thank you. Thank you."

"I should be thanking you. After all, if you hadn't made all that money I wouldn't have come to the city and met August. But you know what? Much as I love him, I don't talk to him the way I talk to you. It's not the same. I need you both."

Frieda couldn't speak. Here was the girl she knew so well, that everyone had always loved. And rightfully so.

Bea said, "So, what will you do now?"

With one hand Frieda pushed away tears, lifted her cup, and swallowed a sip of coffee that burned on its way down. Her throat was too dry. With her other hand she squeezed back. She dared not delve too deeply into what might lie ahead and all that would be missing now from her life. "I suppose I'll work on boat engines. I need to make a living, but I want nothing more to do with rumrunning."

"Understandable," said Bea.

Her vision blurred by tears, Frieda looked deep into her sister's eyes. "I was so stupid . . ."

"There's plenty of blame to go around. I never tried to stop you, not really. I lived off what you made, and truth is I enjoyed the money. It was hard to resist, and no one's perfect. We're all just . . . people, you know."

After that they held each other's hands in a silence of simple understanding.

Bea finally spoke. "I want you to stand up for me at the wedding."

Frieda blinked hard. "I . . . I'd be honored." She hadn't thought of anything happy, such as a wedding, in . . . forever. A moment later she almost managed a smile. "You can even choose my dress."

Bea gave her *that* look. "Yes, please."

A short while later Frieda walked through the city, her thoughts a jumble of past memories and regrets, hopes and dreams. Two little girls left orphaned by the dockside had survived after all, and one was happy, which made the other happier. It was time to go back home. But her heart had other plans and drew her to the one place she shouldn't go. But then again, hadn't she always known she would do this? Hadn't she always known that she would seek some answers before closing this chapter of her life?

...ing in front of Charles's family townhouse, she had no idea who would answer. It could be one of his parents, a servant—or no one at all. The house sat still and quiet. She waited for a long moment, her heart racing, before ringing the bell. But she wasn't surprised when Charles answered the door.

He was dressed casually in fashionable baggy slacks and a striped shirt. His curious gaze softened when he laid eyes on her, and it was as if he'd been bathed in a big wave of relief. "Dear Frieda, I knew you would come for me. I knew I could count on you. What took you so long?" Without waiting for her response, he said, "Please come in."

She moved not an inch. But her stomach swayed with the impact of seeing him again. His beauty still stole her breath, but the memory of him swimming away wouldn't leave her mind and never would. She had been so clouded by his beauty and his need that she hadn't seen what everyone else had so easily seen. Falling in love with him had been like plunging into a pit of ignorance, unwarranted hopefulness fueling her fall. He hadn't taken them seriously. He had played with her for a while and then left her. She would never forget the moments when it was good, but it had—in the end—been simply a summer fling.

Despite it all she missed him. She had not yet completely subdued her feelings for him. She looked softly into those eyes she'd once adored. "I only came to tell you that Rudy will live. His burns are healing, and he'll be taken care of."

He nodded. "Good to know."

There was no trace of remorse, hysteria, or guilt. His cool, confident, classy costume was back on, perhaps for good. This was her answer. Charles was an unfathomable person. Perhaps he was an island unto himself. An island whose winds would soon blow away any trace of her. And yet he was human. She could hurt him.

He said, "Terrible thing that happened out there. But don't ask me to regret any of it. If I hadn't gone there, we would never have met." She lost herself back in that night, and all she saw were the arcs of his arms as he swam away, and all she could hear were the splashes he'd made as he left the three of them on their own. Such a selfish flight, such a tragic flight.

"Yes," she finally said.

He must have known what she was thinking, because he said, "I warned you about me. I told you all along I wasn't worth your adoration. And still you fell for me, dear girl." He opened the door wider. "Come in. I'll make you a drink and we can catch up."

So he hadn't come for her, but now that she'd come to him, he was willing to resume the relationship? She hadn't been worth seeking out, but now that she'd made it easy he was capable of carrying on?

Somehow her feet stayed glued to the stoop. She had not loved him less because of his shortcomings; his flaws had only made her want him more—he was vulnerable and in need of her love. Doesn't a part of everyone want to bring out the best in another? Doesn't that same part of everyone want to save another from themselves, to see that person rise higher, lifted by the power of love?

But love had slipped away like a dream that drifts just beyond your grasp, and nothing can bring it back. And just because something didn't last, it didn't mean it had no value. Charles had opened the world to her and made it bigger. He had opened her mind. She would always be grateful for that. But she didn't want him any longer. Not only because of that night but also because the love she wanted was not the kind he was able to give. However, she could forgive him. How could she ever have asked him to be more than he was capable of being? He was who he was. With no malice or bitterness whatsoever, she said simply, "Good-bye, Charles."

It took a few days for a quiet calm to settle over her.

She was free.

CHAPTER
TWENTY-NINE

A week later, the day bloomed with lemon sun and sweet air, another example of Indian summer perfection. Overhead a flock of ducks flew in V formation, going south to a better place for the winter. At first she felt forsaken, watching them leave. But then something broke free in Frieda's ragged heart. She suddenly felt glad to be alive at that minute, able to see something as simple as the flight of birds.

She walked down the pier and into the moment when her memory had first simmered to life when she was about four years old. With her mother beside her, she had stood very still on this very pier and really *seen* the ocean for the first time. She had gazed at the distant swells, gulls swooping overhead, sparks of light waltzing on the peaks between troughs, and the sea moving like a billowing bolt of silk.

She remembered nothing of what had happened before or after this moment—just this one intense speck in time, and what she was left with forever after—how huge, eternal, and magnetic was that water, and how much she loved it then . . . and still did.

* * *

Hicks stood waiting at the *Wren*. He said through a long exhalation, "Frieda."

"Hicks."

He smiled, and a rush of something sweet and warm and lovely settled over her skin like a layer of the finest sand. She let it sink in from skin all the way to bone. It sent her back to very old feelings that had become lost behind the curtain of everyday struggles—a belief in honor, a longing for something shared, a solid shoulder to lean on, the touch of a caring hand. Could it be that love had always stood before her but she had been too foolish to see it? In a frenzy she had focused her attentions in the wrong direction, on the wrong person, when a man more worthy, kind, and loving had always stood right beside her. He had taught her so many things—including the importance of being yourself. At one time she had known who she was, then lost it, and now she had to learn it all over again. With the gentlest of touches Hicks had guided her back. He had waited for her a long time. But she could not come to him now, not in this weakness. She would come to him only in strength, only strength.

Would he wait longer?

He said, "Are you ever going to call me by my given name?"

Frieda looked away, toward the sea. There was no such thing as stagnation there. Even if the surface was calm, the underworld was swirling with life. Fish came out of rocks to hunt, dolphins swam, and farther out, whale-giants of the sea surfaced to breathe. Perhaps the idea of change could keep her afloat for now. And maybe someday she would be able to shine the light of forgiveness on herself.

Stepping up to help her on board, he asked, "Are you ready?"

She grasped his hand. "Take me out, Sam."

ACKNOWLEDGMENTS

I am deeply indebted to many wonderful people who have assisted in bringing this novel to life. Lisa Erbach Vance, my agent—you are an author's dream representative. Jodi Warshaw, my editor at Lake Union—your support and guidance made the book possible. Amara Holstein—your excellent suggestions and guidance helped make the book stronger. Marcus Trower—your copyediting was meticulous. The team at Lake Union Publishing—thanks for support during every step along the way.

Many fine resources contributed to the preparation of this novel, among them *Capital of the World: A Portrait of New York City in the Roaring Twenties* by David Wallace, *The Black Ships: Rumrunners of Prohibition* by Everett S. Allen, *The Confessions of a Rum-Runner* by James Barbican, and *Rum Row: The Liquor Fleet That Fueled the Roaring Twenties* by Robert Carse.

As always, to my friends, family, and Joe a special thanks for putting up with me throughout it all.

ABOUT THE AUTHOR

Ann Howard Creel was born in Austin, Texas, and worked as a registered nurse before becoming a full-time writer. She is the author of numerous children's and young adult books as well as fiction for adults. Her children's books have won several awards, and her novel *The Magic of Ordinary Days* was made into a Hallmark Hall of Fame movie for CBS. Creel currently lives and writes in Chicago.